YOU AND ME AND HIM

by Kris Dinnison

Houghton Mifflin Harcourt

Boston New York

All rights reserved. For information about permission to reproduce selections from
this book, write to Permissions, Houghton Mifflin Harcourt Publishing Company,
215 Park Avenue South, New York, New York 10003.

www.hmhco.com

The text of this book is set in Adobe Garamond Pro.
Book design by Susanna Vagt.

Library of Congress Cataloging-in-Publication Data is on file.
ISBN: 978-0-544-30112-2

Manufactured in United States of America
DOC 10 9 8 7 6 5 4 3 2 1
4500531807

For Andy and Kate

CHAPTER 1

Let's get one thing straight from the very beginning: I am not one of those shrinking-violet fat girls. I don't sit alone in my bedroom playing Billie Holiday albums while drowning my sorrows in a carton of ice cream. Okay, once—maybe twice—a year, but not every weekend. I have friends, a great job in a vintage record store, and even some minor social status. But I am an overweight teenage girl going to an American high school. It doesn't take a clairvoyant to figure out there are going to be some issues.

The current issue: Which outfit will maximize the four and half pounds I lost this summer and minimize the remaining flesh? As usual, my mom's annual summer diet plan for me didn't result in any magical transformations, so for the debut of my junior year, I decide on my flowy hippie-chick skirt and a black T-shirt with sleeves too long for the heat of early September. I don't love this outfit. But it fits, kind of. And it's not hideous. Most of the clothes in my size look like they were designed for retirees in Miami Beach, Florida. I do not like my shirts bedazzled in any way. Someone in the plus-size fashion industry thinks if you put shiny stuff on a T-shirt, no one will notice the size of the person underneath. This particular first-day outfit is nothing tragic, but it's more of a fashion whisper than a fashion statement.

I climb on the bus and make a beeline for Nash.

"Maggie." He gives me a slight wave, then covers it by smoothing down his rockabilly sideburns. (He grooms them, no lie, with mustache wax.) I slide into the seat beside him. Nash shifts upward as the seat sags in my direction.

"Move your skinny ass over," I say.

"Like my skinny ass has a choice?" He moves. "Nice skirt." Nash squinches up his face like something smells bad.

I sigh. Nash is all about edgy, and my sixties Woodstock wear does not scream edgy. I feel a trickle of sweat drip down between my shoulder blades.

"Nice hair," I say.

Nash pats his shellacked do, making sure it has kept its height through the bus ride. Finding all the follicles in place, he turns his attention to me. He fishes a peppermint lip balm out of his pocket and hands it over. He then picks three or four of my long, brown hairs off my shirt. Nash always grooms me like some fastidious chimpanzee mother. Finally, he straightens the silver charm on its chain around my neck. The charm was Nash's gift to me on the first day of high school. It's this cool spiral; he says it's to remind me that he's got my back. Always. I pretty much never take the thing off.

"Thanks," I say when he's done making me presentable.

Nash holds out his hand. "Did you bring the goods?"

I dig in my bag and pull out a Ziploc baggie. Inside is one of my signature breakfast bars, tailored especially for Nash: cash-ews, chunky peanut butter, oats, cinnamon, dried cherries, and a few dark chocolate chips. I know. Shocking, right? A fat girl who bakes. So cliché. But I started making these bars for Nash a few years back when his dad left and things went to shit at his house. He was living on ramen noodles and cold cereal, so now the bars are part of our morning routine.

I wave the baggie over my head, keeping his breakfast just out of reach. "Who loves you, baby?"

He snatches the bag from my hand and pinches off a corner of the bar, popping it in his mouth. "Mmmmmm." His mouth is full. "What's different?"

"A little cardamom. Fewer cherries. It was too sweet."

"Well done, Mags."

I wait as he chews, looking out the window at the rows of identical cedar split-levels lining the streets. It's a decent neigh-borhood, but it's in between: not new, but not old enough or cool enough to be vintage, either.

As soon as he finishes breakfast, Nash glances around to see if anyone is listening and leans in close. "Check out the hottie in row two."

I tilt my head up above the back of the seats and catch a glimpse of tousled, longish brown hair in the left-hand seat. Ducking back down, I ask, "Who is it?" without letting my lips move.

Nash shrugs, and we fan ourselves with our hands. Nash and I have the same taste in almost everything: teachers, music, art, literature, and boys. The good news is we can mock anyone who doesn't share our aesthetic. The bad news is we have to lay claim to guys we both crush on. There just aren't that many crush-worthy possibilities in Cedar Ridge.

"Dibs!" we say at the same time.

Nash narrows his eyes at me. We've been doing the dibs thing since elementary school, but we didn't start using it on boys until seventh grade. It's kind of a running joke with us, this idea that we can have a guy just by claiming him. Never once have any of the crushes reciprocated, but the ritual allows the one with dibs to discuss the object of his or her affection as if romance was a realistic possibility.

"Okay." I hold my hands up against Nash's world-famous death stare. "You can have him." Not a big deal. I'm long past believing in the fairy tale of the handsome stranger who sees past my not-quite-modelesque figure to discover the fabulous Maggie within. After all, that would be some headline: "FAT GIRL SNAGS NEW GUY." I gaze out the window as the bus turns the corner and rolls along the lakefront. The evergreens still cast long shadows a good distance into the lake from the shore. But starting about thirty feet out, the water glitters with early morning sunlight. I steal another glance at the new guy and cross my fingers that Nash has an actual chance with this one.

When the bus rolls to a stop in the parking lot, we descend into the bustling fray. The kids who drive start streaming in from student parking. I link arms with Nash and move in their direction, hoping to blend into the stream and avoid the shame of being bussies. But Nash stops short, which yanks me to a stop. I look up and see New Guy. He's a little taller than Nash, with sandy brown hair, tan, freckled skin, and these grass-green eyes casting around for something to hold on to. Nash steers us in his direction, and we come to a halt right in front of him.

"Hi," Nash says. "You lost?"

The New Guy just looks at Nash.

"Nash Taylor." He hooks his thumb in my direction. "Maggie Bower. Welcome to Cedar Ridge," he adds, releasing my arm and giving a little bow. "This way." Nash sweeps his arm in front of him, ushering New Guy in the direction of the main building. They start to move off, leaving me alone, the current of students flowing around me.

I'm not sure if I should follow, but as Nash chats up the New Guy, he gives a surreptitious head jerk, the universal sign for "get your ass up here." New Guy doesn't seem bothered by Nash's bossiness or by Nash leading him around. That fact alone is surprising. Maybe this one will break our losing streak.

CHAPTER 2

My first-day jitters turn to first-day boredom as the teachers drone on about rules, deadlines, grading policies, and the joy of learning. The only bright spot is third period English. My friend Cece is already there. If Nash wasn't my bestie, Cece would probably fill that slot. She's one of the smartest kids at Cedar Ridge: destined to escape our small Northwest town via the Ivy League. She waves me over, and I slide into the seat behind her.

"I'm so glad you took AP." She turns around to talk to me. "Everybody took regular English this year. It seems like I never end up in the same class with anyone." She looks around. "Is Nash taking any AP classes?" Her voice is casual, but I can hear the hope sliding underneath her words.

"He's taking AP English, but I'm not sure which period."

Cece sags a little, but then leans in. "Who's the boy you and Nash were with before school?"

I doodle on my notebook. At this rate, the cover will be filled by lunch. "New guy." I start filling in a spiral I've drawn on the cover. "He was on the bus and Nash swooped. I don't even know his name yet."

"Nash seemed pretty psyched," Cece says.

I never really know what to say when Cece talks about Nash. The only place Cece is dumber than me: guys. Not only has she never had a boyfriend; she is nursing a two-year (and counting) crush on Nash. Yep. Cece has a crush on my terminally gay best friend. It's sad, really, and it annoys the shit out of Nash, but I understand what it's like to want something you can't have.

"Maggie!" Nash sort of hurls himself into a desk next to me. "Hey, Cece. Okay, cool. I was thinking I wouldn't have any classes with you, Mags. That would be a tragic first."

"Hey, Nash." Cece's trying to be casual, but she has this goofy look on her face that can't be denied. "I like your shirt."

"Thanks!" Nash looks down like he doesn't know exactly which shirt he spent an hour deciding on that morning. "You like Pollock?"

"Yeah. Obviously. Who doesn't?" Cece starts chewing on her pencil like a nervous hamster.

"Most of the art establishment, for one. At least when he was alive," Nash says.

"Of course. I just meant . . ." Cece flounders in the confusion of her own crush.

"You should definitely watch the biopic they did about him. So cool. I can loan it to you if you want?" Nash waits.

Cece's face goes bright red. She nods, but this kindness on Nash's part appears to have made speech impossible for her.

I throw Cece a life raft. "So Cece was just asking me about the new guy."

"Yeah." She clings to it, grateful. "He's cute. What's his story?"

"His name's Tom." Nash takes the bait. My little magpie! "He just moved here from . . . Oh, shit. I don't remember where now. But somewhere fabulous . . ." Ms. Shone starts class, interrupting Nash. But Nash gives me a grin that says he has a lot more to tell me about the new guy.

After a morning of rules and syllabi, I say a silent thank-you to the universe when Ms. Shone discards the usual first-day litany and has us write a poem about one moment in our summer.

My poem's about lying on the dock at my grandparents' cabin watching the Perseid meteor showers. The trees lining the lakeshore were inky black, creating a perfect frame for the brighter dark of the night sky. I searched the skies for a couple hours, listening to music until the batteries died. Hundreds of stars fell that night, way too many for wishes. It was one of the few times in my life that I've ever felt small. I turn in my poem, crossing my fingers we won't have to present them tomorrow.

By lunch I'm almost comatose. Usually Nash and I meet at his locker, which is near the cafeteria door. But when I get close, he is already walking toward the lunchroom with New Guy, or Tom, I guess. I stop short, but before I can decide to turn around and hide in the library for lunch, Nash waves me over, smiling the smile of the newly smitten. Following them, I only half listen to Nash's tutorial on lunchroom etiquette and the pecking order. Tom nods, looking around the room as we wind through the line and find a spot at the end of a table. Tom draws some curious looks, because he's new and because he's with Nash and me. But Nash is putting it on, making the most of his dibs.

"Tom was telling me about all the amazing places he's lived," Nash says as we sit down. "Atlanta, Chicago, Honolulu, Las Vegas." Nash puts up a finger for each one. "Nine different schools!"

"I'm going for an even dozen." Tom gives me a smile that I am pretty sure has broken hearts in every one of those places.

"So are you some sort of fugitive?" I pull the top off my yogurt. "Or do you have some rare geographical ADD condition?"

Tom laughs, a throaty chuckle that makes my stomach do a little flip. I remind myself that Nash has dibs and try to ignore the flush of heat climbing my neck.

"No, nothing sinister or medical. And if anyone has ADD in my family, it's my dad. Let's just say he has a short attention span where employment is concerned. He's kind of a computer whiz. Does consulting for all these different companies. He takes a job, finishes a project or gets bored with it, and then moves on to the next best thing. We get dragged along in his wake."

"That must be so cool," Nash says.

"That must be tough," I say at the same time. We look at each other, laughing. "It's just . . . I've lived here my whole life. It's weird to think of being always new, always unknown."

"But that's the beauty of it!" Nash says. "You're always mysterious. You get to reinvent yourself every time you move.

Nobody knows who you are, or who your parents are, or anything about your life."

I know Nash is thinking about his own family. And the thing about living in a town the size of Cedar Ridge is everyone knows Nash's story, or thinks they do. He can't escape it.

Cece and her friend Mike come to the table. No trays. Mike's got a brown bag and Cece's holding her Pokémon lunch box. I've never figured out if the lunch box is ironic or an authentically geeky move on Cece's part.

"Hey, Maggie. Hi, Nash," Cece says. She glances at Tom, but really only has eyes for Nash.

I make the introductions. "Cece. Mike. This is Tom."

"I like your lunch box." Tom flashes her that smile. I wonder if he's making fun of her, but it seems like he's sincere.

"Thanks." Cece goes bright red.

"Is it vintage?" Tom asks.

"If by vintage you mean I've had it since elementary school."

"Cool," Tom says.

Cece waits, fiddling with the yellow plastic handle, Mike lurking behind her. Mike doesn't seem pleased with the stop at Nash's table. He's been not so secretly in love with Cece for a long time, but she's oblivious to this fact. Mike likes Cece, who likes Nash, who likes Tom, who likes . . . ? Who knows who Tom likes? The endless cycle of high school romance is like that mythological snake eating its own tail.

"We can make room if you guys want to sit down," I say, grateful for a chance to not be the third wheel.

Nash gives me a look that makes it clear he doesn't want Cece sitting down. Not today.

Mike gives Cece a similar look.

"Thanks, but we're going to eat on the steps. I want to enjoy the sunshine while I can," Cece says. "Call me later, Maggie?"

I nod and turn my attention back to Tom and Nash.

"Maggie and I are going to travel after we graduate, get out of this town. Aren't we, Mags?" Nash says, picking up the conversation right where Cece interrupted it.

"That's the plan," I say, dipping my spoon into my yogurt and taking a bite.

"Really? Where do you want to go?" Tom asks me, but Nash answers.

"We are definitely going to Paris, for one. And London. God save the queen! Far away. Anywhere but here."

Nash and I discuss this plan all the time, and I know it keeps him from wanting to throw himself off a bridge when Cedar Ridge threatens to crush him under its small-town weight. I do want to travel, to all those places and more, but I don't ache to leave like he does.

"I went to England a couple years ago," Tom says.

"Really?" Nash says. "Did you hear that, Maggie?"

I nod, trying to fly under the radar, stay small.

Nash grabs a napkin and starts sketching. He does that when he's nervous sometimes. Nash is one of those natural artists, so even a napkin drawing from him is worth keeping.

"I'm dying to visit London, soak up all that British Invasion, punk rock vibe. I bet you can tell us all the cool places to go." Nash is in full gush mode, sketching and rambling, and he doesn't notice the creep of pink climbing up Tom's neck and cheeks. He finishes his drawing: the queen standing in front of the London Eye and holding a pint of beer. He hands it to Tom, who grins.

"Wow! This is amazing! Thanks." He smoothes out the napkin and sets it next to his lunch.

"So what did you do when you were there?" Nash asks.

"I, um, well, I was kind of young, only eleven." The blush is back, and Tom sputters a little. He starts gnawing on the nail on his middle finger. He's trying hard to avoid saying something.

Nash and I both wait. Nash because he asked the question, and me because I am curious about what Tom's hiding.

Finally Tom spills. "Um, we saw lots of medieval stuff—you know, the Tower of London, knights, castles, that kind of thing." He's looking at us like he hopes we'll fill in the blanks and save him from having to explain the rest.

We're nodding, but it's clear we aren't getting it.

Tom sighs. "I was in sort of a Dungeons and Dragons stage, pretty much obsessed with the Middle Ages, weapons, armor, all that. Every guy goes through that, right?"

Tom and I both look at Nash, realizing at the same time that this phase of adolescent manhood passed him by.

"Okay, maybe not everyone, but I grew out of it. I'm not into D&D anymore. I quit after I got passed over as Dungeon Master."

"Dungeon Master?" Nash and I ask at the same time, but Tom holds up a hand.

"That's a story for another time," he says. "I've already humiliated myself enough for a first day of school, and I should know—I've had nine of them." He points his finger back and forth at Nash and me. "Besides, now you both owe me." He leans back, crossing his arms like he's won some kind of prize.

Nash and I exchange glances.

"Owe you?" I ask.

"An embarrassing story or fact about yourself. One each."

Nash starts to protest, but Tom puts one hand on Nash's arm and holds up his other one to silence him. Nash stops talking. Typically nobody can shush him.

"Not now, but soon," Tom says.

Nash looks at Tom's hand on his arm and nods. They start talking about other things: plans for after school, which teachers to avoid.

I keep watching Tom. He's pretty, but there's something more going on under there, something different. He's really listening to Nash, leaning in, keeping eye contact. He's not looking around for an escape route or scoping out his other options. Not yet. A guy who's been to that many schools knows that hanging with Nash and me is not the best he could do. Yet here he is. Why? That's what I want to know. I stare at Tom, mulling over his motivations, when I hear my name.

"Maggie?" The voice comes from behind me.

I recognize it right away, even though I haven't heard it in a while: Kayla Hill.

"Maggie, is that you?" she says, like we haven't gone to the same school for a decade.

"Kayla," I say, my voice cautious. Kayla is at the top of the food chain, no mistake. Her end-of-summer tan stands out against a bright yellow sundress that hugs her curves. Her whole being screams popular. I wonder why she's decided to go slumming by talking to Nash and me—then I see her wide brown eyes laser-focused over my head at Tom.

"How have you been?" Kayla coos. "It's been so long!"

"Yeah," I say. "About four years."

Kayla laughs this little laugh that sounds like a bell ringing and kind of swats at my arm like I'm a real kidder. But we both know it's been at least that long since Kayla and I spoke.

"Hi, Nash," she says, polite but not friendly, then reaches out her hand to Tom. "And I don't believe we've met," she says. "I'm Kayla." Tom shakes her hand.

"Tom." He smiles that killer smile. "Nice to meet you."

"You're new, right? I'm on the new student orientation committee." Kayla smiles back at Tom, and their combined wattage is overpowering. "If you need anything, you let me know." Her voice is warm and inviting, like caramel, and I remember for a moment what it feels like to bask in Kayla's glow.

"Will do," Tom says.

"Bye for now," she says, waving, and sashays over to some long-lost friends at another table. We all watch her walk away. This is her superpower. It's like she excretes some sort of mind-numbing pheromone that encourages lesser beings to follow her every move and forget everyone else around them. What surprises me is the bristle of anger and jealousy that runs across my scalp as Tom checks her out.

Kayla and I were sort of friends through sixth grade. I guess everyone in our class kind of got along until then. But around that time, someone made the decision that Kayla was boy-girl party, A-list material and I wasn't. Lines were drawn, and I landed on the wrong side of the cool/not cool divide.

Kayla decided to go along with the horde and dropped me like I was a rabid hedgehog. She just stopped knowing me. And she stopped being the kind of person I wanted to know.

"Maggie," Nash says, snapping his fingers in front of my face. "Earth to Maggie."

"Huh?" I say. They are both looking at me.

"Tom was asking you about your afternoon schedule," Nash says through somewhat clenched teeth. He's irritated that I haven't been hanging on their every word.

"Oh, um, honors bio and PE."

"Me too," Tom says, bumping me with his shoulder. "Cool!"

I wince at the thought of another tortuous semester of PE, and Tom's expression changes. Nash kicks me under the table.

"Sorry. It's not you. One of the PE teachers loathes me." I kick Nash back. Tom nods, but he doesn't look convinced.

CHAPTER 3

By the time lunch is over, I'm ready to escape to my locker, but Tom asks if he can walk to bio with me. People stop to look at him, so we have to navigate the halls by dodging gawking clusters of the curious.

"Small town," I say by way of explanation.

He hovers his hand protectively near my back and leans in so he can hear my running commentary. I see why Nash laid claim to this one.

"Don't worry about it. I've been the new guy a lot." We sit down at one of the back lab tables.

"No way!" I hear Kayla Hill's voice for the second time that day. "We have another class together, Maggie?" We had history together before lunch. Kayla ignored me in that class.

"Yeah." I dig in my bag for a pencil. "Cool."

"Hey, Tom, I don't have a lab partner yet." Kayla indicates an empty table up front.

"Oh, thanks, but I'm going to partner with Maggie," Tom says.

"That's great." Kayla smiles at me but wilts a little. "As long as you're taken care of."

"I think Maggie will take good care of me," Tom says. Now they are both smiling at me like it's my turn to say something.

"Uh, yeah," I say. "Totally taken care of."

"Okay, well, see you!" Kayla waves her little wave and takes her perky little butt back to her seat. I rummage around in my bag again, this time searching for my calculator. When I look up, Tom's eyes are on me, his lips twitching like he's trying not to laugh.

"What?" I say, rubbing my face and running my tongue over my teeth in case I have remnants of yogurt lingering.

"Nothing. Just trying to figure things out."

"Figure things out?"

"Yeah. New town. New school. It takes a couple days to put it all together."

"Only a couple days?" I'm hoping Tom won't be one of those guys who decide who you are in the first five minutes.

"Usually," he says. "Sometimes a little longer."

"I've lived here my whole life, and I'm still trying to figure things out. Must be nice to understand it all in less than a week."

"I didn't say I'd understand it all. But schools start to look alike after a while, and so do the people."

"Flattering," I say. "So we're all just clones of people you knew at other schools?"

"Not exactly clones. And there are always exceptions. Nash, for example. And you. You're definitely not a clone."

I stare at him, wavering between pleasure at not being lumped in with the other Cedar Ridge robots and irritation that he thinks he's already figured me out.

"Maybe if you took longer than thirty seconds to get to know people, they might surprise you." I open my notebook, flipping through the pages. The pen sitting on the notebook flies up, arcing over Tom and hitting the floor.

"Good." Tom picks up the pen and hands it to me with a flourish. "I love surprises."

Tom falls into step beside me as we swing into the hallway after class. "Look, I'm sorry if I—"

"Don't sweat it," I say, smiling and speeding up a bit. I can't be late to PE on my first day.

"You in a hurry?" Tom says, matching my pace. "I thought you hated PE?"

"I do. But I hate detention more, and Ms. Perry despises me. If I suit up late, she sends me straight down—do not pass 'go,' do not collect two hundred dollars."

"Ah, the bitchy PE teacher. A high school archetype," Tom says.

"The skinny, bitchy PE teacher who exercises excessively to make herself forget that what she really wants is a brownie. With nuts."

"So, why does she hate you?"

I know why Ms. Perry hates me. She hates me because I'm one of those girls who eat the brownie. I glance at him, squeezing my science notebook tight against my body. Nash claimed

Tom, so there's no need for me to impress him. That doesn't mean I'm going to freely discuss my flaws and nutritional choices with a cute guy I just met.

"Who knows? Maybe she's scared of my intellectual prowess. Maybe she can't handle my epic dance moves. Who cares? She's crazy." I stop at the entrance to the girls' locker room. "You're down there. Next door on the right. The one that says 'Boys,'" I add.

"Good to know." Tom backs down the hall a few paces. "See you inside."

He pauses at the next door, pointing; his eyebrows raise in question. I give him a thumbs-up and descend into the PE locker room, which may not be actual high school hell, but it's certainly one of its waiting rooms.

The locker room is already full of half-dressed hard-bodies when I get there. I make my way to a semi-hidden corner behind some lockers and heft my backpack onto the bench. Next comes my best version of what my old swim team coach used to call a deck change. I put the gym clothes on, then wriggle my street clothes out from under them, thereby exposing the least possible surface area of skin and undergarments.

This may seem like a lot of effort to avoid a few seconds of vulnerability, but it's a necessary survival mechanism. We've been dressing down for PE for four years, but it only took two weeks to figure out that the girls' locker room is fraught with dangers. And don't even get me started on the subtle art of using technology to reveal other girls' dirty little secrets. Cell phones are officially banned but constantly in use. Expose your body in that room, and you better be sure that the only thing that gets out there is that you are perfect in every way.

Once changed, I file out with the other girls, tugging my shorts and shirt over my widest parts. Tom stands with some sophomore and junior boys, and he waves when I walk in the gym. I wave back but line up near the door.

Ms. Perry grimaces when she sees me, checking my name off the list on her clipboard. She raises her whistle to her mouth with a skeletal arm. One shrill blast and the chitchat dies down. We line up, count off, and go to our respective corners. I look around for Tom. He's headed right for me, grinning. He gives me a thumbs-up and plants himself next to me. Some of the other kids are looking at him and whispering, but that comes to an abrupt halt at the sound of Ms. Perry's whistle.

"These will be your activity groups for the semester," Ms. Perry shouts. The four teachers begin to move to the four corners.

I close my eyes and say a silent prayer to the PE gods: *Not Perry. Not Perry. Not Perry . . .* When I open my eyes, Ms. Perry is standing in front of our group, her clipboard out, whistle clenched between her teeth, and her eyes on me. She blows the whistle. I flinch.

"This group's with me. Fall in for three laps around the field, and meet me by the north soccer goal in eight minutes. Go!"

Students leap into action, streaming around Ms. Perry and filing out the door and into the sunshine. In Ms. Perry's presence, I am like a hunted rabbit, frightened and frozen. Tom and I end up at the back of the pack. By the time we pass her, she is already shaking her head and making marks on her clip-board.

"Wow, she really likes that whistle," Tom says, loping beside me.

"You have no idea." I try not to pant as I lumber through the first few hundred yards of the run. You wouldn't think it to look at me, but I am actually a pretty active person. I was a competitive swimmer for four years, until the end of eighth grade, followed by a brief, obsessive volleyball phase during freshman year. I walk and hike for hours in the cedar and fir forests that surround our town and hardly break a sweat. But running has always been my downfall. Any fitness or strength I gain through other activities exits my body the minute I ac-celerate to even a slow jog. Watch me run and you'll assume I'm one of those kids who lie on the couch eating Cheez Doodles and watching reruns of *Saved by the Bell*. When I run, I sweat. I wheeze. I clump around like my legs are formed from lead.

I do not want Tom to see me at my worst. "Hey, listen, save yourself! She said eight minutes, and we're already behind. Running: not my forte. Making Ms. Perry like me: also not my forte. No reason to hitch your wagon to my falling star. That's PE suicide." I am breathing heavier now, and beads of sweat start to form on my forehead, under my bra, behind my knees.

"No, I'm good," Tom says, jogging beside me, not a drop of perspiration on him.

I look around. We aren't at the very back of the pack—some of the girls are walking—but we aren't going to make the eight-minute mark either. I put my head down, working to keep my breath even and think of a way to avoid becoming a panting, red, sweaty mess in front of Tom. No go. Even if he ran ahead, he would be there waiting at the end. Oh well. If the sight of me post-exercise grosses him out, he can suck it. "You really should go faster. There's still a chance Ms. Perry won't hate you."

"Nope. I'm fine. Just enjoying a leisurely run with my new best friend."

"New best friend? Seriously? Doesn't all this new-kid-with-a-heart-of-gold shit get old?"

Tom laughs. "Too much?"

"Yeah. Maybe a little. Are you always this friendly?"

"I guess so. It sort of becomes automatic when you've moved as much as I have. You learn to make a good first impression."

"Ahhh, so this isn't the real you? After a few days, you'll turn into a total jerk?"

"Maybe not a total jerk. I think I'm only occasionally jerky."

"Doesn't it wear you out to be so charming?"

"You have no idea."

We jog for a bit without talking, the only sound my laboring lungs sucking in air.

"If you lift your chin up instead of looking at the ground, you'll get more oxygen," Tom says.

I pretend to ignore him, but after a minute I lift my chin and find my breathing sounds and feels a little less desperate. After a few hundred yards of actual oxygen intake, my legs feel stronger too. And with my chin up, I can see the hillside of evergreen trees sloping behind the school and smell the late summer blooms from the hedge of heather growing along the fence line.

We finish the run in silence, and in spite of how it began, it isn't the worst three laps I have ever run. We don't make it in under eight minutes, and most of the rest of the class is waiting in the bleachers, bored, watching us down the home stretch. Some varsity wrestlers moo when I cross the finish line.

Tom stops, staring at them. He glances at me to see if I heard. I roll my eyes and sit on the bottom row of bleachers.

Tom climbs a couple rows up the bleachers toward the wrestlers. "Hi," he says. "Did you just moo at me?"

The wrestlers look confused.

"Is this some sort of Northwest welcome? Should I moo back?" he asks. "Or maybe some other farm animal sound is more appropriate. A pig, maybe? Or a chicken?" Tom clucks at them, and they shift from confused to pissed off. A couple people snicker. Tom turns his back on them and sits down on the bleachers next to me. Ms. Perry says nothing, but I can see her draw two large zeroes on her clipboard.

CHAPTER 4

It is almost seven when my mom walks in the kitchen that night. She kicks off her heels, drops her keys in the owl-shaped bowl on the counter, and hangs her bag on the back of one of the kitchen chairs. It tips over backwards, spilling her files out on the kitchen floor.

"Bring a little work home?" I say, watching her gather the folders and shove them back into the bag.

She puts it by the living room door, rights the chair, and collapses into it, rubbing her feet through her stockings.

I pour her a glass of wine and bring it to the table, kissing the top of her head.

"Thanks, honey. Yes, a little. I take the files for a ride in my car, then take them right back to work the next day. There's never enough time to get all my students' papers graded. Not if I want to do it right." She sips the wine, closes her eyes, and sighs.

Her eyes pop open. "How was your first day? Tell me all about it. Who'd you see? What did you learn?" She watches me pull a pan of my homemade mac and cheese from the oven.

The bread crumbs are golden, and the pale cheese bubbles around the edges of the glass baking dish.

Mom frowns. "Mac and cheese? It looks great, honey. But I think we need to start eating healthier, don't you?"

I pull a bag of mixed greens from the fridge and pour them into a bowl. "Salad." I turn my back on her and start banging around the kitchen, getting the rest of the meal ready. "Could you tell Dad it's time to eat?" I say, not looking at her. I feel her hand on my shoulder.

"I'm sorry, honey. I am so grateful that you made dinner, and that you help out so much. But I know how hard you worked this summer. And you lost a little weight. I don't want you to slip back into old habits."

I turn to face her. "Mom, I lost four pounds this summer. Four pounds! Not exactly a before-and-after story!" I slam the plates on the counter and toss the forks down next to them. They skitter across the orange Formica, banging against the backsplash.

"Maggie, don't . . . Come on."

"Mom. Listen. I know you're trying to help. You're always trying to help. But I think it's best if we accept the inevitable and stop talking about this." I move the casserole from the stovetop to a trivet on the counter and shove the serving spoon into it. "Daaaa-ad! Dinner!" I yell.

Mom starts in on her standard speech. I'm sure you know the one. Pretty face. Great personality. If you'd lose some weight. Blah, blah, blah.

"Mom!" I interrupt. "Give it a rest!" I start to dish up some mac and cheese and discover I have lost my appetite. Putting the plate on the counter, I wipe my hands on the dishtowel and stomp upstairs.

I throw myself on the bed, fuming at my mom's oblivious efforts to reform me. I have been hearing this shit my whole life. And I mean my whole entire life. As a baby my cheeks curved like peaches. By the time I was walking, my legs drew affectionate pinches from my mother's friends. But as I got older, the baby fat everyone hoped I would shed began to look like it was going to take up permanent residence around my middle, my thighs, my chins, and anywhere else it could take hold. When puberty hit about three years earlier than it did for most of the girls I know, hips and boobs rearranged the bulk a little, but the overall effect was the same. I have been on diets. I've seen doctors and nutritionists and counselors, and anyone else who might turn the cellulite tide. The thing is, I don't remember a time when I didn't take up more room than almost every other kid I knew.

And it wasn't that I was lazy. I was always busy. I roamed our neighborhood, riding bikes, playing in vacant lots, torturing my Barbies with a neighbor kid's Tonka trucks. During the summer I'd swim for hours in the local pool, but even with double workouts and swim meets every other weekend, my fat cells defended their territory.

So for seventeen years, my mom has expounded all the positive self-esteem crap that parents are told is good for their kids. And for the most part, it's worked. I feel pretty darn good about myself, much better than most of the bulimic coat hangers who occupy the top of my high school hierarchy. But Mom can't help mentioning the big "but," or should I say my big butt? I want to be thin. Of course I do. Who would want to go through life fat? And I like who I am except for that one detail. But it's a detail that nobody else seems to be able to see past.

I lie on the bed awhile longer, scuttling back and forth between anger and angst. Then I realize. I'm not hungry. I sit upright and plant my feet on the floor. I passed up mac and cheese. *Homemade* mac and cheese. My own secret recipe homemade mac and cheese. I scan my memory, trying to figure out when was the last time I skipped a meal. When was the last time I didn't feel like eating? Maybe when I got the stomach flu in eighth grade?

I pace, cracking my knuckles as I process this new information. As someone who has tried every diet in the book, I am highly attuned to the combination of hope and fear that flutters around the beginnings of any weight-loss possibility. But then, as I pace, I start to think about the mac and cheese. And then my stomach rumbles and the moment passes. I flop back on the bed, trying to recapture that feeling—or lack of feeling, I guess—but it's gone. I roll sideways, kick on my slippers, and pad downstairs for a bowl of pasta.

The door to my parents' room is shut, so I know Mom's in there with her work. When she has stuff to do, she locks herself in the bedroom, sits up on their king-size bed, and spreads the piles of papers all around her. She wears those noise-canceling headphones, but she never has any music playing on them. She puts them on to keep out all the other noise.

Dad is putting plates in the dishwasher. My dad is one of the only people I know who makes me feel physically small.

He's not overweight; but he's built on a larger scale than the rest of the world. He used to play football, and even though he's a little softer now than he was back then, he's still a pretty impressive guy.

"Hey, Monkey," he says as I slide onto one of the stools. "What's up?"

I sigh, resting my elbow on the counter, my chin in my hand.

"First day give you trouble?" Dad asks.

I shrug.

"Mom give you trouble?"

I push back the cuticles of my right hand with my thumb.

"She worries," Dad says.

"Why can't she just shut it about my weight? It always ends with a fight."

"Your mom loves you, Maggie. You know that."

"You love me. You never make me feel like shit," I say.

"Maggie, watch the language."

"Sorry. You don't make me feel like crap." I pick at a glob of dried cheese on the counter. "Do you worry about me?"

Dad is silent for a few moments, and this is a bit of a shocker. Things are always easy with Dad. It never occurred to me that he might be worried too.

I scrape at the cheese harder, avoiding his eyes.

"Like your mom does?" he says finally. "No. But I worry that you and your mom will miss knowing each other. I worry that you won't see how amazing you are, or how amazing she is. I worry that you don't give yourself or her enough credit."

He looks at me, and I feel like I'm eight years old, before all this stuff mattered, because I know that's how he sees me. The tears come, and Dad leans across the counter toward me. He takes a tissue and dabs at the corners of my eyes, like he did when I was little.

I give him a sad smile. "Thanks, Dad."

He dishes up a small plateful of macaroni and pops it in the microwave. When it's hot, he grabs a fork and napkin, lays them on the counter, and presents me with the plate of steaming, fragrant mac and cheese, swirling it under his arm first in what is supposed to be a fancy waiter move.

"Mademoiselle," he says in this French accent that sounds more like someone from a former Russian republic. "Tonight we have a delicious pasta with zee fromage and zee crumbs of bread on zee top."

Then we both put on our best Julia Child and say, *"Bon appétit!"*

I laugh and dig in. It's delicious, if I do say so myself.

"Remember," Dad says. "You're smart and strong and brave!"

"You always say that."

"And I always mean it." He puts his hands on my shoulders, kisses my cheek, and heads for his workshop.

I try to finish my homework, but my mind keeps hopping around, from my fight with Mom, to my dad's concern, to wondering about Tom and Nash, to trying to figure out what Kayla is up to. After a useless half-hour, I toss my pre-calculus

book on the floor and go downstairs. I can hear Dad banging around in his workshop, fine-tuning one of his inventions.
Mom's door is cracked open.

"Maggie," she says as I walk past.

I stick my head in the door.

Mom is lying in a nest of papers. She shifts her headphones
off her ears. "Honey, I'm sorry about earlier."

I shake my head. "No biggie."

"Still, I'm sorry. And dinner was delicious."

"Thanks," I say, and head to the kitchen.

I turn on the oven and start pulling out the ingredients for
oatmeal cookies. I can't play an instrument, and I can't draw
like Nash, but I can make damn good cookies. I learned from
the best; my grandma was a master cookie maker. Like her, I
get creative with the recipes. I invent all kinds of combinations,
making up new versions of old cookies. I don't want to eat all
those cookies myself; I just like making them.

So I give them away. I hand them out to people at school
or people who come into Square Peg Records, where I work.
I'm sure half of them throw the cookies away. If I'm honest, I
probably wouldn't eat something a stranger gave me in a record
store. But that part doesn't matter. I love seeing the surprise as
it dawns on someone that I've given them something delicious
for no reason at all.

Tonight I'm going to make oatmeal with extra cinnamon,
sunflower seeds, and something else. I haven't decided about
the something else yet. I'm blending the eggs and butter together when my phone rings.

"Hi, Cece," I say, adding some sugar to the bowl. "What's up?"

"I thought you were going to call me," she says.

"Sorry," I say. "My mom started going off and I forgot. What are you doing?"

"Homework," she says. "You?"

"Baking cookies."

"Oooooh! What kind?" Cece will eat as many cookies as I'll let her. She's one of those thin, waifish, smart girls who never gain a pound. Cece could be stunning if she wanted to play it up. But she has better things to do.

"Oatmeal," I say. "And something. I haven't decided yet."

"My favorite!" she says.

"They're all your favorites."

"True! So what did your mom and you fight about?"

"Oh, you know, the usual. Not meeting her rigorous standards."

"Yeah, I know the feeling," Cece says. "I'm glad you and Nash are in English. It would be so boring without you. I was thinking about reading a biography on Jackson Pollock for my first outside reading book. Do you know any good ones?"

"Cece, don't do that just because Nash was a little intense today."

"I'm not. I'm really interested. Nash was telling me more about Pollock in calculus. You know he really changed the face of modern art."

"Okay. Cool. I just don't want you doing stuff just because—" I stop, not sure how much to say. "There are a lot of good books out there. Make sure you choose one that's right for you."

"Sure. Of course." She's quiet for a minute, but I know she's still on the line. I can hear her breathing. "Soooo, Tom seems nice."

"Yeah," I say. "He's okay, I guess." I know where she's going with this.

"You guys all seemed like you were really hitting it off," she says. "So does Nash . . ." she starts. "I mean, is Nash . . . interested in Tom?"

I let out a long breath. "Cece, Nash hardly knows the guy."

"Oh, okay," Cece says. "Right."

"Cece, I'm sorry, but Nash is . . . You know you can't expect—"

"No, no. I'm good." I can almost see her holding up her hands to ward off whatever she thought I was going to say. "So are you going to bring me cookies tomorrow?"

"Of course," I say. "In English. See you then." She hangs up and I finish the batter. I decide to put dried apples in the mix, knowing they'll taste sweet against the extra cinnamon. I wrap the cookies individually—it makes them easier to hand out—and put them in a bag for the morning. I save one, put it on a plate, and pour myself a glass of milk. The cookie is still warm, and the apple pieces are soft and tart on my tongue. I am happy with the result, but even as I eat it, I am thinking about my mom. I'm a fat girl eating a cookie: Will anyone ever see more than that?

CHAPTER 5

My second day of school consists of the same classes, same kids, same awkward lunch with Nash and Tom, same humiliating PE session with Ms. Perry. I have a sinking feeling that junior year is notorious more for the mind-numbing tedium than the challenging content. I usually love school, but sometimes I think the teachers go out of their way to make it tortuous. I know some of the kids do.

I hand out most of the cookies, but I'm pretty careful about which Cedar Ridge students get to sample my creations. Lots of people beg, but only a few are worthy. The jerks from PE asked for some during lunch. Denied. They went on to make unimaginative comments about there not being enough cookies in the world for them to consider getting with me. As if.

After school Nash and I pass through the door of Square Peg Records, and I let out a breath I don't even realize I'd been holding. My boss, Quinn, gave me this job only after I came in begging three times a week for most of my freshman year. He really doesn't need the help, but he got tired of telling me no. Basically, Quinn lets me work there out of the kindness of his heart. The record shop is a life-saving oasis in the cultural desert that is my town. My days at Square Peg are the best of my week.

Quinn is straight up the coolest adult on the planet. He was born in Cedar Ridge but left for a brief, lucrative brush with fame when his postpunk band got some attention in the eighties. The band didn't last long. I never got the full story, but I know Quinn got his heart broken in the fray. Anyway, the residual cash was enough for him to move back here and open a record store that would be legendary in Seattle but can't possibly be making money here in Cedar Ridge. When we arrive, Quinn's grooving to the Smiths' *Louder Than Bombs,* singing along like he always does.

"How do you do that?" Nash asks.

"Do what?" Quinn says.

"Know every lyric to every record you play in this place? You even know the B-sides. It's freakish and slightly unnerving."

"It's a gift," Quinn says. "And maybe an occupational hazard."

Nash heads right for the import bins. On days I'm working, he usually hangs at Square Peg awhile, then plants himself at one of the downtown coffee shops until I'm done, anything to postpone going home.

I throw my loaded backpack under the counter and start looking through a stack of records Quinn has sitting out.

"Those just came in," Quinn says, looking at something on his laptop screen. "From a divorce, I think. They had a garage sale, but the vinyl didn't sell. I'm looking up the Lou Reed album to see if it's worth anything."

I pull the album out of the stack and ease the record from its paper sleeve, holding it by the edges like Quinn taught me. "No scratches or warping," I say, flipping it to side two. "A slight nick in the first track on side two, but nothing major."

Quinn puts on his reading glasses, which he keeps hanging from a chain around his neck like he's some kind of 1950's librarian. He bends down and examines the record from my angle. "Good eye," he says. "I missed that."

He takes the record and slides it back in the sleeve. Quinn goes back to searching the Internet while I sort through the rest of the stack.

I pull out R.E.M. and put it on the turntable.

Quinn glances at me, but I see the corners of his mouth pull into a slight smile.

The music begins and I crank the volume, singing along and dancing around behind the counter. The store is empty, except for Nash, so by the time Michael Stipe is belting out the chorus of "It's the End of the World as We Know It," we are all three flailing and pogo dancing like crazy people, screaming right along with him. I catch a movement out of the corner of my eye and stop mid-gyration as I realize Tom has come in and is dancing with us. Then the song is over and the guys are cracking up, breathless and happy for a moment.

Quinn follows my stare. "Sorry about that! Just trying out some of the new merchandise. Best way to sell it is to know it firsthand." He replaces R.E.M. with another Smiths album and returns to searching for info on the Lou Reed record.

"Tom!" Nash pats his hair and straightens his shirt. "When did you get here?"

"Sometime mid–dance party," he says. "Is that a regularly scheduled thing? Or did I get lucky?"

"You got lucky," I say.

Tom walks over to Quinn, holding out his hand. "I'm Tom."

Quinn looks confused.

"New guy," Tom adds.

Quinn nods, shaking Tom's hand, but I see he's trying to put the pieces together.

"What are you doing here?" I ask before Quinn can start wheedling information out of Tom. My voice sounds squeaky, and I let out this ridiculous little giggle that sounds like I've stepped on a herd of mice hiding behind the counter. Quinn stares at me. I clear my throat and will my voice to a deeper range. "So, what brings you to Square Peg?"

"Nash is going to show me around. I came downtown early to explore a little on my own."

"Oh." I look at Nash. He didn't mention Tom was coming by or that they had plans.

Tom is waiting.

I guess it's my turn to say something. "Cookie?"

"Huh?" Tom asks.

"You made cookies?" Quinn holds out both hands. "Gimme!"

I hand him one of the last three wrapped oatmeal cookies, toss one to Nash, then offer one to Tom.

Tom takes it, nodding, then holds it up to his nose, inhaling deeply. "Mmmmmm," he says. "Smells amazing."

"I think this cookie is my soul mate," Quinn mumbles.

Tom takes a slow bite, and his face rearranges into an expression I would bake all day to see. "Maggie, you clearly have a gift," he says, spraying a few oatmeal crumbs onto the counter. He wipes them off with his sleeve. "Sorry," he says. "They're . . . I mean, seriously . . . Wow!"

The three of them chew in silence as the Smiths sing "This Charming Man." Looking at Tom, I know the kind of man they mean.

"So." Tom wads up the plastic wrap and looks around the store. "Slow day?"

Quinn lets out a little snort. "You could say that. Slow day, week, month, decade."

"Well, vinyl's a hard sell," Tom says, setting down his backpack and starting to peruse the records in the sale bin. "But some of us understand its appeal." He holds up a record and flips it over to look at the tracks.

I smile. "So, Tom, you a big fan of tribal fertility chants?"

Tom plops the record on the counter. "Yep," he says. "I'll take this one. And do you have any of the song stylings of Mr. Tom Jones? My mother says I was named after my great-grandfather, but my dad told me the name was actually in honor of Tom Jones."

I show him the Pop Music section, and Nash joins him there. They stand, heads together, looking at records and talking. I can't hear them over the music, but Nash lets out an occasional staccato giggle I know is his nervous laugh. I return to the counter, and Quinn pounces.

"Sooooooo? Cute. New. Available?"

"Shhhhhh!" I whisper back. "Nash has dibs."

"You should go talk to him. Maybe Nash isn't his type."

"News flash, Quinn: Neither am I."

"News flash, Maggie: Tom's clearly a practiced flirt. *Anyone* could be his type."

Tom and Nash arrive at the counter with two more albums and a Square Peg Records T-shirt.

"Find what you wanted?" I ask, bagging up the records.

"I think so." Tom rests against the counter and leans in close.

I can smell the cherry cough drop he's been sucking on.

"Okay," he says. "What do I need to know about Cedar Ridge?"

"Not much to know," I say. "Smallish town. Smallish minds. A place people move to, to keep their kids safe from the temptations of Seattle."

"And what do Cedar . . . Ridgians? Ridgites? Ridgers? What do people here do for fun?"

"I'll go with Cedar Ridgians," I say. "And Nash will tell you there's nothing fun to do here."

"True story," Nash says, his face grim. He hops onto the counter, sitting next to where Tom's leaning. Tom elbows Nash's knee, and Nash gives him a gentle kick.

"And what would Maggie say?" Tom asks. He starts picking up things off the counter and putting them in different spots.

"Maggie would say she doesn't know." I return each item to its original location.

"There must be something?" Tom grabs a bundle of pens and starts arranging them into a spiked bouquet.

I remove the pens from his hands and throw them back into the cup on the counter with a tiny bit more force than is technically necessary. Persistence may be admirable, but it can also be damn annoying.

"I read. Hike. Work here," I say, flashing Quinn a sycophantic smile.

"You hike?" Tom sounds a little surprised.

"Ughhhh!" Nash groans. "Please don't tell me you're a hiker. How can you be a hiker when you've lived in all those lovely, non-nature-infested cities?"

"Sorry to disappoint, but living in cities has made me love being outdoors more," Tom says.

Nash gives a shudder. "Well, Maggie's your girl, then. Hiking's almost an illness with her." They both eyeball me as if trying to make this piece of information fit the image before them.

I know the nice thing to do is invite him along. I like to hike alone, but he's new and probably bored and lonely. And he's trying. Shit.

Quinn gives me a look, the one he gives when I need to be nicer to customers.

"Um, I'm hiking to the waterfall this weekend," I say. "I, uh, I guess you can come if you want?" But my heart isn't in the invitation.

"Great! Where should I meet you?"

I give him the details, and Nash and Tom leave the store, Tom whistling "It's Not Unusual" in a perky, annoying way that also makes me a little fluttery in my chestal region.

"Hmmmmm," Quinn says as the door closes behind Tom.

"What?" I say, but before he can answer, the bell rings and Kayla Hill walks through the door.

"You've got to be kidding me," I mutter under my breath.

I would be shocked if Kayla knew a turntable from a trampoline. And I'm surprised to see she's alone. Kayla's a pack animal for the most part. But she says hello.

"Hi." I retreat behind the counter.

She looks around awhile in that disinterested way people do. You can always tell. They flip through the records too fast, moving from section to section without paying real attention.

I watch her while I browse through the milk crate again, looking up and greeting customers as they straggle through the door.

After a bit, Kayla meanders up to the counter with a compilation entitled *Disco Duck*.

I look at the album, then at her. "Really?" I say.

Quinn kicks me under the counter.

"Ow! I mean, will that be everything for you?"

Kayla laughs her tinkling little laugh.

I bag up her album and hand it over.

"Thanks, Maggie," she says.

"Yeah. You're welcome."

She's halfway to the door when she turns around. "We should hang out sometime," she says.

I stare at her.

Quinn clears his throat.

"Um, sure," I say.

Kayla smiles, then turns and leaves, clutching her *Disco Duck* album like it's a solid gold hit.

"That was weird," I say.

"I know," says Quinn. "I've been trying to unload that record for, like, two years."

"Not the record," I say. "Kayla. Talking to me. That's the third time this week. Actually that's the third time in four years."

"Wait, what am I missing? Why shouldn't Little Miss Sunshine talk to you?"

"It's complicated," I mumble, putting Kayla's money in the cash register.

"Tell. Now."

"She doesn't talk to me. We don't talk," I say. "Not since seventh grade."

"And what happened in seventh grade?"

I think for a minute, trying to figure out how to describe what happened that shifted Kayla and me from friends to . . . well, to whatever we are now, which isn't anything, really.

"Well, we were friends, kind of: definitely one of my better friends besides Nash," I say, trying to explain without it sounding stupid, explain it in a way that communicates how much it sucked. "And then in sixth grade everything got weird — people started using the p-word."

"'Popular'?" Quinn says.

I nod. "Anyway, Kayla and I were still okay. Or at least I thought so. Over the summer we hung out a little, but just the two of us, never with her other friends, and I told her some things, about a guy I liked and about . . . other things." Here I get stuck, not sure how to make things clear.

Quinn raises his eyebrows.

"Girl stuff. Kayla and I . . . matured sooner than some of the other girls, so we talked about the ins and outs of our emerging womanhood. I love Nash, but he's useless when it comes to girl parts."

"Understandable, considering he only has boy parts and is only interested in boy parts," Quinn says.

"Still, does he have to cover his ears whenever I mention anything remotely related to my nether regions?" I ask. "Anyway, I couldn't talk to Nash about that, so I told Kayla."

"Uh-oh."

"Yep. Big uh-oh. The first day of seventh grade, all these kids knew about my period, my bra size, the boy, all of it. Turns out everything I told Kayla, she blabbed at a slumber party the weekend before school started."

"That bitch."

"Tell me about it," I say. "It was not an auspicious beginning to my middle school career. And the boy? Tyler? He was in one of my classes — math, I think. He came up to me before class and told me, in front of everyone, that I was crazy if I thought he could ever like a girl who was 'bigger' than him." Even four years later, my face burns hot thinking of Tyler's words.

"Ouch."

"I told him he was crazy if he thought I could ever like a boy who was dumber than me."

"Well done," Quinn says.

"Yeah. But it still ranks up there in my top ten most embarrassing moments. And I've had quite a few to choose from. All because Kayla couldn't keep her mouth shut at some stupid sleepover." I brush imaginary lint off my sleeve. "But whatever, we were twelve . . ."

"That's bad behavior at any age," Quinn says, pursing his lips.

"Anyway, we never really talked about it, never talked about anything, and that was four years ago, and now she's speaking to me again."

"Well, just because she's talking to you doesn't mean you have to listen."

"I know," I say. "But maybe I should give her a chance? She's been going out of her way to be nice. She even said hello in the cafeteria the first day."

"Oooo," Quinn gushes. "In public?"

"It sounds lame, doesn't it? She's probably just after Tom."

"Yep and yep," Quinn says.

"But still, we used to have fun."

"Make nice if you want, but proceed with caution."

I give him a knuckle punch in the arm. "Gotcha, boss."

"So, Nash has the new guy locked up—any worthy young men on the horizon for you in this brand-new school year?"

"Sure! I've been fighting them off with a stick as usual. I mean, how could they resist?" I sweep my hand down my body as if to show off desirable curves.

"Maggie, to the right person your dress size won't be any more important than your shoe size."

"I know that, and you know that," I say. "But nobody else seems to know that."

"Don't make me invoke the wisdom of Billie Holiday!" Quinn warns, shaking a finger at me. Quinn introduced me to Billie Holiday when I first started coming in. She's the ideal soundtrack for my unrequited love life. "What would Billie remind you of if she were here today?" Quinn asks.

"Avoid heroin and teen pregnancy?" I ask.

Quinn crosses his arms and waits.

I sigh and recite, "She would remind me that my lover man is out there somewhere, and it ain't nobody's business what I do."

Quinn nods, satisfied at last.

I pick up the stack of records. "Now, can we please listen to something cool and get back to work?"

Quinn flips through the RTP (records to play) bin by the turntable.

He pulls out an album, places it on the turntable, and drops the needle. Without warning, the chorus of "Rock You Like a Hurricane" by the Scorpions blasts through the store. Quinn is cracking himself up, waiting for a reaction.

I don't oblige. I stand there, records under my arm, waiting.

He stares at me for a minute, then grabs another RTP, drops it, and James Taylor is wailing the opening bars of "You've Got a Friend."

This one gets the merest hint of a smile out of me, but I'm still waiting for something I can work to.

He pulls another record, places the needle, and a rich but scratchy orchestral intro flows into the store. Billie Holiday starts to croon "Embraceable You."

Not what I was expecting, but it works. I make my way down the Classical aisle, my stack of records dwindling as Billie explains that just one look made her heart tipsy. I know how she feels.

CHAPTER 6

Nash calls that night, but between work, homework, and fending off Mom's efforts to enroll me in some sort of hybrid cycling-yoga-torture class with her, I don't have time to chat. I send him a text saying we'll talk at school. Besides, I don't really know what to say about Tom. He's perfectly nice, almost too perfectly. That's kind of what bugs me about him. But during school Tom's presence thwarts any dishy conversation concerning his relative merits.

By the next day, Nash looks like he's going to pop. As we're leaving the cafeteria, he pulls me aside, his voice low. "Our spot. Six o'clock. Come alone."

"Our spot" is the ancient swing set that faces the lake near the boat launch in the Cedar Ridge City Park. About five years ago, the city built a hideous new plastic playground on the other side of the park. They tore out the original playground toys, including an amazing old metal merry-go-round. I used to get that thing going crazy-fast, then jump on, lie down, and hang my head over the edge. Nash hated it, said it made him want to hurl, but he'd keep me spinning once I was on.

The only vintage playground equipment left is the creaky old swing set. Most people never go near it, but Nash and I meet there when we want to be alone, or be left alone. When I get to the park, Nash is already waiting.

"I have been busting to talk to you about Tom. By the way, do not"—at this Nash wags a finger at me—"do not ignore a call from me when you know I am feeling neurotic about a boy. That is Best Friend 101. Page two of the user's manual."

"Duly noted," I say.

"Here's what I've learned: There's the moving around, which you knew. His mom's great. Older brother at UC Berkeley. Dad's gone a lot. No pets. Keeps a journal. Favorite color is green."

"Wow, did you give him a survey or something? What's with all the random factoids?"

"People talk to me, Maggie. It's a gift. Anyway, your turn. Spill. Your impressions of Tom?"

I take my seat, always the swing on the left as we face the lake. "He seems . . ." I search for a word that will be both honest and neutral. "He seems nice," I finish. So much for that SAT vocab we've been doing in English.

Nash blinks. "'Nice'?" He stares at me. When I stay quiet, he gets out his iPod and starts to put in the ear buds, his mouth a hard line. "Okay, 'nice' is nice. If you don't have anything else to say . . ."

"Nash, I'm sorry. He's great. And he seems to like hanging out with you. It's just . . . well . . . don't you find him a little annoying? He's so . . . friendly. To everyone. And he said it usually only takes him a couple days in a new town to figure everyone out. What the hell does that even mean? Do we lack originality to the extent that there are stock versions of us in every town he's ever lived? Anyway, sorry. I didn't want to rain on your New Guy parade."

He takes out the ear buds and stares at me again. "Let me get this straight. You find his pleasant demeanor and interest in people irritating?"

"Yep, in a nutshell."

"Jealous much?" he says. "I admit I wish he was a little more standoffish with some people. Kayla, for instance. I don't trust her as far as I could throw her into a vat of boiling hot lattes. I don't mind if we lose Tom to someone worthy, but I will be more than a little disappointed in the young man if he doesn't see through the Kayla . . . thing. Whatever that is. Anyway, don't worry, Mags. Next new guy is all yours."

Nash smiles. I know as the best friend it's my job to ask the tough question. "So, do you think he's, like, into guys?"

Nash's swing goes still. He turns and stares at the lake for a minute. The light is fading behind the range of tree-spiked hills across the water, the shapes dissolving in those muted shades of purple and gray possible only in that moment between sunset and true dark.

"I honestly have no idea, Maggie." He doesn't look at me. "He's not from here, which means there's a chance, at least more of a chance than I have with any other guy in town. Until I escape Cedar Ridge's clutches, an out-of-towner like Tom is pure catnip for me."

I can tell I've killed his crush-buzz. Crushes are serious business to Nash. He has this book of boys he's fallen for. Nobody knows about it but me, and I've only seen it once. It's not a creepy, stalker kind of thing. It's actually sort of beautiful and sweet. It's more a way for Nash to figure out what he likes about his crushes and what he wants when he finally finds a real boyfriend. Once in a while he'll include a yearbook photo, but most of the time he does a portrait of them from memory. It's amazing what Nash can do with pen and ink. Sometimes we watch those reality shows about tattoo shops. It seems like every other episode someone's coming in to get a portrait tattoo of someone who's died. Nash could knock every one of them out of the park any day of the week.

Anyway, the book doesn't have real names, just nicknames he's given them, though his drawings would be enough to reveal each guy's identity in a heartbeat. But the important part to Nash is what he writes there. He once described it to me as "an anatomical study of unrequited love." He starts with what he likes about the guy, then as the crush evolves he adds to it, until the end, when he writes down why his feelings went away. He says it's a Crushology book, a way for him to know himself well enough to be able to identify the real thing when it comes along someday. When the stars align and he finds his match.

"Anyway, I can't help who I care about," Nash says, his voice quiet and serious now. "And I can't make someone love me back. I survived my dad leaving, and my mom too, in a way. If Tom's not into guys, it won't be the first time someone who mattered to me didn't want me. Or the last. I'll survive it."

Between the two of us, Nash and I have had more unreciprocated crushes than Cedar Ridge has stoplights. And if there's one thing it has taught me, it's that you don't die of a broken heart. Nash is right; he'll survive. We both will. I bump him with my shoulder, and he bumps me back. We swing for a few minutes in silence before going home.

As I pass my parents' bedroom on my way upstairs, my mom calls out, "Maggie, come in here." Mom is propped on the bed, student papers in tidy piles on either side of her. She frowns. "What's wrong?"

I paste on a smile. "Nothing," I say. "Why?"

"You look . . ." She waves a hand up and down at me. "Maybe it's your posture. Stand up straight, honey! It'll take ten pounds off you like that." She snaps her fingers.

I don't say a word.

"Sorry. Where have you been, anyway?" she asks.

"With Nash, in the park," I answer. "Swinging."

"Oh, good. How's Nash?" she says.

"Nash is fine." I wait. "Mom? Did you need something?"

"Hmmm?" she says, already distracted by her papers again. "Oh, your laundry's in the dryer. Make sure you get it out before you go to bed or everything will be wrinkled."

"Yep, I sure will, Mom." I give her a big thumbs-up and a cheesy smile. Pulling the door shut behind me, I wander to the kitchen to see what I missed for dinner. Chicken, veggies, and rice. Again.

I think about baking more cookies, but I have too much homework and my conversation with Nash has made me weary and unsettled. I forage in the cupboards for something starchy and sweet. The closest I come is a box of Cheerios, so I fill a bowl, pour the milk, and scoop sugar on top. Sitting at the counter I think about Nash and Tom until I hear the spoon scraping the bottom of the dish. I don't even remember eating the cereal.

I haul my laundry from the dryer, groaning as I dump it on my bed upstairs. About halfway through folding it, I transfer the pile to my chair and keel over onto my bed. I think about doing my homework, but before I can reach for my backpack, I'm asleep.

CHAPTER 7

Between work and school and listening to Nash ramble on about Tom, the week crawls by. When Saturday arrives, I am more than ready for some time in the woods. The sun reaches through the trees, dappling the road to the trailhead as it winds through the park. I'm half hoping Tom will have gotten lost along the way. I'm not an antisocial person, but I like to hike alone. When I was younger, our chocolate Lab, George, went with me so my parents wouldn't worry. By the time he died a couple years ago, they were so used to me going off into the woods, they kind of forgot that I didn't have a hiking partner anymore.

Rounding the corner to the parking lot, I sigh when I see Tom waving. There's no car, so I wonder how he got up here and realize I should have offered to drive him. I pull Mom's Subaru into a space and kill the engine.

"Hey!" Tom says. "I got here a little early. What a spot!" He's beaming, and I find I'm actually a little psyched to show him the trail.

"How did you get up here?" I ask as I grab my pack from the back seat.

"My dad dropped me at the park entrance. I ran up from there. It's such an amazing morning." He looks around again, his breath puffing little clouds into the sharp fall air. "By the way, you think I could get a ride home after?"

"Oh, yeah, of course," I say. In my mind I'm calculating the alarming amount of alone time I am going to build up with Tom today. "You ready?"

He nods, and we set off through the gate to the trail.

Tom stops to read a sign about bear sightings in the area. "Um, bears?" he asks. "Should I be worried?"

"Only if you think you can't run faster than I can," I say.

He chuckles but falls in next to me. He seems content to walk in silence for a bit, so I let myself find the rhythm of the pace and breathe in the early fall.

"The truth is," I say after a while, "the moose are more of a problem than bears around here."

"Moose?" Tom asks. "They seem pretty docile: kind of like tall cows."

"Have you ever seen a moose?"

"Well, no—I guess in pictures and stuff."

"Well, they're huge, and they can be very territorial, and if you piss them off or threaten their babies, they'll try to stomp you flat."

"Understood," Tom says under his breath. "Avoid pissing off local wildlife."

We follow the level part of the trail along the creek and into the old-growth cedar at the base of the mountain. I point out the occasional wildflower or chipmunk, but otherwise we don't talk much. As we wind up the switchback trail, I can hear Tom start to breathe heavier behind me. It's nice to know that not everything comes easy for him. The Patterson Falls loop is one of my favorite trails, winding uphill through some amazing cedar and fir forest. On the switchbacks, you catch occasional glimpses of the lake and town through the trees. We cross the creek a couple of times, but we don't stop until we're about twenty-five yards from the waterfall.

"Close your eyes," I say.

Tom looks like he's not sure he should trust me near the edge of a cliff.

"Just close them," I say. "It's better if you take it in all at once."

Tom nods, adjusts his pack, and closes his eyes.

I take his elbow and lead him the last few yards up the switchback to the viewpoint. Putting my hands on his shoulders, I position him facing Cedar Ridge and the lake. "Okay, take a deep breath, and open your eyes."

Tom opens them. His head swivels as he takes in the panorama of the mountains, the lake, and the glacial valley all laid out before him. "Wow," he whispers.

"That's Hitchcock Mountain," I say, pointing left over his shoulder. "And Rock Lake and town, of course." He's taller than me, so my arm touches his shoulder as I point. I feel his warmth through two layers of fleece.

Tom nods. "What's that?" he asks, pointing west to a mountain with a bit of snow and ice still visible in a basin below its summit.

"Mount Baker. I know: another amazing geological feature named after an obscure dead white guy. So imaginative."

Tom nods again. "Do you know how lucky you are to live someplace this beautiful?"

"Yeah. I do."

"So, why do we have the trail all to ourselves? Does Nash come up here?"

My laugh comes out in a snort. "Um, never. You heard him the other day. Nash doesn't do nature."

Tom turns and stares at me.

I'm standing so close behind that when he faces me, I can smell peppermint and something earthy, but good, underneath. Cologne, maybe, or some manly hair product?

He holds my eyes, and a small smile curls the corners of his lips. "How can you not 'do nature' when you live someplace this mind-blowing? That's stupid." He shakes his head and turns back to the view.

"Well, yeah, the woods are gorgeous, but Cedar Ridge is Podunk. It can feel a little sad," I say. "But we're close enough to Seattle to get our culture fix when we need to. If you want to see the city, Nash is your guy. He knows Seattle better than half the people who actually live there."

"Yeah, we talked about going sometime," Tom says. "And I don't think Cedar Ridge is Podunk at all. Or if it is, I like it that way. It's one of the best places I've ever lived."

"Then you must have been living in some pretty depressing spots," I say.

"Come on, Maggie," Tom says. "How can you look at this and not love it?"

"Still, I want to leave at some point, see the world and all that."

"Sure. Do it," he says. "But don't think you're going to find something out there that will be better than this. Different, maybe, but not better."

"You haven't even seen the waterfall yet," I say.

"In a minute," he says, turning and drinking in the view a bit more. Then we move up the trail, and Tom is struck silent again. Patterson Falls is narrow but tall—a much taller water-fall than you'd expect to find on such a short hike. "Wow," he says again. "I'm feeling the awe here. I had no idea Cedar Ridge had such hidden treasures." As he says this, he turns his head, and now he's not looking at the waterfall—he's looking at me.

I rub my sternum to calm the flurry of flying insects that have taken up residence in my chest. Walking to the edge of the stream, I bend and splash some water on the back of my neck, trying to push down the creeping heat there.

"You have water?" I ask, still crouched by the stream.

Tom holds up a water bottle.

"Do you want to backtrack or do the loop?" I ask.

"Your call," Tom says.

"Loop, then," I say, and hop across the creek on partially submerged rocks. Tom follows and we start down the trail to-ward the western slope of the hill.

"How often do you hike this?" Tom asks.

"Three or four times a year, maybe? It's my favorite, but there are lots of other good day hikes close in like this."

"Maybe you could take me on some of the other ones?" Tom asks.

"Maybe," I say, and I want to, but I'm wondering how Nash will feel if Tom and I become hiking buddies.

We are a quarter mile from the trailhead, back on the flat of the valley floor, when I hear something big in the brush just east of the trail. "Stop!" I whisper to Tom, and put my hand out.

"Very funny." He walks around my hand.

"Tom, shit, stop!" I whisper again, and this time he does. He turns slowly to face me.

"What is it?" His voice is softer now. A young bull moose comes out of the woods and onto the trail about ten yards behind Tom. It's not the biggest one I've ever seen, but it's big enough to do some damage.

"Moose," I mouth.

Tom's eyes widen.

I motion for him to turn around. He does, and the moose takes a step closer to us.

"Now, back up. Slowly," I whisper. We start inching into the tree line on the edge of the trail. The moose stands his ground but doesn't advance any farther. We make it to a large cedar and position ourselves so it's between the moose and us. I peek around the tree and see the moose still there.

Tom lets out a long breath. "What do we do now?" he asks. I shrug.

"Well, do they stick around awhile or move on or what?" I shrug again, and Tom sighs.

"He's so big!"

"Yep," I say.

After about ten minutes, we hear the moose crash through

the brush away from us. I check, and, sure enough, he's gone. "We can go now," I say.

We return to the trail and hurry down the last bit to my car.

"So what would we have done if he had, like, charged us or whatever?" Tom asks.

"Try not to die, I guess? I don't really know."

"Always a good policy," Tom says. "Try not to die."

We wind down the road to the park entrance, listening to music. After the intensity at the waterfall and the near-death experience with the moose, I'm not really feeling social. But Tom dives right into a mini version of the Spanish Inquisition.

"What's your favorite movie?" he asks.

"*Some Like It Hot*," I say.

"What's that?"

"Marilyn Monroe? Tony Curtis?"

Tom shakes his head.

"It's old," I say.

"Oh, no wonder. I hate old movies."

"How can you hate old movies?"

"I watch them, I get bored, so I hate them."

"What's your favorite movie?"

"*Lord of the Rings*," he says.

"Okay, not terrible. Geeky, but not terrible."

"Favorite band?" he asks.

"Nope. Can't answer that one. It depends."

"On?"

"On everything," I say. "On timing and weather and mood and who I'm with and what we're doing and . . . everything."

"Fair enough," he says. "Favorite place?"

"You just saw it."

He nods.

"You?"

"There's this place outside of Vegas, the Valley of Fire. No trees, no water, nothing but petrified sand dunes and ancient petroglyphs."

"That sounds . . . interesting?"

"I know. It seems like it'd be awful, but it's so strange and really amazing. The colors and the light . . ." He's moving his hands back and forth, like he's trying to clear away whatever's keeping me from seeing this place. "Anyway, that's my favorite."

We're in town now, so Tom gives me directions to his house, and I pull up in front but make no move to get out of the car. Their driveway is full of broken-down moving boxes waiting for the recycling truck. The realty sign, complete with a bright red "SOLD," has been uprooted and is lying on the lawn. The grass underneath is starting to turn brown, and I wonder how many times Tom's family has had a sign-shaped brown spot on their lawn, and whether they've ever stayed anywhere long enough to see it fade. Tom cracks his door open, but then stops and turns to me.

"Thanks for the thoroughly Northwest wilderness experience," he says, putting his hand on mine as it rests on the gearshift. He squeezes my hand lightly. Skin to skin, I feel heat but also a current that fires down my arm and settles itself like an ember, tugging the bottom of my stomach. I know we're not holding hands, not really, but it's as close as I've ever gotten.

He gives my hand one last squeeze and gets out of the car. "I'll always wonder how you convinced that moose to make an appearance." He slams the door and leans in the passenger window.

Now that he's out of the car, I find my voice again. "Ah, well, I keep a stable of trained mooses for just such an occasion."

"Mooses?" Tom asks. "Moose? Mooses? Meese? But seriously, thanks. It's the most fun I've had since I moved here." He waves and walks up the path to his house.

I let out a long breath, calming my heartbeat before I drive away.

At home, Mom is sitting at the counter picking at a salad and drinking a glass of iced tea. A stack of student papers sits in front of her, but I can tell she's not really reading the one she's holding. She smiles when I come in, putting the unread paper back on the stack.

"Maggie! Where have you been?" She takes stock of my dirty shoes and cut-off sweatpants.

"The waterfall," I say, dropping my pack by the door and unlacing my boots.

"Oh, that's great, honey. That's such good exercise."

I look at my mother, my face blank, but she doesn't take the hint. "Yeah." I start gathering my things to make my escape upstairs.

"Did you see anyone?" Mom asks.

I stop with one foot on the stairs. This is tricky stuff here. If I tell her I was hiking with a boy, she'll make a big deal and assume all kinds of savory details. I opt for the adulterated version of the truth. "Um, yeah. I ran into a new kid from school on the trail. And I saw a moose." I take another step up the stairs, my arms loaded down with my hiking boots, but Mom's quick.

"Really, someone new? Boy or girl?"

I cringe. Now I have to give details. "His name's Tom. He's new this year, moved from, well, I can't remember where he lived most recently. I know he's moved a lot. By the way, did you also hear me say I saw a moose? I was nearly trampled! It was right there on the trail . . ."

"You saw a moose?" Dad asks, coming in from the garage. "How big?"

"Tom? I haven't heard you talk about a Tom before. What's he like?" Mom asks.

"Tall. But not as tall as that moose . . ."

"Was it a bull or a cow?" Dad says.

"Oh, Steven! Forget the moose." My mom waves her hand in front of her face. "Was this a date? How did you meet him?"

I whisper, "Tell you later," to Dad, and he retreats to the garage. I turn back to Mom. "Nash and I met him the first day. And no, not a date. Nash likes him."

"Ooooh." Mom nods. "Oh, he's gay."

I consider letting this misconception save me from further interrogation, but I decide to stick with the truth. "Mom, I haven't asked him if he's gay or not, but he is not interested in me. We met at the trailhead. We hiked for a bit. We went our separate ways. Nothing more to report." I head for the stairs before she can speak again. "I've got to take a shower." But as I climb the stairs, I clutch my boots and steady my breath. I haven't been completely honest with Mom, or with myself.

Nash calls right after I get out of the shower. "How was your hike?" he asks without saying hello.

"Fine," I say. "We saw a moose. And the weather was—"

"No outdoorsy details, please. I'm really only interested in Tom-specific information," Nash says, interrupting.

"Um, Tom was . . . excited about the moose, impressed by the waterfall, and thinks Cedar Ridge is a great place to live," I say.

"You've got to be kidding! He said that?"

"He said that. But I told him that was because he hasn't seen Seattle with you. He mentioned you guys already had some kind of plan?" I don't want to be third wheel on Tom and Nash's adventure, but I'm usually Nash's Seattle guinea pig, up for anything he wants to try in the Emerald City. I'm bummed I might miss out on what I am sure will be one of his best itineraries.

"Yes. Definitely. That Monday, the teacher work day or whatever. We're going. I need you to be the designated driver." Nash doesn't drive.

"What, exactly, do you have in mind, Nash?"

"Don't worry, Mags. Nothing nefarious or illegal. Tom doesn't have his license yet. Besides, you always drive when we go to Seattle," Nash says.

"Oh," I say. "Great. I'll ask my mom if I can borrow her car again. I wasn't sure you wanted me to go—"

"Of course you're going!" I can tell from his voice that he never imagined anything else. Nash goes on to outline his plan, demanding my opinion about which options Tom will think are both cool and vaguely romantic. When we hang up, he's feeling more confident, and I feel more like the supportive best friend I want to be.

CHAPTER 8

By Monday the fluttery feeling I get whenever I see Tom seems to have faded a bit. But the next few days, I'm extra careful to give Nash and Tom time together. I eat in the library with Cece a couple times, take extra shifts at Square Peg so I'm busy after school, and make sure Tom and I end up on opposing teams in soccer during PE. Bio is the one place where I can't avoid one-on-one with Tom. It's pretty hard to get through a lab without talking to your lab partner. Besides, Kayla keeps circling. She's not stalking me, so Tom must be her prey. A part of me wonders if I should let Kayla have a shot at him to find out which way that gate swings, but I know letting Kayla close isn't going to help Nash.

The first lab is an onion cell thing to get us used to working with the microscopes. Tom keeps making lame jokes about peeling back the layers of an onion to reveal the complexity inside. I feel bad because he's trying really hard, but I think of Nash and stay focused.

"Oookaayy." Tom sighs. He leans down and looks through the microscope. "Let's get down to business."

I wait.

"Whoa, take a look at this," he says after a minute. He pulls me over and makes me look through the scope.

I do and see not the outline of a dyed onion skin cell but letters. I look at him, but he's filling out the lab report. Stooping, I squint through the lens again and start to pull the focus out so I can see all the letters. I decipher a tiny note written in block letters.

It says, "**be my friend.**" Tom is not making this easy.

I pull the note from the clamps, write, "**okay**" on it, then put it back in. I gesture for him to look through the lens and then sit on the stool doodling on the margins of the lab instructions.

He looks, peers up at me, looks again, and then grins. "Rad!" he says.

"'Rad'?" I smile for the first time all period. "Really? 'Rad'? Is this 1984?"

He ignores me. We whip through the assignment and hand it in just before the bell. We're almost out the door when I hear Tom's name.

"Can I talk to you a second?" Kayla asks him.

"Sure. Go on without me." Tom waves me away. "I'll see you there."

I hesitate for a minute, but I can't exactly lurk in the doorway while they talk, so I head to PE wondering which of Nash's nightmare scenarios is playing out between Tom and Kayla in the biology room.

I don't get a chance to find out until Nash and Tom show up at Square Peg after school. There are storm clouds brewing over

Nash's perfectly coiffed hair. I go on high alert when I see his expression.

He nods at me and heads straight to the Blues corner, as far from Tom as possible.

"How goes the fight, Quinn?" Tom asks. He seems relaxed, but I know he's too smart to have missed Nash's bad mood.

"Today we have exceeded expectations here at Square Peg," Quinn says. "How's that small-town adjustment period going for you?"

"Not bad," Tom says. "I think I already have more of a life here than at my last school, and I lived there for six months."

"Nice," Quinn says. "What's on the social calendar today? I'm sure it can't get any better than hanging with us listening to vintage vinyl."

"I'm actually meeting another friend here." Tom looks at his phone.

I glance at Nash as Tom says this; he's pretending to ignore the conversation. The bell rings and Kayla walks in. A cluster of her friends waits on the sidewalk outside.

"You ready, Tom?"

He nods.

Kayla links elbows with him and draws him to the door. Suddenly she stops like she's forgotten something. "Oh, Maggie. I was thinking we should have coffee sometime. I'd love to catch up." She says it like that's something we do once in a while: catch up over coffee.

I am stunned into silence. My scalp prickles. Everyone's eyes are on me, waiting for me to respond. My head bobs up and down like an involuntary spasm, but it must read as a nod to everyone else in the room.

"Tomorrow? Around six?" she says. The spasm must still be in effect because Kayla and Tom both smile their dazzling smiles like I've given the right answer. They wave and shut the door behind them with a jingle and a click.

"I know I'm several years removed from understanding the intricacies of the social scene at Cedar Ridge High, but that seemed a little weird to me," Quinn says.

"Yeah," I say. "*Twilight Zone* weird." Quinn and I are both still staring at the door when Nash speaks.

"What the hell was that, Maggie?"

I turn and see Nash's face, flushed and wounded. "What?" I say.

"That . . . whatever that was just now. With you and Kayla?" he says, sputtering.

"She's the one who asked Tom out. Personally I think she's barking up the wrong tree, but it's not like we can keep him from making other friends."

"Obviously Tom spending time with Kayla is heinous. But I'm not talking about her asking Tom out. I'm talking about her asking *you* out!"

"Oh, that. Yeah. *That* was unexpected."

"*That* was Kayla Hill!" he says. "You just agreed to hang out with Kayla Hill!"

"I know," I say. "I choked."

"To review: We don't say yes to coffee dates with evil people who tried to ruin our lives."

"Nash, she's not evil—"

"Oh, right, she just does evil things."

"Nash —"

"Do we need to take a walk down memory lane and relive Kayla's past wrongs against you?"

"No. I'm good. I remember."

"Then why?"

"Maybe she's changed?" I say it like I'm trying to convince myself.

Nash shakes his head. "Just be careful, Maggie," he says. "I don't trust her. Not with Tom, and definitely not with you."

"Nash, I'm sure Tom isn't really interested in Kayla."

"When has that ever stopped her from getting what she wants?"

"Tom's way too smart for that."

"I thought you were too smart for that too, but here you are, lining up for round two of the Kayla Hill smack-down." He grabs his book bag and heads out the door.

"You guys are better than reality TV," Quinn says, changing the record out. Over the store speakers, the Cure is singing "Boys Don't Cry," but I don't believe that's true.

I text Nash after work, but he doesn't respond. After my homework, I bake a fresh batch of Nash's breakfast bars; I think he's been sharing them with Tom. And I whip up some rosemary lemon shortbread. I glaze the cookies, placing a couple of rosemary sprigs in the icing on each one. They look plain, but it's amazing how much flavor's going on in each one. They're buttery and herbal, not too sweet.

I wrap the cookies, checking my phone one more time. Cece

called, but nothing from Nash. I put one piece of shortbread on a plate, make myself a cup of tea, and sit at the counter. Mom comes in as I take my first bite.

"Cookies again?" she says, and my jaw clenches.

I put the cookie down and brush the crumbs off the front of my shirt. "I was out of Nash's breakfast cookies, and I wanted to use the last of the rosemary from the garden," I say.

Mom looks at the cookie, but instead of the usual disapproval, her face relaxes into a wistful smile. "Shortbread." She sighs. "Your grandma used to make shortbread. She was famous for it. It was always my favorite."

I have probably only seen my mom eat a half-dozen cookies in my entire seventeen years, so this is a revelation to me. "Have one." I grab one of the wrapped cookies from the bag and offer it to her.

"No, those are for your friends," she says, stepping back.

I lean forward, trying to touch her with the cookie. "Take it, Mom. They're not for anyone in particular. I bake them so I can give them away."

But she takes another step back and shakes her head. "No, thank you, honey," she says. "I'm sure they're delicious, but I . . . I can't." She purses her lips in a tight little line. She thinks *I'm* the one with food issues?

I toss the cookie back in the bag. "I'm going to bed. Good night, Mom." Taking one last swig of my now-cold tea, I leave the mug and my half-eaten shortbread on the counter.

CHAPTER 9

I jump on the bus the next morning and rush down the aisle to Nash. Collapsing onto the seat, I pull out a baggie with a fresh-baked breakfast bar. "Peace offering," I say, handing it to him. "Sorry."

Nash takes the bar and starts eating. "Sorry too," he says, covering the partially masticated cookie with his free hand. "Let's chalk it up to low blood sugar." He indicates the bar.

Putting my head on his shoulder while he eats, I notice Tom isn't on the bus. I wait until Nash is done and has neatly folded the empty baggie and placed it in his backpack before I speak.

"So, what's the plan?" I have no idea where Tom is in the Nash Taylor–crush life cycle at this point.

"Well, we have that trip to Seattle on Monday," Nash says. "And Tom and I are watching some weird Japanese sci-fi movie after school today. He called last night, after he got home from hanging out with you-know-who."

"And?"

"And we talked until after midnight." Nash sighs. "Even over the phone he makes me swoon."

"'Beware of fainting fits. Beware of swoons.'"

"Huh?"

"*Mansfield Park*."

Nash still looks confused.

"Jane Austen?" I say.

"I thought you were over your Austen obsession."

"Just some friendly advice." I give Nash a couple more breakfast bars. "So, you sure you want to keep going? Is he worth it?"

Nash nods, smiling; he's not ready to let go of this one yet.

The bell on the door at Square Peg jingles right before six, and I look up, ready to tell whoever it is that we're closing, but it's Kayla. My whole body tenses. I wasn't actually expecting her to show up. I thought the whole coffee invite had been for Tom's benefit. Now that she'd had her date with him, I didn't expect her to keep pretending she wanted to be friends with me. But she strides up to the counter, says hi to Quinn, and turns to me.

"Maggie? You ready?" she asks.

I look at Quinn, who nods, and grab my stuff. "Let's go."

Kayla and I settle into a booth at Common Groundz, the café nearest Square Peg. I'm always amazed when people incorporate puns into their business names like that. It seems to be rampant among coffee shops and hair salons. Here in Cedar Ridge we have coffee shops called Bean Me Up, Human Beans, Espresso Yourself, and C U Latte. The salons are even worse: Hair of Coarse, Curl Up and Dye, and my personal favorite, Hairanoya.

Kayla grasps her caramel latte in two hands and smiles. Her teeth are perfect and white. They look like Chiclets.

I chug my glass of ice water and then take a sip of my too-hot americano. I look at Kayla.

She looks at me.

I wait.

She waits.

"Awkward" doesn't even begin to cover it.

"Sooo . . ." I begin.

"I know . . ." she says.

"You go ahead," we both say at the same time.

"Jinx!" we both say at the same time again. We stare at each other a minute, and then burst out laughing. Ice officially broken.

"So . . . why are we here?" I ask.

"It's my favorite coffee shop in town."

"No, why are we here together?"

Kayla looks down at the rosette of white steamed milk and brown coffee crema inscribed on the top of her latte, then somehow takes a sip without destroying the design.

"I just," she begins. "I thought it would be nice to get to know you. Again." She smiles, but she's less sure now.

"Seriously, Kayla?" I say. "We've known each other forever, but I don't think you've spoken to me for at least four years. Not since . . . well, not in a long time. Why now?"

Her face morphs through several expressions in a few seconds. I see a flush in her cheeks as her nostrils flare. Her eyebrows scrunch together. She follows this with a smile that doesn't quite make it to her eyes. Around the eyes there's something else, something that makes me think of the Kayla I used to be friends with.

"Look, if you don't want to do this . . ." She looks down and starts fishing for something in her bag.

I don't want to be mean, and I'm beginning to think, even hope, maybe there's more to Kayla's invitation than a power play to get near Tom. "No, wait," I say, putting my hand on her arm. "I didn't say I didn't want to do this. But you have to admit: it's a little out of the blue. I'm just trying to figure out the motivation."

She looks at her coffee cup. "I guess," she starts. "I guess I look around at my friends sometimes and get a little bored. And then I see other people, like you." She glances up. "People who have been around but background noise, you know? And I begin to think I'm missing out."

"Background noise? That's flattering."

"I didn't mean . . ." She starts to apologize, but then she sets her mouth in a tight little line. "Isn't that what my friends and I are to you and Nash? Background noise? You don't know anything more about me or my life than I do about you and yours."

I start pushing at the skin around my cuticles, then rip off a hangnail on my thumb. It starts to ooze blood, so I put it in my mouth and suck on it, tasting the sour tang. Kayla's still waiting for an answer. "Okay," I say, taking the thumb out of my mouth. "Fair enough. Things have changed for both of us since elementary school."

She stares into her coffee like it's some kind of crystal ball. "But we did have some fun back then, didn't we?"

"We did," I say. "At least I did."

"I did too. Sometimes I feel like those last couple years of grade school were as good as life gets. Before things got . . . complicated."

"But we're not eleven anymore. It can't all be about Barbies and board games."

"I know. But when we ended up in a couple classes this year, I remembered . . . Well, I thought maybe we could, you know, be friends. Again." She picks at a flaw in the glaze of her cup.

Sitting there, I remember what it was like to be Kayla's friend, remember what it was like before things like perfect teeth and plus-size jeans mattered. She laughed at my jokes. She listened.

"So," I say. "Where do you see this relationship going?"

She laughs.

"Too soon?"

"Too soon," she says. "No agenda. Let's talk, and if we bond, we'll go from there. If there's no bonding, we've at least removed a little bit of the background noise."

So we talk. For about an hour: the basics, what Nash would call first-date material. I'm surprised she had a horseback-riding phase in middle school, although I remember that she used to have a collection of those Breyer Horses (me too).

She's surprised I watch documentaries and hate strawberry ice cream (her favorite). We are still going strong when I plead homework and have to go home.

"Thanks for this," Kayla says, and I think she means it.

"Thank you," I say. "I'm a little low on female interaction in my life."

"Yeah, it seems like most of your friends are guys, but I wasn't sure."

"Yep. Mostly guys. And I keep adding to the club."

"Some girls would love to be surrounded by guys all the time." Kayla fidgets with her cup, turning it in circles. "I noticed you were getting pretty tight with Tom."

"I've only known him a little over a week, but he's a decent addition to the Cedar Ridge universe, I think."

"We had fun last night," Kayla says. "There were a bunch of us for dinner, but everyone else had homework, so it was just me and Tom for the movie."

That almost sounds like a real date. I don't really want to know if Tom's the kind of guy who would rather hang out with Kayla and her friends than Nash and me.

"I got pretty nervous on the way home," she says. "He's kind of adorable."

"Yep, pretty cute," I say, smiling.

"And I thought I was good at flirting? Tom is a master."

"I've noticed he has some pretty potent skills in that area." I think about the hike and the drive home afterward. I think about Tom's low laugh and the electric current when he touched my hand in the car. But then I think of Nash, and I remember who I'm talking to. "I don't mean he was flirting with me. It seems like he's like that with everyone. He and I are just friends. Obviously."

"Why 'obviously'?"

Irritation tightens the skin around my eyes. She has to know that Tom plus Maggie does not compute.

"That's how it is. Me being who I am, him being who he is."

Kayla looks at me, waiting.

"Well, anyway, he's nice. And he's new. You should get to know him better."

"That's the plan," she says.

"Sure," I say. "He's going to need more friends than just Nash and me." Did I just encourage one of the most beautiful and popular girls at Cedar Ridge to pursue Tom? But Kayla didn't seem to need much encouragement. Whatever. Hanging out with Kayla has been nice, but I've had my quota of female bonding for now.

"I gotta go, Kayla. I'll see you tomorrow." I turn and go through the door and out into the brisk fall night. Being with Kayla was easier, more familiar, than I expected. And it was nice to talk to a girl for a change. There has been entirely too much testosterone in my life lately.

CHAPTER 10

Since Tom hasn't actually spent any time in Seattle, Nash is planning a dawn-until-dark sort of excursion. All the pieces of Nash's itinerary are falling into place. As chauffeur, I have no say in where we go, but I don't mind. We are finalizing plans at lunch on Friday when Cece comes by.

She rests her lunch box on the table but seems unsure about actually sitting down. "So, what are you all doing for the long weekend?"

I look sideways at Nash and Tom. Monday is their deal, so I know I can't invite Cece.

"The usual—you know." Nash fidgets, eyes on his sandwich. "How about you?"

"Mostly homework," she says. Cece's the one fidgeting now. "But I have tickets to the modernist exhibit at the art museum in Seattle. I was wondering if you'd like to go with me on Monday, Nash?" Cece pushes this last bit out of her mouth in one quick rush, so quickly in fact that it takes us a few seconds to catch up with her. Cece's whole face flushes bright red as she waits for his answer.

I marvel at her courage and blind persistence. Tom and I both look at Nash.

"You have tickets for that? I have been dying to go," Nash says.

"My mom got them for me." Cece still isn't meeting Nash's eyes. "I figured you'd be the perfect person to go with. You know so much about art."

"There's supposed to be a Warhol and a Pollock. I would do anything to see that."

Cece's face breaks into a wide smile. "Great. We can go early and—"

"But I can't Monday."

Cece's features fall back into a disappointment that's hard for me to look at.

Tom catches my eye, and I can see he feels the same way.

"Oh, okay," she says. "I'll . . . that's fine. Thanks." She turns to walk away.

"Eat lunch with us," Nash says, throwing her a bone.

She turns toward us. Her smile is back, although not as wide as it was a moment before. She slides into a seat next to Tom, and we spend the rest of lunch talking about what animals our teachers would be if they were animals, smoothing over Cece's hurt feelings. Just before the bell rings, Nash presents Cece with a sketch he did while we were talking. It's Cece, arm outstretched, with a snowy owl perched on her arm.

"You'd be an owl," Nash says. "Get it? Because you're so smart."

Cece takes the sketch, holding it like he's just presented her with a diamond. "Thank you, Nash. It's beautiful."

• • •

Tom asks about it while we're walking to biology. "So Cece?"

I nod. "Cece has a mad crush on Nash. For, like, two years."

"And does she know . . . ?" Tom says.

"Does she know what?"

"That he's gay?"

I look at Tom. This is the closest we've gotten to this topic, and I want to just ask Tom if he likes guys, likes Nash in particular. But I'm also worried about his answer and about finding out something that will burst Nash's bubble. I want us all to be able to enjoy the not-knowing just a little bit longer. "She does and she doesn't," I say. "She knows, but that doesn't keep her from liking him."

"Ouch," Tom says. "Rough."

"Yeah. I never know what to say. Do I do the tough love thing and tell her, 'Nash will never like you that way'? Or do I let her like him and wait for her to figure it out on her own? A day like today, I feel like I should slap her upside the head. Keep her from humiliating herself." We walk in silence for a bit before Tom speaks.

"I don't think she's humiliated," he says. "Not in the way you think. When you like someone, you do what you have to do. I think what she did was brave in a way."

"Yep, the girl has guts," I say. "I don't think I could ever put myself out there like that, not without some guarantees."

"Hormones win every time."

"So you think it's all just physical?"

"No. But we don't get to choose who we fall for."

"Nash said that same thing the other night," I say.

"Nash is a smart guy."

Since we didn't get to finalize all the plans at lunch on Friday, Nash is frantic all weekend. He texts me repeatedly about the schedule, his wardrobe, where we should eat, where we should park. He's in full cruise-director mode, trying to anticipate every detail. Nash is both adorable and exasperating when he has a crush. The whole world becomes about setting up a series of encounters that happen accidentally on purpose. Some of the guys never even realize they're being stalked, and most of the ones who do freak out.

So Nash is putting a lot of eggs in this Seattle trip basket. In a way it's Tom's own fault. Most guys would have blown Nash off by now. They become either consciously or unconsciously uncomfortable with his attentions and push him away or run in the other direction. Tom just keeps hanging out like it's no issue at all. He must have some idea how Nash feels, but Tom is so friendly all the damn time; it's hard to tell what he's thinking. He's given Nash the only thing a crush feeds on, the only thing that keeps a crush from dying: hope.

Late Sunday night, Nash calls for what I sincerely hope will be the last time.

"Okay," he says without saying hello. "I have a checklist."

I yawn, trying to communicate how completely not interested I am in this final neurotic manifestation of Nash's nerves.

"You ready?"

"Yep," I say.

"Gas in car," Nash says.

"Check."

"Kick-ass playlists for trip."

"Check."

"Are you sure?" Nash sounds skeptical. "None of your indie-folk-sensitive this-is-the-soundtrack-of-my-life kind of play-lists. I'm talking about really cool stuff."

"Check!" I say, a little louder.

"Money?"

"Check." I yawn again. "Wait, money for me, or do you need me to bring money for you, too?"

"Both?" Nash says. "Pretty please?"

"Yes, check." I can raid my piggy bank and pay it back out of my next paycheck.

"Thanks, Mags," he says. "I want it all to be . . ."

"It's going to be great, Nash," I say. "He's going to have a great day. We're all going to have a great day."

"Okay, you're right. I know," Nash says. "I just really, really want this to be special."

"It will be special, Nash. But if I don't get some sleep, it will be special because we all die in a fiery car crash when I fall asleep at the wheel. Now, good night."

"Good night, Mags."

I hang up the phone. I try to read, but my mind keeps wandering back to Seattle and Nash's plans. All the questions I have about Tom and Nash and whether my best friend has a chance in hell are front and center, making me restless.

The image of a soft, sweet comforting Twinkie pops into my head, and I wonder briefly if my dad still has some stashed in the garage near his workbench. When my tendency toward tubbiness made itself clear, Mom banned all junk food from the house. No chips, candy, ice cream, and definitely no delicious, spongy, cream-filled snack cakes. Twinkies have always been Dad's favorite, his kryptonite. But our house has been a Hostess-free zone for about six years now. Except for, I discovered one day when I was thirteen, my dad's workshop. There, in a toolbox shoved under the workbench, he kept a few choice snack foods that would make Ms. Perry squirm. And I know for a fact that he stocked up when they briefly stopped making Twinkies a couple years ago, although I have no idea where he's hiding that mother lode.

The promise of some sponge cake to distract me from tomorrow's anxieties propels me into action. I slide off the bed and into my slippers, easing my door open. I pad dowstairs and past the living room, where Dad is watching some gruesome forensics show while Mom grades papers next to him on the couch. When I get into the garage, I grab the flashlight next to the door so I don't have to turn on the overhead light. The cylinder of yellow light makes the darkness around it seem denser somehow. Swinging the beam to the workbench, I bend a little until I find the red steel of the toolbox underneath. I hold the flashlight under my arm, open the box, and there before me are a half-dozen plastic-wrapped packages of emotion-numbing fat and sugar. I grab an individually wrapped Twinkie and then a mini-sleeve of Oreos for good measure.

Back in the house, I slip the packages up the sleeves of my flannel pajamas, hiding them in case my parents look up as I'm walking past. I do not want to have a conversation with my mother about the evils of junk food or my unrealized potential right now. Nor do I want to rat out my dad's secret stash. I'm almost past the door of the living room when Mom looks up.

"Hi, honey. What are you doing?" she asks.

"Nothing, um, just taking my vitamins. I forgot this morning." I keep my arms and snack foods resting quietly at my sides so the plastic wrappers won't crinkle and give me away.

"Good. You should take those every day, especially the calcium."

"Yep. That's why I came downstairs. Thanks, Mom." I hightail it past the living room and back to the privacy of my bedroom, where I can enjoy my junk food in peace.

Pushing the door closed, I plug in my iPod. I find a mellow playlist and start the music. Then I circle my bed and wedge myself between the bed and the wall on the floor. I open the Oreos first, delaying my Twinkie bliss for a few more minutes. The crunchy creaminess and bitter chocolate dull my anxiety a little, and by the time the sleeve is empty, I am ready for the pure pillowy comfort of sponge cake and chemical sweet cream. I go through my ritual, eating the Twinkie from the inside out. And after I have dissected and devoured, I am calmer.

But then I look at the empty food wrappers on my bedroom floor, and my cheeks flush with shame and self-loathing. There's a knock on my door.

"Maggie? You in there?" Mom starts to turn the knob, and I stuff the wrappers under my bed, wipe my mouth, and flop myself on top of the covers just as she opens the door.

"I just wanted to say good night, sweetie. And be safe tomorrow." She leans over to kiss me, and I pray she won't smell the sugar and chocolate on my breath. Mom pauses at the door. "Light on or off?"

"Off. Thanks." She flips off the light and closes the door, and I roll over, breathing a sigh of relief that she didn't catch me.

But the sense of calm I got from the sweets is gone after the narrow escape with Mom. My thoughts wander back to Nash's plan, and Tom's expected role in it, and Cece's disappointment. I lie there for way too long wondering about Tom and Nash and Cece and Kayla and the whole confusing tangle. In some ways I feel lucky to be outside that fray. At least I know that when and if someone ever falls for me, it won't be because they're hot for my bod. I'll know they see something more.

CHAPTER 11

Monday morning comes way too early, and I always spend too much time stressing over what to wear when I go to Seattle. I know it's dumb. The city's full of people I will never see again, but I don't want to look like a total dork. I want to look like I could belong there.

I knock on Tom's door. A woman opens it, tall and slim and lovely in that nonchalant way some women have. Dressed in faded Levi's, pink flip-flops, and a flannel shirt that, judging from the size, was probably borrowed from either Tom or his dad. I tug down my own shirt and straighten my sweater, giving her my best meeting-the-parental-unit smile.

The woman grins as if I'd brought her a winning lottery ticket. "You must be Maggie! Come in, come in!" Boxes are piled high in the living room and near the entrance of the kitchen, but they'd managed to hang some pictures in the entry hall. Two little boys, one slightly older than the other but both very Tom-ish, stare out of frames that line the hall. As Tom's mom leads me to the kitchen, the photos form a timeline, moving from chubby-cheeked babyhood to the most recent one, a portrait in adolescent awkwardness that looks no more than a couple years old. "Tom and his brother, Colin," Tom's mom says. "I'm Jen, by the way." She sticks out her hand.

I shake it and try the parental smile again. "Nice to meet you." I look around the kitchen, which seems fully intact. No sign its contents had recently been in boxes.

"I always unpack the kitchen first," Jen says. "The living room, the guest bathroom, those things can wait. Who are we going to invite over, anyway? But it's not home until there are some spaghetti splatters on the stove." She points to one of the kitchen chairs and I sit. "So, Seattle?" she says. "Anywhere special?"

"Not sure, actually," I say. "Nash is the man with the plan. I'm just transportation."

She gives me a once-over.

"I'm a very safe driver," I add.

"You seem safe," she says.

Safe. It stings a little; I'd like to think of myself as edgy and a little dangerous. But I know in parent-speak she's given me a compliment.

"Maggie." Tom stumbles into the room from a back staircase. "You're here." He runs his fingers through messy hair and wipes a little toothpaste from the corner of his mouth. Grabbing some high-tops from the pile near the back door, he sits at the table and starts lacing them up.

"It's okay," I say. "I'm early. Painfully prompt to most things. Take your time."

Tom tugs at his shoes as Jen leans close to him. "Did you get those new Odor-Eaters I bought you?" she whispers.

"Mom!" Tom stands, grabs his coat, and grimaces at me. "Maggie? You ready?"

We hurry down the hall, the fraternal timeline rewinding so the last thing I see before being ushered through the door is an adorable baby Tom smiling out at me.

I head the car to Nash's house.

"Sorry about that," Tom says. "She's really . . . I don't know what she is."

"She's great," I say.

"Yeah, actually she is. Sometimes I get pissed off having to move so much. But at least I have a built-in way to make friends because of school. It's harder for Mom. But she never complains. And Stephen doesn't even notice."

"Stephen?" I ask.

"My dad."

"You call him Stephen?"

"Yeah." Tom puts his shoe on the dash and reties the laces. "It's kind of . . . I started doing it a couple moves ago. Colin was going to college, and my dad announced another move, and I was totally pissed off. So I stopped calling him 'Dad' and started calling him 'Stephen.'" Tom smiles. "He hates it."

"So moving so much has been—"

"Moving so much has sucked." Tom starts chewing on his cuticles. "Like I said, I've gotten used to it. I've learned how to settle in because I've had to do it so many times. But I'm always aware that I could get home on any given day and my dad could say we're moving again. So I never really . . . I guess I never really invest, you know what I mean?"

I nod. "One foot out the door all the time?"

"Exactly!" Tom says. "That's it exactly."

We ride in silence for a minute. "So, the Odor-Eaters?" I say.

"Bad," he says.

I give him a skeptical glance.

"Really, really bad," he says. "Toxic Avenger bad. So bad you can taste it bad."

"Ewww! Taste it? Really?"

"Yep," he says. "Sexy, right?"

"Dead sexy."

"Dead fish sexy."

"Just don't tell Nash," I say. "He has sort of a smell . . . thing. As in he doesn't like things to smell. At all. Ever."

"Good to know," Tom says. "Speaking of which: Nash bailed."

"What?" My head swivels, and I stare at Tom. "What do you mean, 'Nash bailed'?"

"I mean bailed, flaked, ditched."

"Why?" I ask.

"Not sure."

"Well, what did he say, exactly?"

"Something about chores he forgot and going to his mom's doctor's appointment?"

I nod. These are standard Nash codes. What they really mean is that his mom got plastered and he has to either clean up the mess, nurse her hangover, or both.

"Why didn't he call me?"

"No idea."

And now I'm not sure what I'm supposed to do. Did Nash call Tom instead of me because he wants me to take Tom to

Seattle anyway, and he knew if he called me, I'd find a way to postpone? Or did he call Tom instead of me thinking I would automatically know that he didn't want me to carry on without him and would come up with an excuse on my own? I find I'm not up to the task of reading Nash's lovesick mind at the moment, so I turn into a parking lot and grab my phone.

"What's up?" Tom asks.

"I need to just—I need to check something." I text Nash. **What's going on? Why aren't you coming?**

Mom. Why else? Nash texts back.

We'll wait and go when you can come too.

No. Go without me.

No. No way. I'm not letting her wreck this for you.

Nash doesn't text back.

I'm coming over. I'm coming to get you.

Don't you dare! She's bad today. I do not want Tom here!

"Everything okay?" Tom asks.

"Yeah, just asking Nash about his plan for Seattle. Don't want to screw it up." I text Nash again. **I hate that you are going to miss this.**

Me too!

Call you later. Love your guts.

I let my phone rest in my lap, staring at it. Then I toss it into my purse with a little more rage than I intended.

"Okay, so I guess we should get going?" Tom says it as a question, giving me the chance to back out.

But I nod, put the car into gear, and pull back into traffic. We're almost out of town before either of us speaks again.

"Nash and his mom seem really close," Tom says.

I glance at him. Nash's shit is Nash's shit, and I'm not sure if I should say anything. But Tom has clearly picked up on some of the nuances of Nash's family relationships. My thumbs are tapping a spastic Morse code on the steering wheel. "She can be a little needy," I say.

Tom's still waiting for an explanation.

I sigh, then spill. "So the short version is that Nash's dad disappeared a few years back, leaving a gigantic crater in their lives. His mom's tried to fill the hole with booze ever since." I'm all in now so I forge ahead. "I guess Nash sort of blames himself for his dad leaving, so when his mom is bad, his guilt kicks in and he feels like he should take care of her."

Tom watches the road for a minute. "That's sweet," Tom says. "That's actually really cool."

"Yeah, but she's bad a lot," I say. "And none of this is Nash's fault. I wish he didn't have to miss so much of his own life trying to put hers back together."

"So missing today will bum him out?"

"Catastrophically," I say.

"You still want to go, though, right?"

We're stopped at a red light, and I glance over at him. He looks so hopeful, like a kid who's been waiting all week for a trip to the candy store, which I guess he kind of is.

I sigh. "Sure. Of course I want to go," I say. "If you want to. It won't be as much fun without Nash."

"I'll never know the difference," Tom says. "Besides, Maggie Bower, you're my source for fun in Cedar Ridge."

"Yeah," I say. "I am famous in lab partner circles as being on the cutting edge of fun." I turn to look at him, expecting him to share the joke, but he's not laughing.

He's looking at me with those green eyes, his head tilted a bit, like he's thinking about something.

My face gets hot, but I don't look away. I like looking at Tom looking at me. It's like fingers brushing my cheek—the touch is gentle, but it brings goose bumps anyway.

I hear a honk behind me. The light is green. I accelerate and change lanes so I can make the turn that will get us down to I-5 South.

Tom takes in the scenery as we leave Cedar Ridge's punch-bowl valley behind and descend into the flat near the freeway. After a while he picks up my iPod and puts on a playlist I titled "Weekend." This is not one of the playlists Nash would approve of. It's pretty mellow, but it's one of my favorites. After a couple songs, Tom laughs to himself.

"I love it," he says, chuckling.

"What?" I say, a little defensive. "Change it if you don't like it."

"No, no. I really do love it," he says.

"Explain yourself."

"I love that your idea of 'Weekend' is not some raging party mix, but this soulful, quirky, folkish kind of thing."

"Sorry. Nash told me not to play that one. I'm not a party animal. Never got invited, never wanted to."

"See, there. That's what I'm talking about," he says, as if he'd made his point perfectly.

I stare at the road for a minute, trying to figure out if I missed something, but I'm pretty sure I didn't.

"You are 'a riddle wrapped in a mystery inside an enigma.'"

I stare at him for a beat longer than is technically safe at highway speeds. "Bullshit," I say.

"I'll thank you not to denigrate the sacred words of my namesake in such a fashion," Tom says.

"Tom Jones said that?" I say.

"Winston Churchill," he says.

"What?"

"I am named after Winston Churchill."

"I thought you were named after Tom Jones?" I say.

"My first name is for Tom Jones, my middle for Winston Churchill."

"Ahhhhh."

"Maggie, this is a significant milestone in our friendship. Revealing a middle name is a sacred trust. This should not be entered into lightly."

"You think we're rushing things?"

He shakes his head. "Okay. I'll go first. I kind of already did, but I'll make it official." He takes a deep breath and squares his shoulders. "My name is Thomas Churchill Pierce."

"Wow," I say. "No pressure there. You sound like some eighteenth-century British aristocrat."

"Yeah, it's a little intense, huh?" he says. "Now you."

"Margaret Bower."

Tom clears his throat. "Maggie, I'm not sure you grasp the point of this exercise. I know your first name. I know your last name. The thing that's happening here is I learn your middle name," Tom says. He waits and then tries another tactic. "I showed you mine, now you show me yours."

"Sorry," I say. "No can do. I've only got the two names."

"No middle name?" he says. "Not even an initial?"

"Nope."

"So you tricked me?"

I nod.

"Well played," he says. "Like I said: riddle, mystery, enigma. Full of surprises."

I'm not sure what to say to this, so I change the subject. "Kayla said you had fun the other night." I do a pretty good job of keeping my voice level.

"Yeah, I guess," Tom says. "It was all right. The movie was dumb, but Kayla and her friends seem nice. Not as nice as you, though." He smiles.

I glance at him, and I have to force my eyes away to keep from drifting right off the road into that smile. Tom turns up the music, singing along with some of the songs, asking questions about bands he doesn't recognize. By the time we start passing the exits in north Seattle, I realize I have no idea where we're going. Nash planned the itinerary. I want to stay far, far away from romantic, and cool is out of my reach, so I basically have to pick spots that are quintessentially non-Nash. I spot the exit for the Woodland Park Zoo and change lanes. I don't ask Tom if he likes zoos. Nash hates them: something about the cocktail of large animals, whiny children, and acres of dung. Which means I never go when I come to Seattle with Nash. The zoo is neither cool nor romantic, but I love it, so why not?

The gates have just opened, so the zoo parking lot is only about one-quarter full.

"Excellent," Tom says when he sees the sign. No sarcasm or disappointment detectable. I park the car, and we walk toward the entrance. "Come here often?" Tom asks.

"Not that often," I say. "Not often enough. You like zoos?"

"Yep," he says. "I think I want to study biology. Something with animals." Tom pays for our tickets. "You bought gas!" he says when I argue. We look over the map, and Tom asks, "Are you feeling Africa or the rain forest?"

I always do the rain forest first and save my favorite, the elephants, for last. "Rain forest?"

"Good call." He grins. "Save the best for last."

"The best being . . . ?" I can't decide if I'm hoping he will or won't say elephants.

"Giraffes, duh! With those necks and those crazy black prehensile tongues? What other animal has that kind of insane morphology?"

"Did you really use 'morphology' in casual conversation?" I ask. "Besides, the elephants are the best, and we will be saving them for last."

"First of all, we are both AP bio students, so I hardly think my use of 'morphology' was obscure. Second of all: Did you hear me? Necks? Prehensile tongues?"

"Tusks? Trunks? Largest land mammal?" I fire back.

He shakes his head but he's smiling. "We shall see, Margaret no-middle-name Bower. We shall see."

CHAPTER 12

Hungry?" Tom says as we walk through the exit turnstile at the zoo. "I'm starving."

"You good with Asian?" A no-brainer in Seattle.

"Always," Tom says.

We get back on the freeway and drive south to the International District. There's an Asian grocery store there called Uwajimaya. It's good. It's cheap. There's parking. And I know where it is.

I lead Tom into an area that wouldn't fill the inside of most McDonald's.

"Wow, a food court." Tom looks around. "Not what I was expecting."

"I know. It sounds heinous, but you have to trust me on this," I say. "Besides, you said you liked Asian; they have Hawaiian, Korean, Thai, Vietnamese, Japanese, Chinese, bubble tea . . . and it all kicks ass." Tom still looks skeptical. "Trust me. I'll meet you at this table in ten minutes."

Tom picks the Korean place, and I get us both bubble tea plus a steaming bowl of pho for me. We sit down and open our chopsticks. On each of our trays is a place mat covered with the animals in the Chinese horoscope.

"Which one are you?" I ask Tom, pointing at the place mat.

"Do they have a giraffe?"

I shake my head, laughing.

"Bummer. Then . . ." He looks over the dates. "I guess I'm an Ox," he says. "Which sign are you? I don't see an elephant."

"Guess."

Tom starts reading the descriptions, muttering to himself. "Not a Sheep or a Rat. Not a Tiger, either. Too old to be a Dragon. Hmmm." He taps his chopsticks against the side of his plastic bowl, contemplating the choices. "I'm going to say Rabbit. No, Ox! You're an Ox, like me."

He's right. But I don't tell him he's right. Not yet. "Why?" I ask. I hope he doesn't think I just seem ox-ish.

"Well, there's the dependable, hard-working thing," he says, looking over the Ox description. "But there's also the part about being picky about relationships." I must look a little confused, because he tries to explain. "I can see that lots of people like you: Nash, of course, but also Kayla, and Cece, and teachers."

"Not Ms. Perry," I say.

"No, not Ms. Perry," Tom agrees. "Anyway, it seems like you've been pretty selective about who gets to know Maggie, who gets close. That's all I mean. I'm the same way, really. I just don't see the point of getting all wrapped up when I know I'm probably leaving. I've moved too many times to relive the same bullshit with people over and over."

I nod. "But what about all that first impressions, Mr.

Charming McFlirty-pants stuff you were rocking the first few days you were here? Isn't that a form of that same old bullshit?"

"Yeah, I guess that's true, but I'm trying to move past that now. At least with you." He raises his bubble tea, and we tap the plastic glasses together in a toast. "To Oxes! Oxen? Whatever!"

"To Oxen!" I say, and we slurp the first tapioca pearls into our oversize straws.

"What's Nash?" Tom says.

"Nash is pure Tiger."

"'Fierce, unpredictable, fearless in a fight,'" Tom reads from the place mat. "Yeah, that sounds about right."

"And loyal as hell. My best friend is a moody man. His pendulum swings far and wide: big blow-ups, wonderful reunions. But when I need someone for the tough stuff, Nash is my guy."

"He sounds like a great friend to have," Tom says.

"I don't expect to ever find a better one."

"Lucky you. Lucky Nash. I hope I have that some day."

"You've never had a bestie?"

"Not really. I always know I'm leaving so . . ."

"So you never commit."

"You make it sound like it's my fault." Tom fiddles with his chopsticks, not meeting my eyes.

"No. Not fault. But you don't earn a friendship like I have with Nash by playing it safe. You have to be willing to put yourself out there. It's a risk."

"Easier said than done."

"Believe me, I know." We're silent for a bit, letting our words settle and come to rest between us gently. It's not an argument, but I leave it there so it doesn't become one.

"Okay, let's eat! I'm starved." Tom digs in and closes his eyes for a minute as he chews. "Sooooooo good." Tom moans after a couple bites of his bibimbap. I sip some of the pho broth and nod.

"I see you had them hold the meat?" I say.

He nods, still chewing.

"So you're anti-carnivore?"

"Not at all," Tom says. "I love carnivores. But I decided I didn't want to be one myself." He takes a bite of carrot.

"How long have you vegged-out?"

"I flirted with it throughout middle school, but it was a ninth grade research paper on endangered species that tipped me into a full-time herbivore." He takes a long draw on his bubble tea and continues. "My paper was on gorillas. Clearly an intelligent animal, but when I read about the poachers killing the gorillas for bush meat, I got really grossed out. After that I really just couldn't eat meat anymore."

I let a strip of beef fall from my chopsticks and push my bowl away.

"Sorry," he says. "I should know better than to tell that story while people are eating."

"Don't worry about it." I sip my bubble tea. The tapioca jams in the straw, and I have to suck hard to dislodge it. "I may never get the image of gorilla meat out of my head completely, but I asked." I drink my tea as Tom finishes his lunch. "You want to look around?"

He nods so we dump our trays and roam the bookstore for a while. Tom buys a couple of Japanese graphic novels I've never heard of, further cementing his geek status, and we move on to the grocery store to look at the bizarre fruits and veggies.

"Can your delicate plant-eating self bear to look at the seafood section?" I ask.

Tom rolls his eyes. "Is that how it's going to be, Maggie? I share my heartfelt vegetarian conversion story with you, and you mock me? I expected more."

"You'll learn not to." We make our way to the lobster tanks, pausing to look at the googly-eyed spiny fish in the large tank, but I save the best for last. "Ever seen a geoduck?"

"A what-a-what?" Tom asks. "Do I want to?"

I smile and lead him to the last tank. It's filled with large clamshells stuffed with foot-long, yellow-brown clams that extend obscenely from their protective covering.

Tom stops, mouth hanging open. "That's just . . . wrong," he says finally, and his face flushes red. "What . . . what are these things called?"

"Geoducks," I say. I can't stop from giggling a little. It's nice to not be the one blushing for once.

"Gooey-ducks." He's still staring at the clams.

I nod.

"Thanks, Maggie. Payback. Now you've given me an image I won't be able to get out of my head." He stares a minute more. "Okay." He claps his hands together, prying his eyes away from the tank. "Where to now?"

"We have to buy some fortune cookies to take back to Nash," I say. "A consolation prize."

"The Tiger likes cookies, huh?"

"Actually he hates the cookies, but he loves to read the fortunes," I say. "He saves them and tapes the ones he likes around the mirror in his bedroom. He even saves mine when he likes them, although he says technically they're not transferable."

We make our way back to the car, and I sit for a minute trying to think of what else to show Tom.

"Troll or gum wall?" I ask, suddenly inspired.

Tom's face splits into a wide grin. "Both!" He bounces up and down like a giddy ten-year-old.

I shake my head and wonder if Nash has seen this side of Tom. Nash doesn't fit into the American high school male ideal, but he does his not-fitting-in with a definite sense of style. I have never known him to be particularly attracted to any member of the nerd herd. Tom, in spite of having shoulders like a battleship and eyes that could melt chocolate, is, if not a part of the herd himself, deep in nerd territory.

By some miracle we find parking in the lots below Pike Place Market and climb to the top level. We pass tables full of silver jewelry, organic honey, smoked meats, leather bags, and Nepalese sweaters knitted by refugees who, the sign assures us, will receive most of the proceeds directly from the man selling the sweaters. I lead Tom through the crowded market to the south end.

"Watch out." I pull Tom out of the way as a guy in waders catches a large salmon thrown from behind the fish counter. The crowd cheers, and the guy tosses the fish to another guy standing by the Dungeness crabs.

"We are not in Kansas anymore, Toto," Tom says, but I can see he's enjoying it.

I'm sad Nash is missing this, but I'm glad to be the one showing Tom a different side of the city. We wind through the crowd and around a few corners.

"Close your eyes," I say.

Tom looks at me. "Why are you always making me close my eyes before you show me stuff? How do I know this isn't some sort of unpleasant Seattle hazing ritual?"

"Close them, or I won't show you!"

"No tricks?"

I shake my head.

Tom sighs, holds out his hand, and closes his eyes.

I grab his hand; it's rough, and his fingers are longer than I expect. I lead him around the last corner, and I'm glad to see there's nobody else in the alley. I position Tom in front of the wall, with his nose about six inches away.

"Ready?" I say. "Open!"

Tom squints at the wall, trying to get his bearings. He takes a step back, and another, and then spreads his arms wide as he backs all the way to the other side of the alley so he can take in the whole wall. The brick on the east side of the alley is a huge textured Pollock painting of chewed, discarded pieces of gum. The colors range from the grayish white of Doublemint to the fluorescent greens and purples of Bubblicious.

"Stellar," Tom says, with what I consider to be an appropriate amount of reverence.

I dig in my purse and fish out some Bazooka bubble gum.

"Can we?" he asks.

I nod.

"Well then, at the risk of offending, I have my own." He pulls a pack of clove gum out of his pocket. He offers me some, but I hold up my Bazooka and shake my head.

We unwrap and start to chew. Over the sugary bubble gum smell of Bazooka, I catch whiffs of clove. We work our respective gums in silence until they are soft enough to stick.

"Ready?" I ask.

Tom nods. Stepping to the wall, we pick our spots. I take my gum out and hold it up. Tom does the same.

"One, two, three!" I press my pink wad of gum into the wall between two green ones. Tom's gum lands in the middle of a patch of white globs.

"Awesome," he says, giving me a smile. "And can I just say, Maggie no-middle-name Bower, it's not every girl who would show a guy her disgusting, chewed-up bubble gum on a first date."

I stare at Tom, processing the word "date." This can't be a date. There's the Nash factor, of course. And obviously there's the reality that I'm, well, I'm me. I look at Tom to see if it was a joke, but he's fiddling with his phone.

"Time to document the moment." Tom poses us in front of our additions to the wall, leaning his cheek in so it touches mine. The camera clicks, and Tom checks to make sure the photo worked. "Perfect," he says.

I lead Tom out onto First Avenue. First is where the seedy side of downtown sort of butts up against the scenic side of downtown, where the homeless and the tourists overlap. As soon as we hit the sidewalk, I can feel Tom tense up.

"Maggie, maybe we should go back the other way."

"No, it's all right. I always come here when I'm in town."

"Hey. It's the cookie lady!" I hear after a few steps up First. A guy approaches, and Tom hesitates. The guy has clearly been on the street awhile, but I pull out a couple of wrapped cookies and hand them over. "What kind?" he asks.

"Peanut butter chocolate chip," I say.

"Ooh, girl, I think I'm in love!"

I smile and we move on. I hand out cookies all along the block. Word spreads fast, and by the time we're back at the market, I'm out of baked goods.

Tom hasn't said a word the whole time, and I wonder just how much I freaked him out. We start down the stairs to the car before he speaks.

"You realize you've sent me right back to pondering the riddle-mystery-enigma thing?" he says.

I smile like an enigma should: mysteriously, without saying a word.

"How long have you been Saint Maggie of the Cookies?"

"I like to bake."

"Maggie, it's one thing to give your stuff away to suburban high school kids. But this . . . You really made some people happy today. And one of them is me." He stops and turns to face me. He's on a lower step, so our heads are almost level and I am looking right into those grassy eyes. "Thank you, Saint Maggie."

I hold his gaze as long as I can, but it's too much. I dig for my keys. "We're going to get a ticket," I say. "And the Troll is waiting."

CHAPTER 13

We walk through Fremont, making our way to the Troll, a huge cement sculpture emerging from underneath a bridge. Tom climbs all over it, scaling the head, resting between the giant troll hands. He makes me take a ridiculous number of pictures of him in various poses.

I text one of them to Nash. He doesn't respond.

By the time we get back on the freeway heading north, we are both exhausted but happy. The traffic lightens up a couple miles out of the city.

"Favorite part of the day?" I ask.

Tom rubs his chin, then starts ticking off things on his fingers. "The zoo, lunch, geoducks, gum wall, cookies, and the Troll."

"In that order?"

"No, those are my favorites."

"But that's everything," I say.

"Yep."

I check my phone again to see if Nash has answered yet.

"Do you think he's mad?" Tom asks.

"Probably."

"You and Nash seem really different. I mean, from each other."

"That's true."

"So can I ask?"

"How come we're friends?"

"Yeah."

"We just are." Drops of rain start to freckle the windshield, so I turn the wipers on. "The way my dad tells it, when we were little, Nash and I were on the monkey bars at the same time, coming at each other from opposite ends. When we met in the middle, Nash stared me down, expecting me to drop off and let him by. But I just smiled and kept going, grabbing the outside bar to get myself around him. He followed me around the playground the rest of the day, and by the time we left the park, Nash and I were friends."

"I find a child-size version of Nash a little terrifying," Tom says.

I laugh. "Most people do. He wasn't exactly the poster child for American boyhood."

"Yeah, I kind of got that. I'm guessing he got teased a bit?"

"Kids knew he was different, even before we were old enough to understand about gay and straight and everything in between. But Nash is a fighter, and it didn't take long before kids looked for victims who weren't quite so feisty."

"Still, it seems like people are okay with him now."

"I guess. It's not so much that Cedar Ridge is open-minded. I think people just got tired of the wrath of Nash descending on anyone who harassed him. The man has some rage."

"I kind of got that, too," Tom says. "But you seem to have tamed the Tiger."

"Being friends with him is a skill I have mastered through trial and error. A lot of error."

"Saint Maggie."

"No," I say. "Not a saint. You're not getting it. Nash is . . . He helps me see the good things in myself when I have trouble remembering. He does that for his mom too."

Tom looks skeptical.

"I know you think it's the other way around, that I prop him up. And I do sometimes. But our friendship is . . ." I flip through words in my head, but none of them convey what I want Tom to understand about Nash.

"Symbiotic?" Tom offers.

I smile. "Wow, more AP bio vocab! Impressive. But, yes. Thanks. Symbiotic. It's good for both of us."

"Well, then, you are both saintly and lucky." Tom turns to the window, and I realize fully that Tom's never had what I have with Nash.

He still has on my "Weekend" playlist, and it flips to Billie singing "All of Me."

I'm not really sure I'm ready to explain Billie to Tom, so I skip to the next song as fast as I can.

"No, wait. Switch it back," Tom says. "What was that?"

"What? Oh, um, Billie Holiday, I think?" I'm feigning in-difference, but Tom persists.

"Let's listen to it."

I give in and flip back to the song. Billie starts singing again, and I look sideways at Tom. He has his head cocked, listening like a Labrador or something, letting the music wash over him. When the song ends, he sort of shakes his head.

"Jazz. Not really my thing," he says.

"Not really your thing?" I take the bait.

"Nope. Too sappy, too old. Not my thing."

"Don't make me pull this car over."

"So, change my mind, then. How did you get into this kind of music?"

"I'm more into Billie than jazz in general."

"Oh, you're on a first-name basis?"

"Definitely. We're like this." I cross my fingers. "Anyway, Quinn was playing her one day in the store, and I loved her voice. Simple as that. But then when I listened to the lyrics . . . they're so melancholy, but also so hopeful. They just . . . they feel true." I keep my focus on the road. Another song comes on. I can feel Tom studying me.

"Yeah, that fits," he says.

"What fits?"

"Melancholy but hopeful. That's a good way to describe the music. And I think that's how it feels when you're in love."

"I wouldn't know." The words are out of my mouth before I can think. I pray silently that Tom will leave it at that, but I know he won't.

"You've never been in love?" he asks.

I shake my head. I do not want to have this conversation. Not now. Not with Tom.

"Never had a boyfriend?"

I shake my head again. I'm choking the steering wheel, my knuckles white.

"Okay, that's weird."

"Thanks a lot." I accelerate without meaning to, then force myself to let off the gas a little.

"Sorry," Tom says. "I didn't mean that to sound . . . I just can't believe some guy hasn't . . . It's hard to believe, that's all."

My mouth goes dry, and neither of us speaks for a mile or two. "What about you?" I ask. "When have you experienced the melancholy hopefulness of love?"

"I haven't," Tom says. "Of course I've hung out with people I liked, but I've moved so much. It makes things hard."

"So you've never had a relationship? And you're flipping me shit about being weird?"

"You didn't ask me if I've ever had a relationship. You asked me if I've ever been in love. I've gone out with people. And I thought I was in love once. But I was wrong."

"You were wrong? What does that mean?"

Tom looks out the side window.

"Okay, no. You can't drop a tidbit like that into the conversation and leave it unexplained," I say. "Give me the abridged version if you don't want to go into detail, but you can't leave that hanging out there." We're coming to the outskirts of town now, but there's no real traffic. I fake stop at a couple stop signs before Tom decides to tell me.

"It wasn't my last school, but the one before that. Walnut Creek, California, east of San Francisco. Anyway, Dad was working in the city, and my parents were hoping to keep me there for all four years of high school. We did stay there the longest of any of my schools, three semesters plus a few weeks," he says. "So I was there long enough to sort of find my footing and make some actual friends. That's where I met Jamie. Jamie was gorgeous. Black hair—you know in comic books how characters with the black hair are always drawn with kind of blue highlights?"

I nod.

"That's how dark it was. We started hanging out, and I was a goner. Before long I was spending pretty much every waking moment with Jamie."

"Sounds great," I say. "What happened?"

"Well, turns out Jamie's waking moments were split between me and another guy."

I wince. "Oh, sorry. That sucks."

"Yeah. It did suck. It sucked for a long time," he says.

I silently curse Jamie for having a name that doesn't give me a clue about his or her gender. "And now?" I ask.

"And now . . . I think my pride was hurt more than anything. When I think about it, there really wasn't all that much to it. We partied a lot. But we spent most of our time . . ."

I feel him look at me as I realize what they spent their time doing.

"Well, anyway, it wasn't love. And it taught me to be a lot more selective about who I spend time with."

I glance over and he's looking right at me. Our eyes lock for a split second before I turn them back to the road. "Flustered" doesn't even begin to cover it. I take a deep breath, trying to keep my cool. And I realize it would be stupid and obvious to ask about Jamie's gender now. Nash will not be happy I let this opportunity whoosh by me.

Pulling up to the curb at Tom's house, I set the parking

brake and wait for him to get out. But he doesn't. It starts to rain harder. Droplets obscure the windows before Tom speaks.

"Thanks, Maggie."

My hand is on the gearshift, and Tom places his over it again, like he did when we went hiking. I feel clammy and hot, and I need some air. He seems to be waiting for me to do or say something. I don't want to disappoint him, but anything I think of sounds wrong. I pull my hand away to turn on the windshield wipers. Being able to see out of the car again helps my composure.

"Yeah. You too." At least my vocal chords work.

"Can we . . ." He hesitates. "I hope we can do more stuff like this."

"Yeah, me too. And next time Nash can come, which will be so much better. He really knows the good stuff in the city."

Tom smiles at me and gives my hand that little squeeze again. "Going with Nash will be fun," he says. "But there's no way it could be better." He gets out of the car, leaning in to wave one last time. "Hasta la bye-bye!"

I roll my eyes. Suddenly I can breathe. Tom slams the door, and I don't wait for him to walk up the steps before I accelerate. In my rearview mirror, I see him standing on the curb, watching me drive away.

CHAPTER 14

I've only been home a few minutes when Nash calls.

"Tell me!" he says.

"Are you okay?" I ask. "I am so sorry about today! And so pissed at your mom. I really just wanted to come rescue you!"

"Yeah. She's not my favorite right now. But it could have been worse. And at least Tom still got his day in the city."

"Why does she do that? It's not fair!"

"Granted," he says.

"And why tell Tom instead of me? When he said you weren't coming, I didn't know what you wanted me to do. A simple text saying 'go without me' would have been helpful."

"Fine," he says. "I'm sorry I didn't communicate with you directly. My mom did what my mom does, so there's that. I didn't want to disappoint Tom, and I was afraid you would chicken out if you knew you had to go alone. So I called him, not you."

"I am not a chicken!" I say. "And I went, didn't I?"

"Yes. You went. You were very brave, Maggie. Now quit stalling and tell me about Seattle. Every moment rendered in detail, if you please," Nash says.

So I tell him. I can almost hear Nash's eyes rolling over the phone.

"You took him to the zoo? And the gum wall? Were you trying to take a tour of Seattle's most unsanitary places?"

"When you go to Seattle with Tom, you can take him where you want. This was Tom and Maggie's excellent adventure. Besides, Tom seemed to like it."

"I'm sure he was just being polite. He's probably burned his clothes and sanitized everything else by now. Did you do anything cool?"

"I passed out cookies," I say.

"I can't bear it," Nash says. "No more details about your bizarre activities. Tell me about Tom. What did he reveal?"

"He wants to be a biologist," I say. "And he's a vegetarian."

"So cool," Nash says.

"He chews clove gum. And he had never seen a geoduck."

"Maggie! You didn't show him the geoducks!" Nash says, laughing. "You tramp!"

"Yep. I felt it was important to continue my theme of showing him Northwest wildlife. On the hike it was the moose. That set the bar pretty high. I thought a prehistoric bivalve was the only decent follow-up. Anyway, he was speechless."

"I'm sure he was."

"And he loved the Troll. Did you get the photo?"

"Yes. I'm jealous, okay? What else?"

"Oh! He's been in a relationship with someone named Jamie," I say.

"Boy or girl?" Nash asks.

"I don't know."

"Maggie!"

"He never said and then the moment was gone."

"I can't believe you! You get an opportunity for a little reconnaissance and let it pass?"

"I know. Sorry. But grilling people about their love lives is harder than it sounds."

"Did you find out anything useful?"

"They were pretty hot and heavy, and then the mysterious Jamie cheated and broke Tom's heart."

"Poor Tom. Maybe he's on the rebound?"

"Doubtful. It was a couple of schools ago."

"Did he say what he liked about this mysterious person?"

"He mentioned comic-book black hair."

"I guess I could dye mine."

"And he mentioned a lot of partying and a lot of—" I stop, not really knowing what to say about the rest of what Tom said.

"Oh. Well, I can't dull my straight edge, even for Tom, but as for the other part: I'd be willing."

"Nash! Who's the tramp now?"

"I'm just saying." Nash sighs. "Anything else?"

"He talked about Kayla."

"Kayla? What about Kayla?"

"Well, they had that date." I kick myself for mentioning it. "It seems like they had fun, but I couldn't tell if he was being nice or if he actually liked hanging out with her."

"God, Kayla Hill is like my own personal train wreck."

"What do you mean?"

"She's messing with you and with Tom," he says. "I want her to leave my friends alone."

"She's not messing with me, Nash. We had coffee. And I had fun, kind of. That's not a mess."

"Maggie, I hope I'm not the only one who remembers seventh grade," Nash says. "I did the repair work last time. It was not pretty. Please don't tell me the girl can buy you one frappuccino and all is forgiven."

"It was an americano, and I bought it myself."

"Whatever. I'm just saying, she's not worth it."

"Nash, I get it. You're mad that she asked Tom out," I say. "But you can't expect him to survive with only us as friends."

"I don't expect that. But I hoped both of you would have better taste."

"Kayla can offer him access to a whole different world."

"A world where the lovely and vapid go to play."

"I'll give you lovely, but Kayla's not vapid."

"Okay, fine, not vapid. Unimaginative?" Nash says. "And why are you defending her, anyway?"

"Why are you dumping on her?"

"Because she's a bitch who tried to destroy my best friend and I don't want her doing it again."

"You never liked Kayla."

"That's not true, Maggie. I never cared about Kayla. There's a difference."

"What difference?" I ask.

"I don't care about her, so she can't hurt me. You, however, seem determined to relive your painful past."

"Nash, I know you're trying to protect me. And I can never repay you for holding my hand through all my crazy when Kayla crushed me in middle school."

"Obliterated you is more like it. And it took more than just some hand-holding to bring you back."

"I know, Nash. You are the best friend I've ever had."

"The feeling is so very mutual. But please remember: I like my Maggie intact and fabulous, as you were meant to be."

"I try. I try."

"Seriously, Mags. I don't understand why you would risk letting her near you again."

"Masochism? Morbid curiosity? Take your pick." All at once I'm sick to death of talking about Kayla and Tom and Nash and all of it. "Listen, I have to go. Long day."

"Well, don't come running to me when Little Miss Perfect Cheekbones curb-stomps you again." He hangs up.

"Arrrrgh!" I put my phone in a death grip and shake it in front of me, strangling Nash in my mind. He's successfully killed my happy Seattle buzz. I need a distraction, and I gave away all the cookies today, so it's time to bake. I think about Tom and the smell of his gum at the gum wall. I pull out molasses, ginger, and clove and get to work. Soon the smell fills the kitchen and draws my dad in from his workshop.

"You know your Grandma Mary baked cookies all the time," he says, settling his broad frame onto one of the stools at the counter.

"Yeah, Dad. Who do you think got me started?" I say. "Mom said Grandma was famous for her shortbread."

"Shortbread was her specialty, but all her cookies were works of art. Once I started dating your mom, I would get regular care packages from her, full of cookies."

"Grandma Mary died when I was only six," I say. "I don't remember much, except helping her make gingerbread people."

"At Christmastime she made these special spice cookies. She'd put together huge platters of them to give away at church."

"She did?" I didn't know that about her, and I like the idea that I'm continuing her legacy in my own way.

"She gave away a lot more cookies than she kept over the years. It's like baking itself was important to her, not the cookies."

"Yeah. That's what it's like for me." I lift the first batch of ginger cookies off the pan and onto the rack to cool. The spicy scent wafts between Dad and me, making us both smile. I pour two glasses of milk and put two cookies on a plate. Joining him at the counter, I offer one to him. We bite into them, and the clove goes to work on my lips and tongue right away, numbing them slightly. The smell makes me remember Tom at the gum wall again, and I wonder if his clove gum would make my lips numb if I kissed him.

"These are delicious, Maggie." Dad's voice brings me back to the warm kitchen. "Your grandmother would be proud."

I shake my head and raise my glass. "To Grandma Mary."

"To Grandma Mary," Dad says.

CHAPTER 15

Nash is distant the next day, but I don't think he's really mad. I steer clear at lunch, giving him some Tom time. Cece's already in the library when I walk in.

"Hey, Maggie," she says. "How was your weekend?"

"Mostly the usual." I drop my bag with a clunk. "Did you go to the art museum?"

"Yeah," she sighs. "My mom went with me."

"I wish I had a mom I wanted to hang out with."

"Well, sometimes there aren't any other options." She pinches off the crust of her sandwich bit by bit, discarding it onto her napkin. I'm not sure I've ever seen Cece so down.

"Tom and I went to Seattle too," I say. "Yesterday."

Cece perks up a little at this. "Just you and Tom?"

"Just me and Tom," I say. "Nash had to . . . help his mom."

Cece nods. She's smiling a little and takes a bite of her now-crustless sandwich. "That's great."

We finish lunch, chatting until I'm almost late for biology. Tom is already at our lab table. Kayla's in my seat, laughing and tossing her curls off her shoulder. Tom leans in, hands gesturing as he talks softly to her.

I feel a little stab of jealousy seeing them together. Then I remind myself to be jealous on Nash's behalf.

Kayla waves, and Tom stands up, smiling, like he's been waiting for me.

"Hey, Maggie," Kayla says. "Tom's been giving me a rundown of his most embarrassing moments."

"Not the *most* embarrassing," Tom corrects her. "You'll have to earn those."

"Well, if they're like the stories you just told me, I'd do anything to hear them." Kayla leans in a little, touching Tom's arm and flashing those white Chiclets at him. The bell rings. "See you later."

"Definitely," Tom says.

Kayla leaves and I move around to my side of the table, not meeting Tom's eyes. I haven't actually talked to him since I dropped him off.

"You weren't at lunch," Tom says.

It's a statement, but there's a question underneath. I throw my backpack down and climb onto the stool.

I'm deciding whether to be evasive or honest when he says, "Nash seems kinda pissed at you."

"He does? How pissed?" I put my head down on the cool black surface of the lab table. It feels good. "Did he tell you why?" I say into the table.

"He didn't. And I'm not sure I'm qualified to assess the different levels of Nash's emotional turmoil quite yet," Tom says. "But if I had to take a guess, I'd put it at a five or six?"

I lift my head. "Is that all?" I say. "And we're talking a scale of one to ten here?"

Tom nods.

"That's a relief." I know from experience that a five on the Nash scale feels bigger than it is, and that the anger is usually short-lived. A Tiger all the way.

Mr. Smythe shows a movie about the sexual organs of plants.

"I never knew sex could be so boring!" Tom whispers, throwing his book into his backpack at the end of class.

"Personally I was riveted. Stamen and angiosperm? That's serious stuff!" We both turn toward the gym and the dreaded Ms. Perry. My mood collapses.

"You know you shouldn't let her get to you," Tom says, falling into step beside me.

"Oh, okay. Wow, I never thought of that. Don't let her get to me. Thanks."

"I know, easy to say, but she is twisted. She's clearly got some sort of eating disorder and an unhealthy fear of . . . um . . ." Tom shifts his eyes away from me.

My face burns as I realize what Tom was going to say. "Fat?" I supply. "Were you going to say 'fat'?" I clutch my notebook a little tighter and speed up. Tom is so good at making people feel at ease that I'd almost convinced myself he didn't notice or care about what I look like. I feel stupid for letting myself think that even for a moment. My throat tightens unpleasantly as I pass a garbage can, and I consider whether or not I might need to stop and throw up into it.

"Look, it's not a secret and it's nothing new. I've been dealing with this shit my whole life. Believe me, if I could tune out the Ms. Perrys of the world, I would, but they are everywhere. They're an occupational hazard for people like me." We're still walking, but I feel Tom's hand on my arm and I stop. "What?" I say, the prick of tears behind my eyes.

"Breathe." He puts his hands on my shoulders. "In and out. For just a minute. Breathe." He closes his eyes as if to demonstrate the kind of Zen breathing he wants me to do.

I roll my eyes. I breathe. After a few seconds, my heartbeat starts to slow and my cheeks don't feel quite as hot.

"Listen for a minute." Tom's hands are still on my shoulders, and now that I am not quite so absorbed in my own pity party, I become aware of the warm, gentle pressure of his thumbs resting on the bare skin on either side of my neck. "To clarify, I don't think you're fat," he begins.

"Yeah, right." I avoid looking at him. "Then why did you have such a hard time saying it?"

"Nash told me you were sensitive about—"

"Nash told you? Nash? Told you?" I step away from him, shaking off his hands. What else had Nash told him? "Jesus, we've only known you like a minute and a half, and you've got Nash and me both spilling the deep stuff. What else has Nash said about me? No, never mind. I don't want to know." I start toward PE again. "I'm going to be late, and Ms. Perry does not make a habit of extending her minute reserves of compassion to me."

Tom starts to follow, but I change course, veering to the exit doors that lead to the back parking lot.

"Where are you going?" he says. "Maggie, wait, don't . . . I didn't mean to . . ." He trails off as I bust through the double doors and into the golden light.

I walk as fast as I can to a hole in the back fence, praying I can still fit through it. I haven't left school this way since early freshman year. Squeezing through, I head down a side street away from the school. I'm not sure where I'm going, just away. The tears are still threatening. One minute I'm walking to class with a nice guy that my best friend is crushing on; the next minute we are having some sort of impromptu counseling session about my body image issues.

"Screw that," I say, startling a woman walking by with her dog. I head for the mini-mart on the next corner. Inside, I roam the aisles for a couple minutes pretending to look for something I need. I pick up some lip balm and a can of Diet Coke and take them up to the counter to pay.

I don't want to see anyone, so I choose one path in the maze of trails running along the hillside that divides our small city into the upper town and the lower town. You could do a whole year's worth of after-school specials about the kids on the bluff. The stoners, the kids having sex with their boyfriends and girl-friends, the kids having sex with other people's boyfriends and girlfriends, the LARP kids roaming the trails, challenging one another to sword fights with fake swords wrapped in foam. The trees offer plenty of places to hide and party, so I run the risk of bumping into stoned gamer geeks having wild sex among the pines, but it's early yet, so I'll probably be left alone.

I find a patch of moss and fallen pine needles under a tama-rack that's starting to turn golden. The sun is shining on the lake, but there's a bite of fall in the air. It won't be long before it's too cold to sit outside like this.

I remove the lip balm, put some on, and slip it in my pocket. Then I take out the Diet Coke, pop the top, and take a sip. I passed out most of the ginger cookies at school, but I find a couple more in my bag. The idea of the soft, sweet cookie is more soothing than the astringent fizz of the Diet Coke. Unwrapping a cookie, I raise it to my lips, inhaling the ginger and clove. Then I hear voices. I scoot back up the hill under the trees. Below me a couple of tiny, blond women come into view, power walking down the trail. The sound of their voices drifts up to me as they race by, but the wind chops up the words.

I let out a breath and look at the cookie in my hand. I take a slow bite and try to swallow, but the mash of molasses and flour sticks in my throat. I toss the remaining cookies into the trees. Maybe some lucky stoner will find them and think the marijuana gods have granted him an instant munchies cure.

I look out at the water and the patches of yellow tamarack on the distant hillsides. Nash is mad at me. Tom thinks I'm fat. And who knows what Kayla has in mind. The cookies are gone, and my tears are too close to the surface, so I let them come, slow and silent. No racking sobs or hysterics. Just a little of my sadness leaking down my face and leaving wet polka dots in my lap.

CHAPTER 16

By the time I make it to Square Peg, ten minutes after my shift starts, Quinn is picking up the phone to call me. He's having a full-on hissy fit.

"What the hell?" he starts in, putting down the phone. "Where have you been? I was worried!"

I toss my bag under the counter. "Sorry," I say. "I was on the bluff and lost track of time."

Quinn gives me the look he calls "the hairy eyeball."

"What?" I say. "I'm never late. Why are you so mad about this one time?"

"That's why I'm so mad," he says. "You're never late, and so when you are, I'm extra worried." He goes to the turntable to change the record. "The bluff, huh? What were you doing there?"

I move closer so Quinn can scrutinize my eyes. "See? Not bloodshot." I breathe on him. "And no skunky pot breath, either."

"Okay, okay. I was just wondering. You know the bluff has been the place to party since I was at Cedar Ridge."

I sometimes forget Quinn is a product of my hometown. The idea is so unlikely that my brain refuses to hold on to that tidbit of information. But it also gives me some hope. For me and for Nash. "How did you ever survive growing up in this town?" I ask. I want to know; I *need* to know. If Quinn has the keys to the kingdom, I hope to God he's in the mood to share them.

"Tough skin and good hair," he says.

I wait for a real answer.

Quinn sighs. "Someday Uncle Quinn will tell you all about it, sweetie, but right now you need to get to work!" He hands me a pile of albums from the RAP (records already played) bin, and I start down the aisle putting them back in the inventory.

A thought stops me in my tracks, and I turn and look at him. "What would you have done if I had been stoned?"

Quinn thinks for a moment, looking at me. "Look, that's not you. It's not who you are. So I would have told you to stop being someone you aren't."

"Oh, the 'be yourself' speech. Heard it. Hate it." I turn back to my work.

"No," Quinn says, and there is an edge to his voice that demands my attention. "Not the 'be yourself' speech." He rubs his hands back and forth across his balding scalp, trying to gather the strings of what he's trying to say. "Look, Maggie, you're a strange kid."

I stare at him.

He backpedals a bit. "That sounded wrong. I just mean you aren't normal." He holds up his hands. "No. Wait."

I have the uncomfortable impulse to laugh, but Quinn takes a deep breath.

"You are . . . you. And if you did the stereotypical movie-of-the-week teenager stuff, like smoking pot or lying to your parents, it wouldn't fit."

"Thanks, Quinn." I run my fingers along the soft edges of the album covers. "I think I needed that."

Quinn lets out a breath and I go back to filing records, and the room starts to feel like the home away from home I've come to expect.

"By the way," Quinn says, his voice casual. "Tom came by to see you earlier."

I stop what I'm doing and spin back to Quinn. "What? Why didn't you tell me?"

"Didn't realize you cared," Quinn says, watching me.

I steady my voice, but my stomach clenches as I remember our conversation this afternoon. "What did he want?" I ask.

"You, I guess."

"Did he say anything— I mean, what did he say?"

"Said he'll be back later. And to tell you to 'breathe.'" Quinn finishes sorting the bin and sits down at the computer to enter some inventory. "It's good advice," he adds.

"Easier said than done," I mumble. But then I do breathe. I take a big breath, in and out, and then another. And I feel better.

It isn't long before Tom comes back. He scans the store, but I am in the far corner, restocking Jazz W–Z, so he doesn't see me right away. I scrunch down and try to hide behind the stack of records I have clutched to my chest. When he finally spots me, he comes right over. His face is pulled together in a worried, questioning sort of way. I brace myself for niceness.

"Hi," Tom says, stopping across from me in the next aisle over.

There are two record-bin widths between us, but I feel cornered anyway.

Quinn puts on a new record, and Billie Holiday comes over the speakers singing "Them There Eyes" and how they are going to get her in trouble.

I glare at Quinn until he turns it down.

"You okay?" Tom asks, and when I look up at his eyes, I can still hear Billie's warning. Those eyes could cause a lot of problems.

"Yeah." I flip through the records. "Sorry about losing it like that."

"Sorry if I crossed a line I shouldn't have crossed."

"Yeah, what's up with that?" I ask. "Does your body produce some sort of truth serum or something? You skipped over a lot of the getting-to-know-you stuff and went right for the jugular. What else did Nash tell you?"

"I know. I have this habit of going directly to the juicy bits."

"And yet you share nothing about yourself."

"I share stuff. Sometimes. But people just tend to want to talk to me, and sometimes they tell me things they didn't mean to. Sorry. I know that's not everyone's favorite."

"Ding, ding, ding. We have a winner!" I say, and Tom finally smiles, but his eyes are stuck in worry mode.

"So, do you hate me? Or does the new guy get another chance?" The words sound like he's joking, but I get the sense he's afraid he's blown it. He's chewing gum, and his jaw works the gum a little faster as he waits for my answer.

I decide to give the guy a break. "It's your lucky day!" I say. "Two-fer Tuesday at Square Peg Records means you get two fabulous albums for the price of one. In your case, you get two chances." I lean over the bins, and Tom leans in too, and our faces are close enough that I can smell the clove. I wag my finger at him, emphasizing each word. "Limited. Time. Offer."

He nods and reaches both his hands out over the bins, grabbing my hand.

I look at his hands holding mine, and I feel that little tremor of electricity. The bell rings and our eyes go to the door.

Kayla's standing in the doorway. She's staring right at us, but I can't read her face. She's still there when the bell rings again.

Now Nash is behind Kayla, eyes darting from her to us and back again. His face pinches like he's eaten some bad sushi. They're both staring at our clasped hands, and I realize too late what this must look like to both of them.

I drop Tom's hands and go back to returning the records to their bins.

Quinn assesses the situation in an instant. "Nash!" he says. "I have that live Clash album you've been asking for. Came out of an estate sale. A suicide, I think." Quinn gives an involuntary shiver. "Come on back. I've been holding it for you." Nash gives us another glance but allows the diversion.

"Hey, guys." Kayla gives a little wave. Her voice is bright and warm, like honey drizzling over us, trying to make everything sweet again. She sidles over to one of the bins near the door and starts looking at the sale albums. Every few seconds she glances up at us. I'm not sure if she's here to see me or Tom, but either way, with Nash on the premises it would be best to get her gone before Quinn is done with him.

"Look, it's Kayla," I say to Tom. "You should go talk to her."

But Tom, a little slow on the uptake, stays where he is. As I flip the records back and forth, trying to find the proper spot for the album in my hand, he pushes them back before I have a chance to drop the record.

"Quit!" I hiss at Tom, but I'm trying not to laugh. When he won't stop, I march the unfiled records back over to the RAP box, sliding them in while glancing at the office where Nash and Quinn are examining an album.

Tom follows me, and Kayla follows him, standing closer to Tom than is strictly necessary. But he doesn't seem to mind. He bumps shoulders with her, she bumps back, and pretty soon they are laughing and jostling for space at the counter.

"You win!" Tom says, holding up his hands.

"I usually do! Remember that," Kayla says. "Maggie, I wanted to double-check: You're coming over on Saturday to work on that history project?"

"Yeah, I'm in."

"Great. Come around ten. I might still be in my PJs, but I'll be ready to work."

"Sounds good," I say.

"Do you need directions?" Kayla asks.

"No. I remember."

Kayla turns on her thousand-watt smile. "What are you up to, Tom?" she asks. "I was going to go get some frozen yogurt."

"Tempting," he says. "But I have plans. Thanks."

"Okay. Another time?"

"Definitely."

Kayla leaves, the bell jangling behind her.

I start straightening things on the counter that don't need to be straightened. I want to ask what his plans are. Tom leans against the counter smiling this Cheshire cat smile. It simultaneously makes my eyes roll and my toes curl. Nash and Quinn emerge from the office, Nash clutching the album in front of him like a shield.

"Hey, Nash." I make a stab at nonchalance, but he's clearly miffed, probably about Kayla. And the fact that she showed up at Square Peg, a place she never comes — or at least never did until Tom moved to town — just confirms all of Nash's fears.

"Nash, what's up?" Tom says, throwing his arm over Nash's shoulder.

Nash puts on a smile for Tom. "Picking up an album I've been wanting. What about you?"

"Oh, making the rounds. Thought I'd come in and say hi to everyone."

"Really?" Nash says, his voice moving in rapid-fire fluctuations between hurt and anger. "I looked for you guys after school today."

"I had a minor breakdown before PE and fled the building," I say.

"You seem fine now." Nash adjusts the watch and bracelets on his arm.

"Just a bout of teenage angst combined with a completely rational fear of Ms. Perry. Tom was concerned, but you would have slapped me right out of my amateur hysterics. Disaster averted by Diet Coke, new lip balm, and skipping my last class." I smile at Nash, and he nods. But I can tell he's still trying to decipher the array of information he saw when he first walked in to Square Peg.

"Interesting," he says.

"Actually," Tom says, "Maggie and I were hoping you'd come to dinner with us after she gets off work."

I stare at him. Tom flicks my wrist with his fingernail, and I catch on enough to play along.

"We were," I say. "Totally hoping."

"I can't go to dinner," Nash says to Tom, ignoring me. "But we could hang out until then."

"Maybe Maggie could meet us after work?" Tom says, as Nash drags him to the door. It's futile to fight Nash when he's got a plan. Tom shakes his head and gives in. The bell rings, the door slams, and the empty shop is quiet and still.

"Nash owes me for that record," Quinn says, still looking at the door. "And what the hell just happened here?"

"Kayla Hill just happened here," I say. "Ancient middle school feuds happened here. Nash's jealousy happened here."

"Ahhh, that's why he was such an ice king," Quinn says. "Well done, Mags."

"What do you mean?" I say. "I have been flawlessly following the best friend guidelines, trying to give Nash and Tom every opportunity to establish a relationship while simultaneously running interference by keeping Kayla occupied." I collapse on the stool and put my head in my hands. "Why isn't it working? I'm doing everything right."

"Well, let me ask you this," Quinn says, stroking the divot in his chin like he does whenever he's trying to solve a big problem. "You've been doing all this work to preserve Nash's claim. And that's to be commended. But who does Tom like?"

"That's part of the problem. He's not giving off the usual signs."

"What are the usual signs?"

"Well, typically the object of Nash's affection runs away, avoids him, and makes it clear that he is not interested in dating Nash, ever."

"That kind of clarity would make things easier," Quinn says.

"But Tom's kind of a flirt."

"Definitely a flirt."

"With everyone."

"I've noticed."

"It makes it hard to tell if he's being charming or if he's really interested. When he's with Kayla, he flirts with Kayla. He kind of even flirts with me, if that can be believed. But when he's with Nash, I think he really could like Nash."

Quinn shakes his head. "Honey, that dog won't hunt."

"Huh?"

"Tom does not like Nash."

"What?" I say. "You've only known Tom for like ten seconds."

"Trust me on this one. When you've been gay as long as I have, you get a sense for these things," Quinn says. "And perfect, smiling Kayla seems a little obvious for a man of Tom's apparent taste and wisdom."

I nod. And then it hits me what Quinn's hinting at. "Puh-lease!" I say, and grab the same stack of records for the third time.

"Okay, let's try this another way. Boy meets boy. Boy meets girl."

"Boy likes boy," I say.

"Not gonna happen, sweetie!"

"You don't know that. How can you know that?"

"Years of experience punctuated by painful trial and error."

"And even if you're right, that doesn't mean—" I start to object but Quinn holds up his hand.

"I know what's in front of me, Maggie," Quinn says. "And right now it looks like Tom and Maggie sitting in a tree."

"Quinn, seriously," I say. "I'll admit to some moments of wishful thinking in this case, but in the real world, guys like Tom do not go for girls like me."

"You can believe what you want, Maggie, but that boy sees you, and he likes what he sees."

I head back to Jazz with the records.

"Just think about it," Quinn says, turning to the computer. "You and Nash don't get to make all the rules."

CHAPTER 17

Tom comes back to Square Peg at closing time. "Where are we going?"

"How am I supposed to know? This is your party."

Tom laughs. "Do you guys have any good Vietnamese around here?"

"There's PhePhiPho."

"Mmmmmm. Hot noodles on a cold night? Lead the way."

We walk toward the restaurant, tucking our chins against the chill.

"How was your time with Nash?" I ask.

"Good," he says. "Confusing. He seemed mad, but not at me. I kind of thought it was at you, and that made me a little mad." He rubs the back of his head, like he's trying to stimulate his brain. "But I don't really know why anyone would be mad."

"Nash is . . ." I search for the right word. "Passionate . . . about his art, his friendships, loyalty."

"Has someone been disloyal?" Tom asks.

I shake my head. "No, not really," I say. "But he feels . . . threatened? Uncertain, I guess?"

"About me?"

I stop, not sure how to answer, then start walking again without looking at him. "Nash thinks you're great." I tiptoe across the words so I don't make a misstep. "What do you think of Nash?"

"I think Nash is great," he says. "I think you're great. Kayla's great. I really can't complain about anyone I've met in Cedar Ridge." He takes a deep breath, and I see the cloud his breath forms as he blows it out. "Look, usually I have a strong belief that conversations about friendships should happen between those two people."

"Fair enough," I say.

"But in this case, well, I'm kind of getting that Nash likes me . . . more than I can like him, if that makes sense?"

I stop and look him in the eye. "So Nash is not your type?"

"Nope."

"And that's because he's too tall?"

"Nope."

"Too sarcastic?"

"No."

My heart sinks. "Too male?"

Tom nods. We walk again, letting that information rattle around us for a bit.

"So my brother's gay," he says.

"Okay. Good to know." I'm wondering if Tom told Nash.

"He got messed with, a lot. You know, every time we moved, he had to go through this whole process with the local brand of bullies."

"That must have been tough."

"It was. And I wasn't always there for him like I wish I'd been. We're okay now, but we weren't for a long time. I was kind of an asshole. A lot."

"So hanging out with Nash——"

"Listen, Nash is fun and smart and interesting. I want to be friends with him." Tom shoves his hands in his pockets. "But yeah, hanging out with Nash might be a little bit about making up for the shit with my brother."

"And that's a problem because . . . ?"

"It's not a problem. But he's very . . . for whatever reason Nash obviously thinks he and I . . . and I'm not . . . That's not happening. That's not my deal."

"'For whatever reason'? Could it be because you are excessively friendly to everything with a pulse?" I ask.

"What? I'm not——"

"Bullshit."

Tom opens his mouth like he wants to argue, then looks away. "Okay. Sorry. I know. It's a bit of a survival mechanism. It tends to accelerate the friend-making thing at a new school."

"And I'm sure this isn't the first time your 'friendliness' has been misunderstood?"

"Yeah, well, no, not exactly. Anyway. You're Nash's best friend. What do I do?"

"If you'd asked me a couple weeks ago, I would have told you not to play with his emotions in the first place."

"I wasn't playing. Not on purpose. But whatever. Now what?"

"You've got to tell him. Soon."

"Then what happens?"

"Shit, Tom, give it some time, I guess. And it's going to be awkward."

"It already is."

"Yeah, well, maybe you should be a little more careful. Clearly flirtation is your superpower. Someone could get hurt."

We walk a couple more blocks along Main Street, turning onto a side street. "Can I ask something slightly more philosophical?"

"Ask away," Tom says.

"Why hang out with Nash and me in the first place?" I ask. "I mean beyond working out unresolved issues with your brother."

"I didn't exactly have a choice. You guys hijacked me that first day."

"True, but you had to know pretty quickly how the Nash thing was going to play out. And anyway, in general, why not aim higher?"

"Maggie, what the hell are you talking about?"

"Seriously. You come to this school, smart, funny, not bad-looking . . ."

Tom grins. "You think I'm good-looking?"

"I said 'not bad-looking.' There's a difference."

He elbows me in the side, almost knocking me off the sidewalk.

"A big difference," I say. "So anyway, you could use your skills to finesse your way into any group of friends in the school. What's with the slumming?"

"Would you rather I defect to the A-list?" he asks.

"No." I shake my head. "But I wonder why you don't. You

said yourself you had fun with Kayla and her friends the other night."

"Well, she asked me out, and I didn't want to be rude," Tom says. "And if I'm honest, she seems like she might be sort of smart under all that giggling and flirting, but I don't have that kind of time. It was okay, not a bad experience. But it's not like when you and I hang out. With you it's different. Normal."

"Normal?" I laugh. "I don't get called that very often. If Nash and I seem normal, you must have run into some real freaks in your travels." Tom laughs too, and for a minute it feels like Seattle again. "So, what you're saying is that all your moving around has taught you the wisdom of shunning the popular in favor of the drastically less popular?"

"Let's say my experiences have taught me that assholes come in all shapes, sizes, and social classes."

"Ah, yes, your vast and worldly experiences."

"Well, I think I can claim a little more of that than someone who's lived in Cedar Ridge her whole life."

"Ouch."

Tom looks at me sideways. "The truth is that I have been to nine new schools in ten years. Every time I moved, I had to make new friends. When you're little, nobody cares about popularity. There are always one or two kids on the outside, the nose-picker or the one who smells funny, but in general everybody's friends with everybody else."

I nod.

"A few years ago, making friends got harder. I had to start . . . positioning myself, I guess, if I wanted to make friends. And I had to start working at it. Had to make myself more lik-

able. Sometimes I set my sights on the 'popular kids' or whatever, sometimes not."

"Did you just use air quotes?" I ask, stopping.

He scowls at me.

"Sorry. Please continue."

"Anyway, I never thought that much about it, until a couple
years back. First day, new school, a nice guy named Jim is the
first one to approach me. Sort of like you and Nash did. He's
kind of dorky, but so am I, so we talk comic books and sci-fi
movies, and things are great. We hang out for a couple days,
and then I meet some other people, people who also seem nice.
I'm having fun and kind of lose track of Jim, but I don't think
much of it since I've hit it off with these other kids."

"The 'popular kids'?" I ask, using air quotes myself.

"Do you want to hear this or not?" Tom stops outside a dark
storefront a couple of blocks from the restaurant.

I clamp my lips together and nod.

"So these other kids seem great and we're all having fun,
and then one day we're in the hall and there's Jim alone by his
locker. I feel the mood shift. The guys I'm with start elbowing
each other and whispering."

"Oh. Not good."

"Yeah. So pretty soon they start saying stuff to Jim. This
wasn't just teasing—this was bad. Crap about his mom, and
things they want to do to his sister, and how he's a fag and
a sicko. They keep going, and I'm talking nasty, awful shit. I
don't say anything, but I don't stop them, either. Jim ignores
them at first, just keeps getting books out of his locker, but
eventually they get to him, and he faces us."

I am still now, hands shoved in my pockets.

"I will never forget the look on his face when he turned around. He was resigned, weary. Like he knew the script and was just waiting for the scene to be over. I'd seen that same look on my brother's face before. But this time I was one of the people making someone feel that way." Tom looks away from me. "Anyway, he said stuff, and they said stuff, and I stood there like an absolute idiot. And then somebody grabbed Jim, pushed him into his open locker, and shut the door. He starts banging right away, but these new 'friends' of mine"—he uses the air quotes again, but I don't tease him this time—"these guys walk away laughing and patting themselves on the back."

"What did you do?" I ask. My voice comes out a little squeaky.

"I just stood there. I was so surprised by it all. It happened so fast. Jim was banging on the inside of the locker and screaming, and the guys were disappearing around the corner, and I just . . . stood there."

"You didn't let him out? You didn't help him?"

"Some girl came down the hall and tried to get Jim out. She had to talk him down enough to get him to give her the combination, and when he got out he was so angry, I thought he might beat the shit out of me. So I left."

"That's it? You left him there?"

"That's it."

"Wow. That's . . . so you didn't even apologize?"

Tom looks away. "Yeah, I know. Not my finest moment. None of those assholes ever talked to me again, and neither did Jim. And I don't blame them."

"So the moral of the story is everyone sucks?" I'm a little confused about how this relates to my original question.

"Not exactly," Tom says. "I guess the moral of the story is social status doesn't make people worthy. It doesn't make them unworthy, either. Since then, I go with my gut and spend time with people who seem interesting, whether they are at the top of the food chain or the bottom."

I nod. Maybe I'm a little suspicious of Kayla because she's popular. I know Nash is. She's been nothing but nice the last few weeks, but it's weird how I keep waiting for the punch line with her. At the same time, I get a little psyched at the idea we could be friends again. If I go with my gut, as Tom suggests, I'm still confused. Part of my gut is telling me it could happen, but another part keeps kicking my brain with steel-toed boots, telling me she's after something more selfish. Tom and I walk along in silence for a bit, and after a while I bump him with my shoulder and say, "Thanks, Tom."

"For what? All I did was reveal, twice in one evening, what a spineless idiot I can be."

"For telling me the truth, and for . . . I guess for thinking I'm interesting enough to spend time with." We stop, and I give an involuntary shiver as the wind pushes some dry leaves up and around us.

Tom takes off his wool coat and wraps it around me, then pulls me into a sort of hug and starts rubbing his hands up and down my back to warm me up. I hope the bulk of our coats will camouflage my body's bumps and lumps enough that Tom doesn't notice them.

I smell his clove gum and the clean woolly scent of his collar.

I have never been this close to a guy before, not anyone besides Nash. And Nash never makes my insides go haywire the way Tom does. That ember is back in the base of my stomach. I feel myself sort of relax into Tom, and he rests his chin on the top of my head.

"Hmmmm," I say. "Thanks."

"Anytime, Maggie." Tom pulls me a little tighter, slowing the pace of his hands. The stroking feels less practical now, more about pleasure than warmth.

I go from relaxed to alert, unsure of what I should do. It seems like Tom is kind of, well, making a move. And I like it, like standing in his arms. Like that my senses are wide awake whenever he touches me. But there are too many things complicating the purity of this moment. Besides, I'm beginning to see Tom has a gift for making whoever he's with feel this way. Still, I let myself enjoy it for a few more seconds.

"Maybe we should go get some food," I say, pulling back from him and handing him his coat. I clench my arms around my torso and turn in the direction of PhePhiPho.

It takes a few seconds, but Tom falls into step alongside me. I don't look, but I can feel that he's watching me as we walk. After half a block of silence, I resort to page one of the dating handbook: I ask him a question about himself.

"So, I am getting to know you well enough to know about your Dungeons and Dragons phase, your torture and locker imprisonment of innocent students—"

"Too soon," Tom says.

"Sorry. Your occasional use of air quotes. But I have one more question that will seal my growing conviction that you are more than just a pretty face: that you could be an authentic dork like me."

"Uh-oh," Tom says, but he's smiling. "What's the question?"

"How many action figures do you own?"

"Oh, no. I've had enough humiliation for one day. Besides, you owe me several embarrassing tidbits about yourself," he says. "Until we even the score a bit, we will not be discussing my action figures."

CHAPTER 18

Nash hasn't contacted me, so when I get on the bus the next morning, I assume he's still angry. My eyes dart to our usual spot. The fall sunlight is slanting in the dirty bus windows, bathing Nash in a diffused glow. He's left room for me to sit next to him, but I stop in the aisle, not sure if I should take the empty seat.

Nash smiles and pats it, inviting me back to my former status quo without a word.

"Hi." I slide into the familiar seat.

"Miss me?" Nash says, squeezing my knee.

"Yeah. Um, why the warm fuzzies after so much cold shoulder?"

"I know. I went off the map. Sorry. It's just— You know me. I get a little—"

"Touchy? Insecure? Unstable?"

Nash drops his head. "Again. I know. But enough about me." He pats my knee again. "How was your dinner with Tom last night?"

I'm not letting him off the hook that easily. It takes a while, but I wait him out.

Nash only tolerates silence if he's the one in control of it. After a minute he sighs. "So, here's the thing: I was really . . . I like him so much, and you guys are getting along so well, and you and Kayla are acting like friends again. I think I could survive Kayla stealing Tom, but I don't want her getting her hooks into you again. She almost destroyed you last time. I can't lose you, Mags. I couldn't bear that." Nash puts his hands on his knees. His knuckles go white for a minute, then relax. He takes a deep breath. "Anyway, I'm sorry. I know you're smarter than that now. I know we're solid." He doesn't look at me, but I can see the last couple days have been as rough on him as on me. Maybe rougher. I'm really all Nash has.

I grab his pinkie with mine, and we do this weird little pinkie handshake we've been doing since fourth grade. Our teacher had us pair up for math that year, and when we got it all sorted, she had us do the pinkie shake and tell our math buddy, "You are my pinkie partner for life!" It was dorky, but Nash and I like dorky, so we're still doing it seven years later.

"Don't worry, Nash," I say. "You are soooo not replaceable, my friend. I admit I'm curious about Kayla's recent overtures, but I'm being cautious. I don't intend to let her crush me this time."

"Good," says Nash. "Because I don't intend to pick up the little Maggie-shaped pieces again. And if Kayla knows what's good for her, she'll back off Tom too. She needs to go back to one of her usual Neanderthals."

I feel a tug to tell Nash what Tom told me last night, that Nash and Tom are not going to live happily ever after, but the bus doesn't seem quite the right setting to share information that will break his heart. I dig into my bag and pull out a breakfast bar.

"You have no idea how happy I am to see that." He bites into it and chews slowly.

"I have a couple more in my bag, but they're probably a little squished."

"Yes, please!" Nash says. I hand them over. Nash looks at me. "Wait, why do you have more than one? Have you been handing these out like they're normal cookies?"

"Never!" I say with mock horror. "These are a Nash Taylor exclusive. Nobody gets these but you." I lean in and whisper, "But I know you've been sharing them with Tom."

Nash covers his mouth and looks up at me through his long dark lashes. "Sorry. Are you mad?"

"Don't be an idiot. Of course not!"

Nash nods, relaxing again. "So, what have you been doing?" You gotta love a guy who jumps from a multiday tiff back into normal peacetime relations with barely a breath in between.

"Oh, the usual: school, work, missing you."

Nash sinks down in his seat and motions for me to do the same. "What are we going to do about Tom?" he whispers.

"What do you see as the main challenge?" I ask, half hoping Nash's crush will pass before I have to break the bad news.

"Twofold," he says. "First: If the usual pattern ensues and he doesn't want to date me, can we bear to remain friends with him? And second: Either way, how do we keep him out of the clutches of Kayla and her minions?"

"Hmmm." I organize my thoughts. "So you really do think Kayla is a threat?"

"Oh, Mags, please!" Nash says. "She's been stalking the guy since noon on the first day of school. And if we leave him battered and bloody, there will be a feeding frenzy. Poor Tom won't know what hit him."

"Well, we can't have that," I say. "He's kind of the innocent bystander here. He comes to this school, the odd couple latches on before he even gets in the door—"

"I prefer 'unique.'"

"Fine, the 'unique' couple become his constant companions, without, I might add, giving him any say in the matter." Nash nods in agreement, his face thoughtful.

"Anyway, the poor guy gets caught up in the very confusing politics of our particular brand of friendship through no fault of his own."

"Not entirely true," Nash interrupts again. "If he weren't so appealing in every single way, this never would have happened."

I roll my eyes, but the bus ride is getting short. "Yes, okay. We can blame him for his general hotness and likability. But Cedar Ridge's overly enthusiastic reaction to that: not his fault."

"True. And I don't think it's right to befriend him and then abandon him the minute he doesn't do our bidding. He's still getting his Cedar Ridge bearings. He's vulnerable. We can't leave him to fend for himself. Not if there are unsavory elements that might lure him into social circles unworthy of his brilliance. I think we have to put our own feelings aside in this case."

"So?" I'm letting Nash take the lead on this one.

"So, we continue to protect young Tom from the influences that might destroy him."

"Agreed," I say.

"And who knows? It might only take a few more days before he comes to his senses about our future together." Nash is smiling now, but my gut clenches as I realize his hope is still alive. I can't crush his dreams on the school bus. That wouldn't be fair.

Nash sees my face and holds up his hand. "Don't burst my bubble, Mags. I need a little something to hang on to right now."

When we get off the bus, we flank Tom like we did the first day. Nash links elbows with him and laughs a little at his surprised look.

"I thought you guys were . . ." Tom doesn't finish the sentence, so Nash does it for him.

"Arguing? Brawling? Cat-fighting?"

"Well . . ." Tom says. "Yeah, kinda."

"We were," Nash says. "But we're over it now." He smiles at me.

"Oh, okay. Great," Tom says, still a little confused by the sudden shift from hostile to happy. Then he frowns. "Wait, is this the part where you tell me you can't hang out with me anymore because it almost ruined your friendship?"

"No, no, no," Nash reassures him. "Nothing like that."

"Oh. Good. 'Cause I hate that part." Tom looks at me, back at Nash, then links his other elbow with mine. We walk up the steps like that but have to disband in order to get through the doors. "See you at lunch!" Tom calls as he walks to his locker.

Nash sighs, watching him go. "Why does he have to be so . . . everything?"

"Be brave, Petit Chou." I put my hand on his shoulder.

"Wait, what does that mean, again?"

"Little cabbage," I say.

"Eww. I thought the French were poetic and romantic? What's romantic about a cabbage?" He gives a little shudder. "Whatever. See you later."

"Gator," I say. Nash gives me a backwards wave as he makes his way down the crowded hall. I let out the breath I've been holding for days.

CHAPTER 19

Kayla's house is one of the sprawling hundred-year-old lakeside mansions built by the Cedar Ridge founding fathers. I'm sure she wouldn't call it a mansion, but the shoe fits. Walking up the driveway on Saturday morning, I have flashbacks of the last time we worked on a project together, the science fair volcano. We used vinegar and baking soda and a little red food dye for the lava. A maid or nanny helped us put together the two-foot-tall mountain because her parents were out of town. I remember feeling kind of creeped out at the idea of being in that big house with no parents around.

Kayla opens the door almost as soon as I knock, like she was waiting on the other side. She smiles and says hi, but keeps playing with the pearl ring she always wears, spinning it around on her finger. We walk through the echoing foyer, past several immaculate, tastefully decorated rooms and into the kitchen.

"You want anything?" Kayla asks. The kitchen is different from how I remember it. It used to be kind of a country kitchen, with a big farm sink and hardwood counters. Now everything's modern and clean. Stainless steel and white tile. I look at the double oven and the professional mixer and imagine getting to bake in this space. But the room has an unused look. I wonder for a minute if they still have a maid.

"Maggie?" Kayla asks again. She turns around and sees me checking out the kitchen. "It's all for show," she says. "We never cook. I don't really know how, and Mom and Dad stay at our condo in Seattle a lot. The microwave gets quite a bit of use." She points at the small microwave in the corner of the kitchen. "Soda? Do you still like root beer?"

"Wow, good memory. No, thanks. Maybe just some water?" I say. "And I brought caramel brownies. I thought I remembered you liked brownies?" I pull the Tupperware out of my bag and open it on the counter. The smell of chocolate and salted caramel wafts out of the container.

"Yeah, when I was twelve." Kayla leans over and smells the brownies. "Oh my god! Um, yeah, I still like them, but I can't . . . I don't eat them anymore. Thanks."

"Suit yourself." I grab one and put the lid back on the Tupperware. It would be fun to whip up some new cookie recipes in a kitchen this nice. "So you don't cook at all?"

"Nope," she says, handing me a glass of cold, filtered water. "I mostly eat take-out." She opens a drawer, pulls out a three-ring binder, and starts flipping through it. It's full of local restaurant menus slipped into clear plastic sleeves. "My favorite is Nacho Momma's. Their fish tacos are amazing! But I order sushi a lot too. Rock'n'Roll has the best tuna rolls, I think." I nod, as she keeps flipping through the menus. "Oh my gosh! I just remembered the first time we tried sushi! Remember? My mom took us?"

"You ordered eel because it was one of the only things they cooked." I laugh.

"I was ten. I didn't want to eat raw fish."

"The tiny fish eggs got stuck in my teeth and kept popping all night."

"The gift that keeps on giving!" We crack up for a minute, but when the laughter dies down, the silence is awkward.

"Are your parents home now?" I ask.

"Seattle for the weekend." She slips the binder back in the drawer. "They have big cases going to trial on Monday. But they stay there even when there isn't something going on at work. I can't remember the last time they stayed here during the week."

"Wow. So no nanny anymore?"

Kayla laughs. "Not since I was about thirteen."

"Don't you get a little freaked out living in this big place all alone?"

Kayla starts twisting her ring with renewed energy. "Not freaked out, really. Not about the house, anyway." She rubs her fingernail across an invisible spot on the counter.

"That's cool," I say. "It must be nice to be able to do your own thing. I could do with a little less parental scrutiny myself."

"Careful what you wish for." Kayla's voice takes on a hard edge. But then she shakes herself and the moment is past. "Okay, let's get to work. We can go to my room. I have art supplies and stuff up there."

Kayla's bedroom is huge and bright, with large windows overlooking the lake and the mountains beyond. I feel a pang of jealousy that she gets to see this view whenever she looks out her window. It's perfect, like something out of a Martha Stewart magazine. I'm actually relieved to see a pile of shoes next to the doorway and discarded clothes making a path to the full-length mirror near the desk. The only thing that looks familiar is the huge mound of stuffed animals covering most of the bed. Some of them have seen better days. I recognize a plush dolphin Kayla got at the Seattle Aquarium on our fourth grade field trip. I also spot the stuffed orangutan I bought her for her birthday in fifth grade.

Last time I was here, Kayla's room was painted white and decorated with framed pictures of flowers picked out by her mother. Now three of the walls are painted this warm yellowish-orange that sort of glows in the midmorning light. But the fourth wall is wallpapered floor to ceiling with photos. Most of them are people I recognize from school, but I see a couple photos of her parents. It's like a giant photo collage shrine to all the people in her life. Across the top in big loopy letters cut out of construction paper it says "Friends Forever." This kind of thing typically rates high on my cheese-o-meter, but the wall is pretty impressive and unexpectedly sincere.

"This is really cool," I say, perusing the wall. "Did you do all this yourself?"

"Yeah."

"It must have taken you a while."

"It did. But I like having people around me," she says. "And this way I'm never really alone, you know?" With all these friends, I wonder again why Kayla is making such an effort with me.

"Seems like you're always surrounded by people."

"Yeah, well, lots of people doesn't necessarily mean lots of friends," she says.

I notice some photos of a dog, a dachshund. Or at least I think they're all the same dog—it's hard to tell with wiener dogs. Kayla's wanted one since grade school. "You finally got a dog?" I ask.

"I wish." Kayla clears a space on the bed. A waterfall of stuffed animals spills off the edge as she pushes them to one side. "I want one, but my parents don't think I'm ready for the responsibility. Plus a dog, in particular a dachshund, 'wouldn't really go with the décor.'"

"So, you're here alone all the time, you want a dog, and your parents won't let you get one because it won't match the couch?"

"Pretty much."

"Bummer." I'm still looking at the photos. I know most of these kids. A lot of the pictures were taken at parties. I don't go to parties, or more accurately I don't really get invited to parties. But there are telltale signs. Kayla and her friends with red plastic cups in someone's basement. Kayla and her friends with red plastic cups at someone's lake cabin, in someone's kitchen, in someone's hot tub. "So do you ever have parties here?" I ask.

Kayla laughs. "No way! My parents are never here, but they're pretty anal about the house. They would know if I had a party; they would not be pleased." She laughs again. "Maybe I should, now that I think of it. That might get their attention." She goes quiet, apparently pondering the possible fallout of surprising her parents with a raging party in their absence.

The photos get older, and Kayla younger, as I scan down the wall. In the lower right-hand corner of the mural, I see a photo of Kayla and me standing next to our science fair volcano. I am covered with red splatters from a particularly enthusiastic eruption, and Kayla is holding the green ribbon we received for participating.

Kayla sees me examining the photo. "We had fun, didn't we?"

"Yep." I straighten up and turn my back on the picture. "That was a good project. I think we should have won."

Kayla's eyes are on the photo, but they have an unfocused look, like she's not really seeing it. "Not just the volcano. All of it." She sighs. "You always made me laugh."

"Yeah, I make a lot of people laugh."

"No, not that way. I did stuff with you I never did with anyone else. That secret book club we had? And the time we dyed your hair with Kool-Aid? What color was that, anyway?"

"Purplesaurus Rex. Not my best idea."

Kayla laughs. "No, probably not. But it was entertaining. Even the weird stuff was fun."

I don't know what to say, so I take another look at the wall. "Yeah. Good times. And ancient history." I glance at her clock. "Speaking of which, we have work to do."

Kayla shakes herself and claps her hands together. "Okay, the Lincoln assassination: a creative interpretation. What are you thinking?"

"I'm thinking puppet show."

CHAPTER 20

I check my phone as I leave Kayla's. There's a text from Tom.
Hike? it says.

It's one of those spectacular, sunny fall days. A hike sounds perfect. A hike is what I need. He sent the text over an hour ago, but I text back anyway.

Where?

Lakeshore trail. I'm already there.

I drive from Kayla's house to the short, flat interpretive trail that follows along the shoreline. I set a good pace the first quarter mile or so, the part of the trail that runs between the lake and waterfront houses like Kayla's. But it isn't long before the houses stop, and the forest takes over.

The sunlight filters through the branches. It's chilly in the shade of the trees despite the clear blue of the sky outside. A flock of Canadian geese makes a noisy landing on the still runway of the water's surface. I breathe in the pine and cedar. Then I round a corner and stop short.

Tom is there, sitting on a bench looking out over the lake.

Seeing him like this, in an unguarded moment, makes me want to leave him undisturbed. His arms are both thrown over the back of the bench, his legs extended and splayed. The slight breeze tosses his hair.

I linger long enough to feel like a bit of a creepster and decide I should announce myself. I clear my throat, but he doesn't hear over the lapping of the lake and the sounds of the geese, so I do it again, louder. Still no luck.

"Hey," I say. My voice carries enough to startle him.

His face breaks into a smile. "Maggie! You made it!" He pats the bench next to him and slides over a bit to make room. "I was going to do the whole trail, but I sat down here and haven't moved since."

I plant myself, looking out at the water. We can see a few rooftops scattered along the town waterfront, but beyond that it's gray granite cliffs dropping into the lake, mounds of hills spiked with trees, and the peak of Hitchcock Mountain in the background, the white snow level already dropping into the tree line.

"I thought you and Nash had plans."

"Yeah, we were supposed to go thrifting, but his mom . . ."

"Ahhh." I'm sad Nash had to ditch Tom on such a beautiful day to baby-sit one of his mom's hangovers.

"Yeah, so anyway, I decided to come out here instead. A day like this . . ." He waves his hand in a way that gathers in the whole scene. We sit in silence for a minute.

I pull the sleeves of my fleece down over my hands and give a little shiver.

Tom's arm drops from the back of the bench down to my shoulder. He rubs until I feel the warmth. "Better?" he asks. He slides a little closer and pulls me into the crook of his arm.

I try to tell myself a little friendly friction on the upper arm is no big deal. But I'm sure Tom can feel my brain buzzing as I lean into him. I take a deep breath in, catching a whiff of soap and mint amid the evergreen and lake smells.

"And look," Tom says. He sits up, turning toward me, and points to a plaque on the back of the bench. "This bench is a memorial. 'To Jane and William Bennett.' Must have been some old couple who liked to come here." Our eyes meet for a brief second before I turn and look at the lake again. Tom drops his arm between us and leaves it on the bench, the back of his hand touching the back of mine. I give another little shiver and tell myself to pull it together. Gripping the seat of the bench, I sit forward a bit.

"So," I say, forcing brightness into my voice. "The other night you said I owed you a tidbit of embarrassing personal history."

"In fact," Tom says, "you owe me several. I have shared much and received little."

"Well, it's time for me to settle my debt."

"I can't wait."

"Okay, let's see . . . when I was five, my parents told me that we were going to Canada and that we would ride a ferry to get there."

"So far not embarrassing or humiliating in any way," Tom says.

"It gets better. I was giddy about the trip, worried about

what I would wear, what the weather would be like — the whole deal was making me frantic. And my parents couldn't figure out why."

"Go on."

"Turns out I thought I was riding a fairy, you know, with wings and magic and the whole thing." I wait for his reaction.

"Super cute, but not at all humiliating," Tom says. "Next."

"Wait, what do you mean? That's embarrassing!" I say. "I'm not sure you understand: I believed I was going to ride an actual fairy. A sprite. A pixie."

"You were five. It's adorable. Next."

I contemplate the volumes of embarrassing incidents I could pull from and decide to bring out some bigger guns. Besides, maybe a solid dose of self-sabotage will pull me back from the abyss of whatever I've let myself imagine is going on with Tom. I take a deep breath and spill.

"All right: sixth grade graduation. Everyone's there. The chorus goes up to sing a song, and I have a solo. It's only a couple lines long, but it's my big moment, you know? Anyway, the time comes, I step forward, and from the first note I know I'm singing in the wrong key. Half the sixth grade class is *oooh*-ing and *ahhh*ing behind me, the other half is watching, and I am not even close. Disaster."

"That's better," Tom says.

"Clincher? I'm beet red; everyone else is horrified by my performance and relieved it's over. As I turn to walk back to my place on the risers, I trip and fall, taking our music teacher and her music stand down with me."

"Wow. That works," Tom says. "Um, did anyone get hurt?"

"Mrs. Harper: whiplash and a sprained wrist. And I had the rare privilege of an entirely public humiliation." I look at Tom. "So are we even? Have I abased myself sufficiently for whatever arcane rules of friendship you live by?"

"Well, it's pretty good—or bad, I guess I should say. But I'm not sure a moment of klutziness when you were eleven is on the same scale as months of immersion in Dungeons and Dragons culture. Just in terms of personal flaws and life choices. I'll have to get back to you on that."

"Failed again," I say. I search my memory for something that will tip the scales. "Third time's a charm. But this one stays here. I need your solemn vow on that."

Tom holds up his right hand. "You, me, and the geese."

"Freshman year I went through a pretty heavy Jane Austen phase. Read the books over and over, repeated viewings of the BBC *Pride and Prejudice* miniseries."

"Repeated viewings of a miniseries?"

"Yeah, well, I was very committed. Anyway, one day I was bored in science and started doodling in my notebook."

"Doodling?"

"Okay, not exactly doodling. I made a list."

"Of?"

"Of my possible Mr. Darcys."

"Who's Mr. Darcy?"

I stare at him. "Seriously?"

"Sorry. Jane Austen falls into the 'old and boring' classification. Not a fan."

"You're making this really difficult."

"Sorry, again."

"Mr. Darcy is the man Elizabeth Bennett—"

"That's you in this scenario?"

"Yes. Anyway, eventually Elizabeth loves him, but for most of the book, they hate each other."

"Ahhhh. Okay, I get it. Continue."

"So I thought of all the guys that I sort of loathed but also thought might be secretly wonderful and put them on my list of Darcys."

"And?"

"And my lab partner saw the list, ripped it out, and spread it all over school."

"Not good."

"Not good at all," I say. "Needless to say, I have not committed a single bit of my inner life to paper since."

"But that's someone else being mean. That's not about you."

"It sure felt like it was about me." A breeze sends riffles down the lake. It disturbs the geese, who ruffle their wings, honking, before resettling into their gentle gliding.

Tom looks at me. "Okay, we're even."

"Finally!" I slap my hands on my knees and stand up. "I'll be able to sleep at night. Well, I have homework to do. Thanks for the, well, not a hike exactly. It was nice. Humbling, but nice." He stands too, close enough for me to register a slight duskiness on his jaw; he didn't shave today.

"I like seeing you in the woods," Tom says.

"Good," I say, "because it's kind of becoming a regular thing."

"You seem more . . . sort of . . . *you* here."

Tom's eyes wander over my face as I try to focus on

homework, geese, anything but Tom's face inches from mine. I feel myself reaching for him, searching over and around the moment, trying to discover a way things could be different, a way that this could work. But there are no cracks, no seams to get ahold of. Tom is the guy my best friend likes, wants, whatever. That means hands off, whether Tom likes Nash or not. And besides, Tom's attention is too universal. I have the feeling anyone standing in this place with Tom would believe they had a chance with him.

But then Tom bends his face to mine and kisses my forehead. His lips are soft, his kisses feathery. I close my eyes, and one of his hands moves lower, pulling my body into the contours of his. I stiffen at first, not wanting Tom touching my fleshy waist, worried he'll regret this when his hands move over my curves and bumps.

And then he's kissing me. Really, really kissing me. Arms around me, tongue in my mouth, kissing me. It's gentle, but there is enough pressure that I know he means it. At first my eyes pop open, and my brain is spinning, and I'm trying to figure out what the hell is happening. But it feels good, so I close my eyes and then I'm kissing him back, and every piece of my body is short-circuiting all at once. I let everything disappear for a moment except the feel of Tom's lips on mine, his hands on my back.

Our bodies touch at a hundred contact points, but somehow he pulls me in even closer, making it a thousand, moving the kiss to another level. I press myself into him, and for once I really don't care that there is more of me than I want there to be. Running my hands between his shoulder blades makes him kiss me even more enthusiastically, which I wouldn't have thought was actually possible. But then the geese spook at something, flapping and honking as they take off from the lake.

We break apart, and I am all at once shy. We stand watching the geese moving away from us over the lake.

"Walk you to your car?"

I nod, and Tom takes my hand as we head back down the trail. I can still feel the pressure of his lips on mine. As we emerge from the trees, the trail narrows and he has to let go of my hand. When we get to the parking lot, my car is the only one there.

"Do you need a ride?" I ask, unlocking my door.

"Nah. I'll walk. Especially since I got distracted from our hike." Tom smiles and my face flushes hot. "But I'll see you later?"

I nod. Watching Tom walk away, I try to hang on to the remnants of the kiss. But the feeling is fading, and thoughts of Nash and Kayla are crowding in. Things just got complicated.

CHAPTER 21

Nash and Tom are both home sick Monday, so I get an extra day to wrestle with my guilt before I have to face them. I'm not working, so Cece and I decide to have coffee after school. It's her idea, and she tries to act casual, but I can tell she really wants to talk about something. I hope it's AP English and not Nash. I order an americano, slide into a booth, and wait. Cece comes in a few minutes later. She orders some blended chocolate, hazelnutty monstrosity with extra whipped cream.

"How can you drink that stuff?" I ask. "You can't even taste the coffee."

"Hence the appeal," Cece says. She takes a long slurp and relaxes into the seat. "So, how are things? Since Tom moved to town, I hardly see you!"

"What do you mean? I don't hang out with Tom that much." I stare into my coffee cup, scared if I meet her eyes, she'll know.

"It's okay," Cece says. "I get it. He's new, and cute, and way more interesting than almost anyone in Cedar Ridge." She takes the straw out of the drink, licks it clean, and then puts it back in. She starts chewing on it. "Is Nash spending a lot of time with Tom?" she asks.

"They've done some hanging out."

Cece nods and gives a little smile. "I guess Nash thinks he's more interesting than anyone in Cedar Ridge too?"

"Cece," I say, but she holds up her hand.

"I know it's dumb to like someone who won't ever like me back, but I don't know how to stop." She smiles again and takes a long drink through her flattened straw.

"Nash is . . . Nash," I say. "I understand the appeal—after all, he's my best friend, so obviously I find him lovable. But honestly, Cece, on the gay-to-straight continuum, Nash is un-ambiguously gay. You're amazing, and I know Nash cares about you, but you simply don't have the right equipment."

Cece blushes at this, and I can't tell if it's because I men-tioned her equipment or because I finally told her to get over Nash. "I know," she says. She slurps down her drink, and I wonder what effect that volume of caffeine and sugar will have on Cece's slight frame. I fold my napkin into a little fan, smooth it out, fold it again.

"Cece, can I ask you something?"

"Sure." Cece licks the last of the whipped cream off the end of the straw.

"Have you ever done something . . . Have you ever made a decision . . . ?"

Cece looks at me, the straw forgotten. "Maggie? What's go-ing on?"

I stare at my coffee and feel my courage leave me like a souf-flé collapsing. I've done something shitty to Nash. And Cece will hate me for hurting him. I can't tell her. I look up to see Kayla through the window. She air-kisses a couple other girls before she comes inside. "Oh look! There's Kayla."

Kayla waves when she sees me. "Mind if I sit?"

Cece looks at me like I'm a box she's trying to unlock. "Be my guest," she says to Kayla. "I have to go anyway." Cece stands up and throws her heavy book bag over her shoulder. "We'll talk later?"

I nod and Cece leaves.

Kayla tosses some shopping bags on the seat and collapses into the booth. "Sorry," she says. "I hope I didn't chase her away?"

"No. She's fine." I'm a little ashamed at how glad I am Cece's gone.

Kayla waits, looking at me like she expects me to say something more.

"You getting coffee?" I ask.

"Maybe later," she says. "I had something with Kelsey and Amy."

I guess it's my turn again. "Did you guys go shopping?" I indicate the bags.

"Picked up a few things on the way down. They gave me a ride from school and Amy had to stop to buy some tights, so I made use of my mom's credit card."

I wonder what it must be like to be able to cruise through a store and know everything will fit.

"So, that was fun on Saturday," I say when Kayla doesn't speak again. "In a few short weeks, we've already tripled the amount of time we've spent together in high school. Kind of weird, huh?"

"What's weird about it?" She picks at a spot of something brown on the table. "I like hanging out with you, and you seem like you could use a friend of the female persuasion right now."

"I have friends, Kayla. Don't do me any favors."

"I know you have friends. That's not what I meant," Kayla says. "The timing seemed good for you, and the vibe seemed good to me, so . . ." She's trying to find words that won't offend me.

"I just don't want to be anyone's good deed." My guilt is making me edgy. I know I'm being an asshole, but I can't seem to stop myself.

Kayla grabs a napkin and wipes Cece's side of the table clean of whipped cream, scrubbing briefly at a spot of chocolate before balling up the napkin and tossing it aside.

"Look, it seems like you've enjoyed hanging out with someone besides Nash," she says. "And personally I'm a little sick of shopping and friends and talking about shopping and friends."

"Yeah, fine. But I'm still not sure what you want from me."

"I'm not sure either," Kayla says. "But I'm trying here. If you can't see that I need this right now too, then maybe we should continue to ignore each other and call it a failed experiment." She grabs her bags and purse and starts to slide out of the booth.

I drop my forehead to the table. "Wait," I say. "Wait. Okay . . . I'm sorry. I'm really bad at this, and I haven't made a new friend for a long, long time. Since, like, third grade? Anyway, I know I can be a little cranky."

Kayla pauses with her butt hovering over the seat. "Cranky?" she asks. She crosses her arms and waits.

I squirm a bit, then give in. "Distant? Guarded? Cautious?"

"I was thinking more along the lines of brutally honest and unreasonably suspicious."

"Okay. Wow."

"Relax, Maggie. I'm kidding. This is called joking around. Ever done it before?"

I force a laugh. Nash and I have been friends so long that we know which buttons to push and which lines not to cross. Feeling this out with someone new is exhausting. Our laughter fades and we sit in awkward silence again.

"Besides, I don't believe that shit about not being good at making friends," Kayla says. "Cece seems nice, and you've certainly hit it off with Tom. So no more false modesty about your social skills." This sounds more like the Kayla I've been talking to the last few weeks. "Maggie, I don't think you realize how much I envy you."

"Envy me?"

"You're so . . . you're always totally and completely yourself. You don't care what people think. I wish I could be more like that."

I watch her for a minute, trying to decide if this is just flattery. "Give me a break, Kayla. You have everything anyone could want," I say, leaning in. "You're thin, and beautiful; you have money, clothes, friends, guys. I, on the other hand, have a less-than-ideal body, I'm hopelessly geeky, and I work in a record store listening to music nobody else has even heard of.

By every possible measure, you have won the jackpot and I didn't even get a lottery ticket."

"How about the measure of happiness?" she asks, her voice so quiet I almost can't hear her.

"Kayla, be serious," I say. "You can't possibly—"

"You don't know what it's like," she interrupts me. "You saw that wall with all those people on it, those 'friends' of mine? And that seems great. But to be with them, I have to be this . . . person. The person you just described. And if I stray from that even a little, if I want to talk about a book I read, or skip a party to study, or make friends with people like you and Nash, I'm out. No friends, no status, nothing." She's spinning her ring like crazy.

"It's not a cult, Kayla."

"It might as well be," she says. I must have looked skeptical. "You don't get it," Kayla says. "It's like chickens."

"Chickens?"

"Yeah. You know how if there's a chicken that's weird, or just not like the other chickens, the whole flock turns on them? They actually peck them to death. You can't be different and survive. It threatens the group."

"Then find a different group."

"I know," she says. "That sounds easy. But what if nobody else wants me? I don't think I could handle being the one on the outside."

"Come on. It can't be that bad. You're here with me, in public. Twice now. And you had me over to your house. Have they threatened to throw you out of the clubhouse?"

The table is clean now, but Kayla starts rubbing her fingernail over the spot where the chocolate used to be.

I press her harder. "What exactly did you tell your friends about why we've been hanging out?"

"I, um . . . I told them we had an extra-credit project to work on for history and that you needed help." She looks away. "It's harder than you think, Maggie. I'm onstage all the time. I am never myself."

"So let me get this straight," I say. "You were so embarrassed to be seen with me that you told your friends you have to hang out with me for extra credit?" I want to kick myself for not listening to Nash and my own intuition. "This is such bullshit!" I start to slide out of the booth.

"No, Maggie, wait! Please!"

I don't look at her. "You didn't used to be like this, Kayla."

"I've always been like this. But I never had to worry about it with you. Being friends with you was easy." She pulls her hair back into a ponytail, then smoothes it down in front. "I'm sorry. I know it's lame. But I'm doing the best I can here. I'm out of practice at how to be . . . real, I guess? I haven't done it in so long. Please, don't leave yet."

I let that sink in, then slide back onto the bench. "Okay. I'll stay." My hand is still clamped on my backpack. "But this is messed up, Kayla. You can't pretend you don't know me. If you have the kind of friends that would kick you to the curb because you hang out with the fat kid, those are some twisted amigos."

She slumps forward and covers her face with her hands. "I know, I know, I know." She sits up, giving me her trademark smile. But I can see it doesn't reach deep. "Can we start over? Talk about something normal?"

"Sure," I say. We sit in silence, and I pick at my cuticles, waiting. I've done enough today; Kayla's going to have to come up with something or I'm out.

"So, tell me more about Tom," she says. If she was looking for a neutral topic, she missed by a mile. "I started sitting next to him in French, and we've hung out a couple times, but I can't seem to get beyond '*comment allez-vous*' with him. What's his story?"

"I'm still trying to figure that out myself."

"He seems like he might be kind of a player."

"He's pretty universally friendly, that's for sure."

"Yeah. I definitely have some new competition as the school flirt. But he's hot, all the same."

"Kayla Hill: Master of the Obvious."

"I know he and I went out, but seeing you guys together, it looks like, well, you must be crushing on him a little?"

I smile to myself, thinking about Tom's goofy grin, Seattle, the hikes, the kiss. One unguarded moment, and Kayla pounces.

"I knew it!" She points at me. "I knew you liked him!" She claps her hands together and rubs them like she's about to hatch some evil plan. "Maggie Bower, you've been thinking naughty thoughts about Tom!"

"No, Kayla," I say, backpedaling wildly. "It's not like that." But I can see she isn't listening. I grab her hands across the table. "Kayla, listen to me!"

She stops, looking at our hands, then up at me.

"Oh, Maggie, chill out! I won't tell anyone," she says. "Your secret's safe with me."

"There's no secret to tell." Kayla's watching me. I feel a bit like a bug watched by a crow. "I'm serious, Kayla!" I say, feeling desperate now. "I don't want people getting the wrong idea. There's nothing between Tom and me. Period. End of story." My heart starts rattling, my fight-or-flight instinct kicking in.

Kayla examines me. I can practically see the wheels turning behind her eyes. "Maggie," she says, her voice coaxing. "Something happened. Tell me."

I start folding my napkin again, but it's wearing thin and starts tearing into strips. I go with it, adapting my fidget to this new reality. I can hear Nash's warning about Kayla, his voice in my head telling me to be cautious. I know I should listen. But the pressure of the kiss with Tom, my first kiss ever, is swelling in my throat like water behind a clogged drain. I have to tell someone, and who else do I have right now? I take a deep breath, let it out.

"Nothing happened." My voice is quiet. I clear my throat. "Really. Nothing."

Kayla looks at her phone, then back at me. I can see she's trying to put things together, her mind clicking and whirring. I feel the dizzying weight of my secret resting on my heart, a secret made of both bubbles and stones.

"Nothing? Nothing at all?" She watches me, then picks up her phone again. "Hey. Whatever. If you don't want to tell me—"

"Look, Kayla. After I left your place yesterday, we met for a hike and—"

"But you like him?"

"Yeah, no, not— It's not like that." I put my head in my hands and feel the heat of my lies creep up my neck and onto my cheeks.

"If you say so, Maggie." Kayla glances at her phone. Sends a text.

"I do. I do say so." I hesitate. Telling Kayla about Nash's crush on Tom could be as big a mistake as the kiss. I understand all at once that my guilt over Nash is only part of my stress. What if Tom was on drugs? What if it was just a rush of errant hormones? What if it was some kind of dare or bet? Kiss the chubby girl, an extra twenty bucks if you do it with tongue? I put my forehead on the table again as it begins to dawn on me what a colossal mistake I have made. "It's complicated."

"Okay, okay. Don't worry. I get it. Just friends." Kayla starts texting again, which makes my heart pump faster.

I cover my panic with a quick retreat. "Okay. Good. Thanks, Kayla." I grab my pack and scoot along the bench. "I have to go. But thanks, again, for this. Sorry I'm not better at it."

"Don't worry." Kayla lays her hand on my forearm. "Life has a way of working out. You'll see."

Leaving the café, I feel like I'm in one of those Whac-A-Mole games. I just keep popping my head up and letting Kayla bash me on the head with her hammer. My stupidity is epic, and all I can do now is sweat it out and hope she doesn't catch on.

The walk home gives me plenty of time to settle down, and the crisp, fall evening cools the heated flush that my moment of panic brought on. Mom is working at the kitchen counter.

She offers me dinner. I want to eat, but not dinner. I want something that will dull the edges of these feelings. Something sweet. Something soft. Not the chicken stir-fry Mom cooked. But I take it anyway. I need to push down the panic with something.

I carry the chicken and rice up to my room to do homework. It's only a few minutes before I hear a knock at my door.

"Can I come in?" Mom says, hovering outside in the hall.

"Sure," I say. "What's up?"

"I was going to ask you that."

I flip through my history book, looking for the chapter I'm supposed to be studying. "What do you mean?"

"You seemed a little agitated when you came in. Anything I can help with?"

"Nope, nothing in particular going on. Life's been sort of a giant hairball of crazy this last month, but that's actually pretty normal for me."

Mom laughs. To her credit, she doesn't act at all surprised or condescending about my bout of teenage angst.

"I'll get through it," I say.

"I know you will, honey. I hope . . . .I want you to enjoy life a little along the way. You deserve that."

I snort. "Sorry, I've been spending a lot more energy surviving than having fun."

"That's too bad." Mom doesn't leave.

I put the history book aside, but I'm glancing through my notes now, avoiding Mom's eyes.

"What can you do to change that?" she asks.

"What do you mean?"

"If your life isn't going the way you want, change what you're doing."

"Who said my life isn't going the way I want?"

"You just said you're barely surviving!"

"I didn't say that. I said I was spending more energy on surviving than on recreation."

"Fine. And is that how you want to live?" Mom's voice rises.

I turn back to my notes, hoping she'll get the hint and leave me alone. She doesn't. "Mom, no offense, but I'm not sure a lecture is really what I need or want at the moment."

Mom takes a deep breath. She starts to massage her forehead with her fingertips. "Then what do you want, Maggie?"

This one stumps me. Mom usually asks me how I feel, or what I want to do about a particular situation. Most often she hands out advice like free peanuts on an airplane. But this question stops me. What do I want?

"Hmmmmm . . ." I say, stalling. "World peace?"

Mom flinches.

"Universal health care?" I try again. "Mom. What's this all about?"

"I'm just trying to help."

"I know, Mom. You're always trying to help."

Mom looks at the floor and sighs. "Look, Maggie, I'm guessing you want a lot of things all at once."

I've stopped shuffling papers now. Mom has my full attention.

She rubs her forehead again. "I know what it's like to want things, and I know what it's like to feel like you don't deserve to have them. Or to feel like you don't deserve to even want them."

Mom looks right at me now. "I spent too much of my own life tossed around on the waves of what other people thought was best for me. I know I've been hard on you at times, but I do it because I can see you're adrift."

"I'm not adrift. I really do want world peace," I say.

Mom sighs. "Joke if you want, Maggie. But I hate seeing you unhappy."

My eyes start to contract as they fill with tears. One drops onto my notes, smearing the blue ink. I kind of hate Mom for being so caring and wise all of a sudden after months of not-so-gentle cluelessness.

She hands me a tissue. "Sorry if I said too much."

I wipe my eyes and blow my nose. "No, it's okay. I know you care."

"Never forget that," she says.

CHAPTER 22

The minute I get on the bus the next morning, I know something's up. Nash crosses his arms and looks out the window, but not before he has given me a momentary death stare. He doesn't make room for me, so I sit across from Tom in the other front seat. I kind of dig how he always sits there. He's just going to school, and he seems blissfully ignorant of the fact that the front seat is designated for king geeks and losers.

I haven't seen him since the weekend, since the kiss. And there are so many questions and not enough answers right now. I can feel my forehead knotting together in the middle as I wait to see if my Kayla stupidity has any consequences. Tom tells me some story about living in Las Vegas and how he found out his friend's mom was a stripper during a sleepover one night. He's acting weird, but in an endearing way, so I don't call him on it.

Out of habit I look around for Nash when I get off the bus. I don't see him until he pushes between Tom and me, knocking us apart. He doesn't say a word or look at us as he stomps into the building.

"Shit," I say under my breath.

"Rough morning, I guess." Tom steps closer and lays his hand on my arm. "He wouldn't talk to me, either."

I look at Tom, a panic rising in my chest. "Any idea why?" I keep my voice neutral, but the answer is already kicking around my brain, trying to get my attention.

"Can we talk? Maybe after school or something?" People are flowing around us into the building. Tom leans in. "You know, about this weekend?"

I almost slap my hand to my own forehead like some Saturday morning cartoon character as I realize the worst has happened: Nash knows about the kiss. "Sure. Whatever. I have to go." I scuttle into the building, putting as much distance as possible between Tom and myself. When I get to my locker, I lean against it, my body heavy with the weight of my confusion. What is going on here? Kayla must have said something, but what, exactly, did she say? Who did she tell? And why? I mean apart from the obvious: she's just that girl. The warning bell rings, echoing the ones going off in my head, and I decide all I can do is play dumb until I have time for more reconnaissance.

Cece is waiting for me outside English. As soon as she sees me, she rushes over, grabs my elbow, and drags me into the girls' bathroom. After checking the stalls and finding them empty, Cece leans her backpack against the door. She's scaring me a little now.

"Nash told me! How could you do this to him?" she says. "He is . . . You are . . . Nash is your best friend. And you throw it away for . . . for what?" Cece's pacing back and forth. She won't look at me.

"Cece—"

"Nash told me!" she says again. She's still pacing. "I knew something was up. You were trying to tell me yesterday."

"Nash told you what, exactly?" I'm speaking softly, trying not to spook her.

"Don't play dumb, Maggie. You and Tom?"

"And where did Nash hear that?"

"Who cares? How could you do this to Nash?"

"I haven't . . . This isn't what you think. Tom and I aren't . . ." But I don't really have a way to explain this away, and Cece knows it.

"You are not who I thought you were, Maggie Bower. Not at all." She grabs her backpack, flings open the door, and marches out into the hallway.

The bell rings before I make it to English. Cece and Nash are huddled together across the room, far from where the three of us usually sit, and Nash shoots me a look that's three parts venom and one part heartbreak. I slide into an empty desk, my stomach already clenching with the ache of isolation.

Just before lunch, I get a note from the office saying Ms. Perry wants to see me. I gather my things and head to the gym, preparing myself for another layer of mortification. Ms. Perry is obviously waiting for me. She waves me in, closes the door, and indicates that I should sit. She seems very cautious, and I have a fleeting impression that she's a little afraid of what I might do.

She sits at her desk, turning her body and leaning forward so we can talk face-to-face.

I press myself into the back of the chair, trying to maintain a safe distance.

"Maggie," Ms. Perry begins, then pauses, like she's trying to decide what to say. "I was wondering how things are going?" Her left leg moves up and down like a sewing machine, and she's rubbing her thumb over each of her fingernails in turn. She waits, I guess hoping I will spill my guts, but I can't help her. There will be no more honesty between me and, well, pretty much anybody in the near or distant future. She waits.

I wait.

I wait longer.

She tries again. "I've been . . . concerned for a while now. About you. I see you're getting teased in class."

I groan. "Ms. Perry, this is really not a good day to have this conversation."

"I know it must be embarrassing for you. Boys can be cruel, especially to a girl like you."

"A girl like me?" I start to get up.

"Sit," she says.

I sit.

"Okay. Let's start over. I've noticed there have been some comments directed toward you in class."

"I've noticed that too."

"I was wondering if you thought we should do anything about that?"

"I've thought of all kinds of things I'd like to do about that."

"Good! Good. Wonderful." She claps her hands together in what I can only assume is relief. "I've also been thinking of how we can change the situation." Ms. Perry digs in her file cabinet, pulling out pamphlets and piling them on her desk.

"How 'we' can change the situation?"

"If you took a few steps to take better care of yourself, I think you'd find those boys wouldn't have anything to tease you about. I have some information here about how to be more active—"

"You've got to be kidding," I say under my breath. I look around at her office, at the posters of buff men and women in athletic gear, tanned muscles shining with oil and airbrushing. Then I look at Ms. Perry, all sharp angles and bony self-denial, and I get brave. "Can I ask you a question?"

"Asking questions is never a bad idea, Maggie. I want students to feel they can talk to me."

"Well, you seem to have it in for the fat kids, and I was wondering why you find us, me, so revolting?"

"I don't—"

"Please, Ms. Perry. I'm not trying to get you in trouble or make you feel bad. Well, maybe I am trying to make you feel a little bad. You obviously have some strong feelings about me, about 'girls like me.' I'm just trying to figure out why?"

"Maggie, my job is to help people be healthier." She leans toward me. "I take that work very seriously. My methods may seem harsh, but I have your best interests at heart." She pushes the pamphlets into my hands. "These have some great information about diet and exercise that could help you—"

"Thanks, Ms. Perry. But I know everything people like you think people like me should do. I was mostly wondering why you're so mean about it. But now, I think I understand. I thought I had a problem, but you're the one with problems."

"Just a minute, young lady!"

My voice has an edge to it that is keeping both my anger and my tears at bay. "I can handle the jerks in PE. So don't worry: you can keep doing what you've been doing, which I guess is nothing." I toss a cookie onto the desk, and she recoils. "Good luck."

Leaving the locker room, I glance through the pamphlets Ms. Perry handed me. Mixed in with the ones on diet and exercise is one on teen pregnancy and another on STDs. I let out a bark of laughter and dump the whole pile in the trash.

I can't stay at school. I have to be outside, to breathe. I stop by my locker, where I shove the rest of my books in my backpack, and race-walk down the hall and through the double doors to the fields in back of the school.

As I make my way to the trees that line the fence at the edge of the school property, I say a silent prayer that the stoner patrol hasn't made their way to the woods yet today. I am not in the mood to deal with the positive vibes of the newly baked. I shiver as I walk among the frosted trees, trying to stay out of sight of the building.

Leaning against a tree, I realize I have gone from never been kissed to boy-stealing ex–best friend in one weekend. I feel somehow both wounded and ashamed. Kayla screwed me.

Again. And I'd like to kick her perky little ass. But I'm the one who kissed Tom. I hurt Nash. And I have no idea how to make it right. I make my way up the ridge toward town, walking until the trees and the fresh air blunt the edges of my frayed nerves.

CHAPTER 23

I can't go back to school, and I can't go home, so I spend most of the day drifting from one coffee shop to another. I slide into Square Peg about five minutes late. My gut roils from too much espresso and a pre-work chocolate-scarfing session. But as the sugar winds through my system, I feel less frantic than I did when I left Cedar Ridge's hallowed halls.

"Hey, Mags," Quinn says, looking up from his computer with a wide smile. He glances at the clock and his smile morphs into a scowl, what he calls his "boss face." "You're late again!"

I look around the empty store. "I'm sorry. Did I leave you in a lurch while you were trying to serve the zombie hoards hungry for vinyl?" I throw my backpack under the counter and lean against the chipped Formica, looking through a milk crate of records. "What's this?" I pull one from the crate, studying the artwork on the worn jacket.

Quinn looks up. "Record collection someone wants to sell. Short on cash, moving, blah, blah, yadda, yadda." He peers at me. "What's that on your face?"

My hand darts to my face, covering as much of it as possible. I wipe at a dab of chocolate smeared above my lip. "Nothing." I turn back to the milk crate. "So what's on the agenda today?"

"The 'agenda' today is pretty much like every day here at Square Peg Records: Pray for customers and winning lottery numbers while listening to rock and roll as it was meant to be heard."

"Um, don't you have to play the lottery to win?" I ask.

"Details, my dear. A technicality." Quinn dismisses me with a wave of his hand. "But come to think, the bathroom could use a bit of a scrub."

The public bathroom at Square Peg is one of the few things Quinn and I totally disagree on. He thinks it keeps people in the store longer, and therefore gives them a higher likelihood of purchasing some quality vinyl from him. I think it gives the losers downtown an opportunity to pretend to be interested in records for about twelve seconds before they lock themselves into the bathroom with the singular intention of trashing it with various body fluids. I have cleaned up pretty much every one of those fluids in that tiny water closet. On occasion I send Quinn e-mails with advertisements for biohazard gear, asking that we purchase some for bathroom cleaning duties, but so far he's declined. We both hold our hands out for Rock, Paper, Scissors, and as usual, I lose.

I grab the bucket full of cleaning supplies.

"Use the gloves!" Quinn calls to me as I disappear into the hallway that holds the bathroom.

The gloves are another point of contention with us. I want

to use them; believe me, the thought of my bare skin against any surface in the Square Peg public bathroom is abhorrent to me. However, the gloves may be, if it's possible, even more disgusting than the bathroom, and Quinn has not replaced them in all the time I've been working here. I know where they've been, and with that history they should have been disposed of long ago with the care given to nuclear waste.

I clean the bathroom, using as much bleach as is safe in an enclosed area. When I emerge several minutes later, gloves still on, my face is hot and I'm sweating from exertion in a confined space. I hack from the bleach fumes, a sound reminiscent of a cat expelling a hairball. When I look up, the store is no longer empty. Nash is there with some friends from an LGBT group he goes to sometimes in Seattle. Nash doesn't like them that much; he says they cause too much drama (hello, pot; meet kettle). Nash goes there if he's feeling lonely and needs to be reminded he's not the only gay teenager in the world, or if they're having a dance and he wants to see if anyone new has emerged from the closet.

I know he called them because he doesn't have anyone else. The fact that he's here, and that he's here with them, is meant to remind me of that. It's a message to me about how serious this is to him, how big a betrayal. And here I stand, looking ridiculous and awful in disgusting gloves, holding a cleaning bucket, sweat pouring down my face. The boys all give me a once-over, and Nash makes a face like he's the one who had to clean the bathroom. Now that they've seen me, there's no point in avoiding things.

"Hey, Nash," I say. "I was going to talk to you earlier but I . . . um . . . I had to leave school unexpectedly."

Nash looks at his friends, then back at me. He's smiling a tight little smile. "I didn't really notice you were gone."

"Yep. Gone for the whole afternoon," I say. "Maybe you could call me after work?"

"I don't think I'll have time." Nash runs his fingers along the edges of the albums in the bin nearest him. His friends are all watching, listening. Quinn looks through the milk crate of records, but I know he's hanging on every word.

"Okay," I say. "Well, when you do have time, I think we should talk."

Nash gives a little head jerk to the boys. They head for the door, and the minute they leave, I make an about-face into the bathroom to pull myself together.

"Trouble in paradise?" Quinn asks when I return.

"There's been some talk about Tom and me . . ." I grab lotion out of my bag and start applying it to the hands I just scrubbed into raw, red blotches in the freshly cleaned bathroom.

"Talk?" Quinn asks.

I shake my head, trying to rid it of the disastrous scenarios that have been dive-bombing my brain all day. "Nash has his panties in a bunch. You know how he can be. It's nothing. It'll blow over." But my stomach is twisting, and I know this time Nash is hurt for real. And I hate that I'm the one who hurt him. I start thinking I need to move, or eat something. I need to distract myself from this awful feeling.

"Didn't look like he's going to get over it to me, but what do I know?" Quinn's still looking at me. "Maggie, you know if you ever need to talk . . ."

"Quinn, we talk all the time." I punch him in the arm super slow-mo.

"I'm glad. But I know how things can be, especially when love and friendship get tangled up." Then he says in an accent I think is supposed to be sort of a New York mobster type, "You want I should rough anybody up for you?" At that moment Tom walks in. Quinn waggles his eyebrows at me and hooks a thumb at Tom. "Like him, maybe?"

I shake my head, giving him a big hug. "You rock," I whisper.

"What was that all about?" Tom asks when I join him in the R&B section.

"Nothing. Quinn's just taking care of me."

"You disappeared today."

"Yep." I avoid his eyes. "I needed a little 'me' time."

"Well, I was worried," he says. "And I had to do the lab with Kayla."

"Oh, poor baby. You had to put up with a gorgeous blonde fawning all over you."

"She didn't fawn. She flirted but didn't fawn."

I can see he's trying to get a reaction, but I don't bite.

"So do you want to get together after work?" he says. "Maybe have a cup of coffee or something? I think we need to talk."

"Tom, listen," I begin, but I'm not sure what I want to say. "Nash knows."

"Maggie, does it really matter? He's not an idiot. He must have already known you were into me."

"Into you? I'm not . . . Okay, whatever. That's not the point." I think I know the answer, but I ask anyway. "Did you tell Nash?"

"No. No. Not all of it."

"What part did you tell him?"

"I was trying to break it to him that I wasn't . . . that I didn't like him, and before I knew it, I was telling him how much I liked hanging out with you. I started out trying to make him feel better, but I guess it kind of backfired."

"Yeah, kind of."

"He'll get over it, though. Right?"

"Nash was here a few minutes ago. He won't even talk to me." Tom still doesn't get it.

"Nash is my best friend. He has been for so long that not talking to him feels like I lost an appendage. A day without Nash is like a day without . . ." I search for something that communicates how basic Nash's presence is to me.

"Is like a day without drama?" Tom offers.

It's the first really snarky thing I've heard him say. I want to congratulate him on shedding the nice-guy thing for once, but my loyalty to Nash won't let me.

"He's really not like that," I mumble.

"Could have fooled me." Tom shoves the record he's holding back into the bin. "I don't get it. I'm not gay. I would never have liked Nash in that way. I think he's cool and all, but I don't really understand what that has to do with us." Tom puts his hands on his head and kicks a bin of sale records near the counter.

"Hey! Gentle with the merchandise!" Quinn says.

Tom takes a deep breath. "Sorry. I honestly don't know what the big deal is, Maggie. All I know is I like being friends with you. Can't we keep hanging out like we have been? You know, just as friends?"

"Just friends?" My skin goes cold, then hot, and I grab the counter, clutching it until my knuckles whiten. I knew this was probably coming, but it stings all the same.

"Yeah." Tom lowers his voice and leans in. "I know I'm the one who kissed you, but I'm not sure what it meant for me. You know, long term?"

"So you're telling me you kissed me, risked the best friendship I have, the best friendship I've ever had, and now you're like 'maybe not'?" I sway a little, reestablishing my grip on the counter. "You have got to be fucking kidding me," I say under my breath.

"Maggie . . ."

"No offense, Tom. But I have friends. I don't need more friends. I need Nash."

"With friends like Nash, who needs enemies?"

"You don't know what you're talking about."

"Well, I know Nash is an idiot if he's mad at you for one little kiss."

"Look," I say. "Did you ever play dibs when you were a kid?"

"Yeah, of course."

"Well, Nash and I have been doing it since probably second grade."

"Maggie, what the hell are you talking about?"

"Nash called dibs."

Tom still looks confused, and then it hits him. "Dibs? On me? That's why he's so mad?" Tom shakes his head. "You guys are unbelievable!"

"I know it sounds stupid. But it's really about being a good friend. Being the kind of friend who doesn't get in the way when the other person really wants something. And now we've kissed, and I blew it. I'm not that kind of friend anymore. And I don't know how to fix it. I don't even know if it can be fixed."

"Whatever. Dibs are for bunk beds or the last chocolate doughnut. You don't dibs people. Call me when you grow up, Maggie." He swings his backpack onto his shoulder and pushes out the door, leaving the bell jangling wildly.

"I am so screwed," I say. It comes out half as a laugh and half a sob.

"Wow, how many people are you going to piss off today?" Quinn stands next to me.

"It's fine. The men in my life must all be PMS-ing." I look at Quinn and smile. "All the men but you, exalted boss and spirit guide."

"So, a question for you: If the tables were turned, if you liked the boy, but the boy liked Nash, what would you do?"

"Tom doesn't like me. Didn't you hear him? He wants to hang out, be friends."

"Whatever. Indulge me for a minute. What would you do?"

"Cry myself to sleep for a few nights, like I do whenever the man of my dreams likes someone else?"

"But what would you do about Nash?" Quinn asks. "Would you blame him? Would you make him choose? Or would you let him have the boy?"

"Well, it's different," I say. "It's harder for Nash to find boys who are . . . compatible. Especially in Cedar Ridge. If Tom liked Nash, I'd be sad for me, but I'd be psyched for him."

"Hmmmm," Quinn says, turning to his ledger.

I wait.

Quinn has something to say on the topic, but he's pretending to be absorbed in the accounts.

"'Hmmmm'?" I say. "'Hmmmm,' what? What does 'hmmmm' mean?"

"Nothing," Quinn says, his voice nonchalant. "But, okay . . . I have to wonder why Nash can't do that for you."

"Do what?"

"What you said you'd do for him. Be psyched because you found someone."

"But it's different—"

"Bullshit," Quinn says. "How many boyfriends has Nash had?"

"None."

"How many have you had?" he asks.

"None."

"Doesn't sound that different to me," Quinn says.

"But I kissed Tom." I pace back and forth inside the tiny square island of counter. "Ultimate betrayal. Nash liked him. I kissed him. How do I fix that?"

"Look, if Tom makes you feel good, if you really like him, even if it's just as friends, then Nash needs to find a way to be okay with that. Even if it hurts him a little." He spins back around to the desk and picks up his pencil. "Now, let me do my work. I think Classic Jazz needs straightening."

I make my way over to the Jazz section. If there was a yearbook category for "Least Likely to Find a Boyfriend at Cedar Ridge," Nash and I would be the clear winners. Either of us finding a guy here, a guy who likes us back, would be a minor miracle: something to be celebrated.

Flipping through the third bin, I find the album I need right away. I go back to the counter, put it on, and drop the needle down on Billie Holiday's "It's the Same Old Story." Quinn doesn't turn around, but he stops writing and sits up to listen. I put my head down and get to work, thinking about Tom and singing along with Billie's mournful voice. Like Billie says, it's an old story, but to me it's brand new, and I don't have a clue about what comes next.

CHAPTER 24

That night I'm stretched out on my bedroom floor, feet on my bed, one arm thrown across my face. What a shit storm of a day.

Checking my phone, I see a text from Tom: **Sorry**. And one from Nash: **Sorry yet?** Like bookends, those two. I don't respond to either text.

My phone buzzes again. It's Nash. And he's calling, not texting, so I pick up.

"Nash!" I say, fumbling the phone a little as I answer.

Nash is silent for a few seconds, but I can hear him breathing. "Maggie, how could you do this?" he says. His voice is quiet, but I can hear a little tremble of anger underneath.

"Nash, I'm not sure what you heard, or who you heard it from." I try to keep my voice level. "But Tom and I aren't together. Talk to Tom if you don't believe me."

"Oh, Tom and I talked already—we talked about a lot of things, hon." The word is sweet, but it drops like a blade. "Last night we talked about how I'm not his type. Right after he spent an eternity raving about the stellar time you two have been having behind my back."

"Stellar time? What, in biology lab? Give me a break."

"Biology? Yeah, nice cover. Hiking? Seattle? Dinner? You were after him all along, and congratulations! Tom wants you, not me."

"Nash, listen, that's not how that happened. You were standing right there when we decided to go hiking. And Seattle was your idea until you bailed and left me to play tour guide. Get a grip!"

"Why would he say that, then?"

"Say what?" I ask. "That we had fun on the hike? Or in Seattle? We did, but that doesn't mean he *likes* likes me." I sound like I'm twelve. "Nash, I know you're sad, but you've got this wrong. Tom and I are not—"

"I would be happy for you if it were any other guy."

"Nash, you have dibs—"

"Fuck dibs, Maggie! When has dibs ever helped either of us in the boy department? Jesus! Grow up! Until now we were both in danger of reaching legal adulthood without being kissed." His voice verges on hysterical now. Nash is unhinged by whatever he imagines is going on between Tom and me.

"No, Nash, it's not . . . We're not . . ." I say, but he isn't hearing me now.

"I should have trusted my instincts. Way back when you said he was too nice to everyone, I should have known you liked him. I should have known!"

"Nash, you're my best friend! You know me—"

"I thought I did, but now I have no idea. We were both in the same boat: seventeen, never been kissed, never had a boyfriend. That sucks, right? But we were in it together, and I thought you would be happy for me when I finally found someone."

"I am—I mean, I will be—" I am crying now, but I don't care. "Nash, you don't understand . . ."

"Don't, Maggie," he snaps. "Seriously. And you know the hardest part? The thing that is really breaking my heart right now? What I want to do most is talk to my best friend. But since she's the one that fucked me over, I guess that won't be happening." He's crying a little now. "You were the only one I could trust, Maggie! The only person who knows all my shit. The only one who's seen how hard it's been. I really can't wrap my brain around how you could do this to me."

"This didn't . . . It's not what you think!" Now I'm crying in that disgusting, gulping, snotty way that can't be controlled, trying to get enough words out to make him see how sorry I am. How much I want to fix this.

"All this shows is that you don't care what I want, as long as you get yours." Nash's voice sounds bitter and brittle.

This poison dart stops my crying immediately. Nash has crossed the line. I remember what Quinn said and take a breath.

"Nash, Tom is not your someone," I say, my voice shaking.

"Thanks to you!" Nash says, and his voice is so whiny it temporarily sucks all the empathy right out of me. I want to reach through the phone and strangle him.

"Tom's not gay, Nash. He's not gay, he's not bi, he's not even bi-curious! He thinks you're a wonderful person, but he doesn't want to be your boyfriend. He will never want to be your boy-friend."

"God, Maggie. No shit!" Nash says. "I know all that. In spite of Tom's ability to make everyone in the room feel like he's in love with them, I still have some pretty good instincts about who's gay and who's not. You really think this is about some guy not loving me back?" I can hear in his voice all the familiar, frustrated longing of years of unrequited love. "This isn't about getting crushed by another crush. It's about friend-ship. It's about loyalty. It's about trust. It's about giving a rat's ass about what your best friend wants and not screwing over the ones you love."

I feel my heart tug toward my best friend's pain, but I recapture my anger and say my piece.

"I would be happy for you if Tom had turned out to be the one."

"Yeah, right."

"And I'm not the one for Tom either. He was pretty clear about that today. But as my friend, since you can't have Tom for yourself, wouldn't it have been nice if you could have been a lit-tle happy he might have liked me? Happy one of us might have a real chance with someone?" I stand and start pacing. "Look, the one-sided crush thing got old in about seventh grade. Tom being into either one of us would have been a hell of a lot better than one of the fucking A-listers getting the guy. Again."

When Nash speaks, he spits the words out with the venom of the recently betrayed. "Maybe I'd be happy for you, if you hadn't been so slutty about the whole thing." He hangs up, and I stand there, holding the phone.

I burst into tears and for a few minutes I try to call Nash back, but he won't pick up. I text him several hundred times. He doesn't respond. Gripping my phone, I pace some more, trying to decide what to do. Nash won't answer, Cece is pissed at me, and calling Tom seems like the worst idea ever. What I'd really like to do is find Kayla and punch her in the head. But I know this is my own fault.

The promise of some cookie dough to ease my pain propels me into action. I slide into my slippers, go downstairs, and pad past the living room, where Dad fiddles with some sort of small motor while Mom peers at her laptop. I do not want to have a conversation with my mother about the evils of junk food or my unrealized potential right now. I'm almost past the door of the living room when she looks up.

"Hi, honey. What are you doing?"

"Nothing, um, just getting a glass of water."

"Water's good for your brain," Mom says. "You know a de-hydrated brain . . ."

". . . Is a cranky brain. Yes, I know, Mom. Thanks." I start to make my escape, but Dad calls me back.

"Mags," Dad says. "Good-night kisses?"

I hesitate in the doorway, but don't see a way out without hurting Dad or making Mom suspicious. I circle behind the couch and lean in for a kiss with each of them, then hightail it out of the living room and head for the kitchen, where I can forget Nash and Tom and everything in a blur of flour and chocolate chips.

Mom comes in while the first batch is still in the oven.

"I thought you were coming in for water?" she says.

"Mom, not now, please?"

"Maggie, whatever the problem is, cookies are not the answer."

"That sounds like a refrigerator magnet." I'm measuring out spoonfuls of dough onto parchment paper. If I stop moving, I might fall apart.

Mom laughs, shaking her head. "You're right," she says. "That's probably where I saw it. But that doesn't mean it's not true."

"Mom, I know. I'm almost done."

She watches me for a minute. "Everything okay, honey?"

"Yeah. Good. All good." I keep my eyes on the balls of dough I'm lining up on the cookie sheet.

"You sure? You seem . . ."

"I'm good, Mom. Really. I'm tired."

She comes around the counter, putting her arm around my shoulder. "I love you, Maggie."

For about five seconds, I consider telling Mom the whole thing, but I drop the last bit of raw dough into place and the moment passes. "Thanks, Mom. Love you, too. Now get out of the way so I can get these things in the oven."

"All right. All right." Mom laughs, retying her robe as she heads back to the living room. "Don't forget to clean up when you're done."

"I always do!" I say, and start washing the mixing bowl. I finish baking and wrapping the cookies: plain chocolate chip tonight—my favorite. Instead of eating my one cookie at the counter as usual, I take four of them back to the privacy of my bedroom, where I can stuff my emotions without witnesses. I load up my most morose playlist, start the music, and sink to the floor, settling into my spot between the bed and the wall. I go through my ritual, breaking the cookies into quarters, then eating them from the inside out, leaving the crunchy, caramelized edges for last. And after I have swallowed the last crumbs, I am kind of okay. The cookies were crunchy and soft, and the bitter chocolate dulls both my anger and my hurt. There's a knock on my door.

"Maggie? You in there?" My mom starts to turn the knob, and I wipe my mouth and scurry onto my bed as she opens the door. "Maggie?" she asks again, and smiles as she sees me clutching my stuffed elephant, Neshie. "You've had that thing for so long!" she says, her eyes getting a little wet.

"Yep," I say, looking at the plush green skin and the bindi I drew with Sharpie on his forehead.

"Your dad says the cookies are delicious."

"Good. Nothing special: chocolate chip."

"Isn't that your favorite?"

"Yeah. How did you know?"

"I'm your mom, Maggie. I know what your favorite cookie is."

Suddenly my eyes are moist and I can't swallow. I hug Neshie tighter.

"I wanted to say good night," she says.

"Night, Mom."

She turns off the light, and I climb into bed. I fall asleep with images of Nash and Tom and Kayla swirling in my sugar-buzzed brain.

• • •

When the alarm clock jangles the next morning, I groan, slapping my hand on the snooze button to stop the electronic beeping. I have thrown off all my covers, but I am clutching Neshie by his trunk, which I have apparently been twisting for a good part of my REM cycles. It's crinkled and frayed looking, and I try to smooth out the damage, kissing Neshie on the bindi as I lay him back on the bed. I feel frayed and crinkled as well, but I suck it up and head to school, determined that today will be better.

CHAPTER 25

As I board the bus, Nash's eyes lock on mine and he scoots to the middle of our seat, leaving no room for me. Tom is in the front row and tries to motion that I should sit with him. I smile but slide into a neutral row halfway between them. The sun is streaming in the windows, and I catch glimpses of the lake and hillsides through the houses. I spin my iPod to my perkiest playlist, psyching myself up for whatever the day has to offer.

English is the worst. Nash and Cece huddle together, whispering like long-lost besties. I say hi as I walk by them to a back row seat. Cece says hi back: courtesy is an instinct with her. Nash just watches me, his face blank. I know this look. It's the look he has when he's so messed up, he can barely keep his seams from unraveling. It's the look he has when he doesn't want to fall apart.

With Nash and me both avoiding Tom, Kayla has stepped into his friendship vacuum. During a brief foray into the cafeteria to buy a Diet Coke from the soda machine, I see Tom sitting with Kayla and her friends. He looks amused, and the girls giggle at something he says. Kayla puts her arm on his forearm, marking her territory for the others. With all his talk of spending time with people "worthy," if Kayla's the best he can do, his standards aren't that high.

One of Kayla's minions notices me and leans in to tell Kayla. Tom spots me. Our eyes lock for a second. He smiles, but his face clouds with worry. Seeing him smile, I feel my chest open, and I breathe for the first time all day. But I also feel naked, vulnerable, like everyone in the cafeteria can see my insides, can see all the pain and anger I've looped through the last couple days. He starts to get up. I reach into my bag for some of the cookies I baked last night, then put my chin up and walk over to the table.

"Hi, Tom," I say, handing him a wrapped cookie.

"Maggie, hey!" he says. He keeps glancing between Kayla and me.

I smile and offer cookies to the skinny girls at the table. They look at me like I offered them freshly harvested rabbit turds.

"I'll take one," Kayla says. She reaches across Tom, rubbing against him to take the cookie I offer. "You know I love your cookies." She places it on the table without unwrapping it.

"Anyone else?" I ask, but the other girls avert their eyes and shake their heads. "Okay, well, I'm off to spread the love elsewhere, then." The girls stifle giggles. I turn and walk away, tossing cookies onto tables like grenades on my way out of the cafeteria.

• • •

I bake like mad the next few days, bringing cookies to school, trying to keep my giving ahead of my excess production. I pass them out three at a time, leave them on teachers' desks. I even offer some to the janitor and give a whole batch to the skaters playing Hacky Sack in the quad.

"Thanks, dude!" they say, and dig right in.

The fall weather is holding, and the mornings are frosty but bright with sun. I walk to and from school so I don't have to be trapped on the bus between Nash and Tom. The walks settle me down and give me time to think about what I'm going to do about the mess Kayla made.

In PE I fake an injury to keep from having to spend a twelve-minute mile in conversation with Tom. Unfortunately this means that when the wrestling jerks finish their runs, I have to sit in the bleachers and listen to their litany of unimaginative, off-color jokes.

"What's brown and white and fat all over?"

"I think I see a moooooooooose!"

"We should ask Tommy Boy if her love handles really work?"

I know I should ignore it, but I find myself thinking surprisingly detailed thoughts about the damage I'd like to do to them.

Bio is a different story.

"Why won't you talk to me?" Tom asks.

"I'm talking to you."

"You're talking to me, but we're not really *talking*."

"I don't know what you're talking about." I start paging through the massive bio book, looking for information on the mitosis lab we're supposed to do the next day.

Tom waits for more, but I'm all business. Eventually he gives up.

Quinn knows something's wrong, so I psych myself up for work in my post-school, pre–Square Peg time. This involves walking the bluff, eating cookies, and blasting my "Angry GRRRRL" playlist. Sonic Youth and Sleater-Kinney howl in my ears, obliterating for a few minutes the dull pain losing Nash has carved into my gut. It's not a permanent solution, but it gets me through my shift.

None of this fools Quinn, but it's better than disintegrating into a weeping pile of sludgy teen angst while I'm trying to help some customer find the album he was listening to when he packed for college, or when she lost her virginity, or whatever other life moments can only be recaptured by experiencing the sound of John Cougar's "Jack and Diane" played on vinyl. Come on, some of these people are tipping into "ancient" on the timeline. Is it even legal for them to subject me to the horrifying imagery that comes with hearing stories that meld their first sexual experience with the crappy music now in heavy rotation on the local classic rock radio station?

After a week or so of my faking it, Quinn draws a line in the sand. Billie is singing "Glad to Be Unhappy," weaving her spell over the store speakers. I ring up some lady's purchase with my now-customary zombie verve. After she leaves, clutching *ELO's Greatest Hits* like it's the fountain of youth, Quinn switches Billie out for some random record in the RTP bin. A classical tune—Mozart, I think—comes over the speakers.

"Hey," I say. "I was listening to that."

Quinn slams the nearly one thousand pages of his collectible record price guide down on the counter. "Stop it, Maggie." He slaps his hand on top of the book. "Just stop it. Enough Billie. Enough wallowing. Enough sad little Maggie." He gets my attention with the potentially lethal price guide, and I glance around to make sure there aren't any customers in the store before I answer.

"Um, Quinn? Are you okay?"

"Compared to you, I'm the picture of mental health," he says.

I get quiet.

"How long have I known you? A year that you've been working here? And then a couple years before that when you were hanging out trying to score some eighties vinyl?"

I straighten the counter, putting pens back in the ceramic fish.

"So about three years? Give or take? And in all that time, have I ever tried to boss you around about your life, or your friends, or about anything that went beyond interested conversation about weather, school, and your slightly disturbing relationship with Nash?"

"Yes," I say.

"Okay, yes, but this is different."

"Quinn, listen . . ." I say, but he shakes his head.

"I know you think you screwed up, that you deserve whatever heaps of agony Nash is dishing out."

"Because I do—"

"But friendship is a two-way street," Quinn says, interrupting. "Denying yourself everything you want does not make you a good friend."

"Neither does kissing the boy my friend likes."

"Okay, okay," Quinn says. "Maybe you have some apologies to make. That's your business. But remember, you deserve to be happy too."

I look away, but Quinn waits for me to meet his eyes before he continues.

"Maggie, you can't see it. I know you can't see it, but you have light. And you spend so much energy shoving that light down, making yourself small inside, and big outside, to hide yourself." Quinn puts his hands on my shoulders and forces me to look him in the eye. "Stop hiding," he whispers.

"I'm fine," I say, twisting away from him, wiping my eyes. "Tears of a clown and all that shit."

"Maggie, don't," Quinn says. "Don't go. Don't run away."

I grab my pack and, pausing in the open doorway, I say, "Thanks, Quinn," and make my escape.

About halfway down the block, I stop and let out a short burst of laughter as I realize that five seconds after Quinn tells me to stop running, I run. I know I'm in danger of becoming that awful cliché—the fat girl who eats her feelings—so I go to the mini-mart near the bluff and buy cigarettes. I have no idea which ones to buy; there's a brand made with organic tobacco. I decide the lack of pesticides will offset some of the other bodily harm, so I buy those and a cheap lighter and take them to the bluff, finding a spot where I can watch the sun sag into the hills around the lake.

Settling in, I unwrap the thin cellophane and take out one of the cigarettes. It has an herbal, almost clean scent, way different from the menthol smoke I remember from sneaking one of Nash's mom's cigarettes in fifth grade. I put the filter in my mouth and light the end, inhaling as I do. After a prolonged hacking fit, I try again. More coughing. I give it one more try before deciding that I'm an absolute idiot.

I have to face the facts: food is my drug of choice. Not as glamorous as cigarettes or as tortured as alcohol. I could probably hang out with the cool kids if I numbed out to one of the more interesting substances. I sigh, stubbing out the cigarette, and pull out my phone. **I miss you**, I text Nash, and send the message out into the universe. I want to remain on the bluff, watch the stars come out, feel small again, like I did last summer on the dock. But it's too cold to stay, and I know I can't hide forever.

CHAPTER 26

B y the time I get home, my throat is raw and scratchy and there's a screaming maw in the region of my stomach. I go to the kitchen, looking for something to feed the beast. The pantry, I realize too late, has turned into a health food market. I slam the door and make a fruitless search in several other cupboards before accepting that my mom has crossed over into eliminating every one of the foods that I need most on a day like today. We're even out of chocolate chips. In desperation I decide to make a stripped-down cookie dough from the butter, raw sugar, eggs, and organic flour my mom still allows in the house.

By the time I get it mixed, I don't feel like actually baking, so I scoop a large clump of dough into a bowl, throwing the rest into the trash can. I clean up after myself; I don't want anyone to notice I've used the kitchen. In my bedroom I put on some vintage Morrissey, the ideal soundtrack for my self-piteous mood. I check my phone. Nothing from Nash. Nothing from anyone. Flopping onto my beanbag chair, I start in on the bowl of soft, raw dough. After a few bites, I feel a little sick, so I put the bowl aside and slip my headphones on, shutting out everything but Morrissey's whiny lyrics.

I fall asleep like that, waking a couple hours later to my dad shaking my shoulder. I start, ripping off the headphones, and then look around sleepy and confused.

"Dad? What . . . ?" I sit up, taking in the bowl of half-eaten cookie dough, the headphones, and see how it must look to my dad.

"Dinner's ready, if you're still hungry," he says.

My gut forms a hard little shame biscuit. "Dad, I . . ." I begin, but what can I say about this?

"Maggie, I wish . . ." he says, his words sticking. "I wish you could see yourself like I see you. I wish you could see . . ." He makes a vague gesture toward me and then lets his hands drop to his sides. "I don't like to see you treat yourself this way." He turns to go, and I let him.

I pull my grandma's quilt off the bed, wrapping myself in its soft cotton, and spend the rest of the evening arcing between sobbing jags and numb lethargy. When sleep comes at last, it descends like a hammer blow, and I'm down hard, my face glued to the beanbag chair with saliva and snot from crying myself to sleep. Too soon the shrieking of the alarm and the glare of the bedside light drag me up through the deep layers, and I'm conscious again.

I slap my hand on the alarm, silencing it on the second try. I don't even try to turn the light off. My fine motor skills were never at their best in the early morning, and my hand tingles, heavy from sleeping on it too long. Groaning, I throw my numb arm over my eyes. After a few minutes, the alarm starts screaming again. I hit the snooze again, with better aim this time, and let one foot fall to the floor. Progress. I'm up. Sort of.

There is a tentative knock on my door. "Honey?" my mom whispers, cracking the door open.

"I'm up."

"Okay, I was worried . . . I heard the alarm." She inches her way through the crack. One foot, one shoulder, her head, the rest of her still outside. I can't tell if she's trying to respect my privacy or provide herself a quick escape. "I missed you yesterday. I didn't see you at all," she says. "How are you?"

I shift my arm off my face enough to give her a dirty look. "Awesome!" I say. "Living the dream!"

"Maggie, come on, honey," she says. "How bad could it be?"

I drop my arm back over my face.

"That bad?" She shifts her weight, still trying to decide if she wants to be in the room or out of it. "Can I help?"

"Mom, I appreciate the parental concern, and you are doing a bang-up job, believe me. But this is something I'm going to have to solve myself."

"There must be something I can do," she says.

"Mom. Sorry, but no. You're going to have to take my word on this one."

She watches me for a moment; I know a big part of her wants to advise me, to organize and arrange my life. "Okay, honey. You let me know if you change your mind." She commits now and comes all the way into my room to kiss my forehead and give my knee a squeeze. "Hang in there, Maggie."

"Excellent advice," I mumble as she leaves. I swing my other leg onto the floor and propel myself up and to the shower.

I'm running late, not enough time to walk to school, so I catch the bus, barely. Nash shows no signs of softening, no sign of letting me in or even letting me get close. The bus empties, and I don't even try to blend with the drivers from the student parking lot. I round the corner to my locker and stop short. Tom is there waiting for me. Looking around, I search for a place to hide, but he sees me before I can escape. Tom lifts his hand in a little half wave. My lips form a little involuntary smile.

"Hi," he says.

"Hi." I set down my pack between us and work on my combination, sending out a silent prayer than my lock will actually open on the first try today. But the locker gods are in trickster mode. I rattle the lock and try again.

"You okay?" he asks.

"I've bounced off the bottom, on my way back up." The combination clicks, and I jerk my locker open. He cranes his head around the locker door.

"Maggie, I know you think we can't be friends because of Nash, but—"

"Listen," I interrupt. "I don't think it; I know it. Nash does not tolerate betrayal." I slam my locker and swing my backpack onto my shoulder. "I don't think it matters now because Nash hates me, but if there is a chance of salvaging my friendship with him I will."

I start to walk away, but Tom calls, "What about me?"

"What do you mean?"

"Don't I get a say in any of this?"

I look around, wishing the hallway was less populated. "I'm guessing you'll get over it. Nash and I were the welcome wagon when you first came, but I'm sure a few weekends of parties with the beautiful people and you'll forget you ever went slumming."

Tom throws himself back against the lockers, kicking one of them hard enough to make it rattle. "You two are unbelievable."

"Yeah, well, sorry about the blow-off. Lifelong friendship trumps the new guy every time," I say.

"Yeah," Tom says, his voice low. "Ditched again. Story of my life."

"Poor Tom."

"I wish you guys had left me alone in the first place. It would have made my life a lot easier."

"Better late than never."

"That's not always true."

"Come on, Tom. You must already have plans with Kayla? All signs point to you guys getting pretty close."

He stares at his feet. "Well, she keeps asking me out."

"Oh, wait. I think I heard this one," I say. "She's nice but you don't have time for all that fake. Now you do?"

"Well, yeah. Nash is being weird and you won't hang out with me, so I have tons of time. Tons of time and no friends."

"Tom, look. You're the handsome, smart, athletic, acceptably dressed new guy who moved to a small town desperate for novelty. You can have your pick of friends. Although if you keep acting dense about this, I may remove 'smart' from the description."

"Acceptably dressed?"

"Really? That whole speech and that's what you want to land on?"

"Well, the rest of it is bullshit, so I won't dignify it with a response."

The bell rings.

"I gotta go," I say. "I have social pariah duties to perform." I don't look back, but I know he's watching as I round the corner to my first class.

Cece is waiting for me outside of English again. She jerks her head toward the bathroom and I follow her in.

"We've got to stop meeting like this."

"Maggie, I don't understand any of this."

"I know, Cece. I'm sorry."

"You're sorry? I don't even know who you are!" Cece says. "I thought you were . . . Well, I thought you were a nice person. But you're . . . you're not."

I drop my bag on the floor and slide down next to it. "Cece, if you think there's anything you could say that will be worse than what I've already said to myself, then you're right, you don't know who I am."

"Nash is so hurt."

"I know. And I know I'm the one who hurt him. I screwed up, and he'll probably never speak to me again." I stand up, pick up my bag, and reach for the door.

Cece grabs my arm. "Wait. What about you and Tom?"

"I'm not with Tom," I say. "He kissed me. Then he said he didn't really feel that way about me. So there's no me and Tom."

Cece waits. "Is that all you have to say about it? Because I think we all know it was more than just a kiss."

"Huh? No it wasn't."

Cece shakes her head and shoulders her backpack.

"Wait, Cece. What have you heard?"

Cece blushes bright red in an instant. "I heard . . . I heard there was more than a kiss. A lot more."

My mouth drops open, and I feel things click into place like the tumblers on a lock. "And that's what Nash heard too?"

Cece nods.

"Look, you may not believe it, but it was only a kiss. That's all. And the kiss was a momentary lapse, an unintentional moment of hormones overrunning my better instincts and my higher brain functions. But even if Tom wanted us to be a couple or whatever, I would have said no. The kiss was a mistake, being Tom's girlfriend would be a betrayal. I couldn't do that to Nash."

Cece looks like something I've said has turned her version of things sideways. She studies me a minute, then she grabs the handle and holds the door open for me.

After school, I walk home. My brain jumps and spins between all the different ways I'd like to hurt Kayla for what she's done. It's bad enough that she spread the news about the kiss. But the fact that all of this has ballooned into something more, into an even bigger betrayal of Nash, makes me sick with shame and rage. The clouds have rolled in during the school day, threatening rain. It's cool and gray, which I love, and windy, which I hate. But the fresh air blows some of the fuzz and anger out of my brain and gets me thinking. Cece had it wrong, but she listened to me, and that gives me some hope maybe Nash will do the same. I stop at the store and pick up a few supplies. I'm going to make breakfast bars for Nash, give him the whole batch, and tell him how much I miss him. I can only hope he's missing me too, or at least missing his breakfast bars.

CHAPTER 27

I pack up Nash's bars and walk to school the next day. By lunchtime I'm having fantasies about becoming an exchange student or being kidnapped by drug runners to work as their mule across the Canadian border rather than face Nash. But when I find myself alone in the hallway with him, it's my sheer desperation that gives me the courage to try. I grab the box of breakfast bars out of my locker and move toward him.

"Nash!"

He doesn't speak or meet my eyes, so I plant myself in the middle of the otherwise empty corridor, cookies in hand. I hold them out.

"I made your bars," I say. "A whole batch."

He keeps walking in my direction, no indication he's heard a word I've said.

"Nash, talk to me. Please. This is killing me." I am not happy to hear my voice quiver a little, and when he doesn't respond or slow down, I square my shoulders and shout, "This isn't fair! You have to talk to me!"

This stops him. He looks me up and down like I'm one of the dead fish we sometimes find on the beach near the swing set. "I? Have to talk to you?" he says. "I don't have to do anything. You are the one who fucked this up, Maggie. And a batch of cookies is not going to fix it." He stops, and a look of pain sweeps over his face. "I can't believe I trusted you. My mistake."

He starts to walk again, but I hold the box of cookies out to block him. He tries to go around, and I move side to side to prevent it.

"Tom doesn't even like me," I say, and my voice sounds so pathetic I stop, taking a deep breath. "Nash, I screwed up. I know. But then I stopped screwing up. And I'm trying to fix it. So please stop acting like I've killed Bambi's mother or told you the Easter Bunny isn't coming this year." I know the clock is ticking. I don't have much time to explain myself. "Yes, Tom kissed me. And I kissed him back. That's all. But no matter how I feel about Tom, or he feels about me, I could never be with him, you know, long term if it hurt you like this. Never. Bottom line. I screwed up, but I didn't keep screwing up. So please don't hate me!"

"Oh, sorry, Maggie. Is my pain and suffering inconvenient for you? Too much drama for your delicate sensibilities?"

"Yes . . . I mean, no. Yes, it's a lot of drama, but no, I don't think you created it."

"Oh, really?" he says, crossing his arms. "Who created it, then?"

"Two words for you, my friend: Kayla Hill."

"I thought you and Kayla were bosom buddies again? You going to turn on her now too?"

"She started all this, Nash. Maybe she misunderstood the situation. Maybe she likes Tom and figured if everyone thought we were together, he'd be embarrassed and run the other way, right into her arms. We haven't had a chance to chat about it."

"She got the idea somewhere."

"Yes, I said enough to Kayla about Tom that she made the leap about the kiss." I hold up my hand. "And before you say it: yes, I know that was absolute stupidity, especially after you warned me. But the rest of the sordid details are pure fiction."

Nash pauses, his eyes scanning my face.

"Come on, Nash. Is it really easier to believe I would screw you over than believe that Kayla would screw us both?"

He shakes his head, discarding my words like a dog sheds water. "I know what I heard, and what I saw. It looked like smoke, so I'm guessing there's fire."

"I guess that's that, then? You're going to throw away ten years of friendship over a guy?"

"I wouldn't, but you did." Nash, arms still crossed, drops his eyes. I can see his chin quivering, can see how hard he's trying to hold it together. Then he takes a deep breath. "Can I go now?" His voice is like tiny splinters of glass.

I step aside, watching his retreating back. Two weeks ago I thought he was the one person who understood me; now I think maybe he doesn't get me at all. And at that moment, I want nothing more than to hurt Nash. At that moment, I know I could do exactly what he's accused me of just to twist the knife. The force of that knowing knocks the wind out of me.

I need to get out of there, but I'm not sure where to go. No time for the bluff before work. It's too public and too far from Square Peg for my current needs. What I want is a centrally located place where I can be alone and settle down before I face Quinn. I rack my brain, but the only place I can come up with is the park near downtown. Even if there are people there, I can lock myself in a bathroom stall and process my conversation with Nash in relative peace and privacy.

When I get there, a couple of young moms sit near the playground, watching their toddlers in the sandbox. I dodge into the bathroom but stop short when I see that all the doors have been removed from the stalls.

"What the hell?" I glance at my cell phone. Twenty minutes to get a grip and walk across downtown to work. Realizing I still have the box of cookies in my hand, I go to the end stall, close the toilet lid, and sit down. I put my backpack on my lap and set the breakfast bars on top, then rip open the package and take a large bite of a bar before I can think about it. They are dense, but I chew just enough to get the cookie down. It sticks like a hard lump in my throat, so I swallow a couple more times to move it along. I don't really want to eat the rest of the bar, but I finish it anyway, gnawing little rabbit nibbles around the center until I'm left with the softest parts, an aggregate of coconut and chocolate and cashews.

By now the initial rush of the food has come and gone, that flooding of my system that makes me lightheaded and then calmer. What's left behind is a film in my mouth and a vague lump in my stomach. Checking my phone, I figure I have time for one more. But if I'm honest, I don't really want to eat it. It's not helping anyway. I hear a noise and straighten as one of the toddlers from outside lurches around the corner of my stall like a drunken sailor. He loses balance and clings to the only stationary object nearby, my knees. We stare at each other for a few endless seconds, then the little boy squeals and reaches a pudgy little hand out for the scrap of breakfast bar I'm still holding.

The kid's enthusiasm and simple trust break the spell. I toss the box and the remaining bar in the trash can and hold the toddler's hand as I lead him out of the bathroom.

"Connor?" I hear the mom calling for the boy, her voice both alarmed and coaxing.

"He's here!" I say, still holding his hand.

"There you are. Come here." She gathers Conner in her arms. "Thank you," she says, looking up at me.

"No problem." I wave at Connor. "He just sort of wandered in."

"Can you say bye-bye, Connor?" The mom flaps his hand up and down, trying to get him to wave.

"Bye," I say, making a tiny little wave at the kid.

Connor smiles and waves back, and so does his mom. And that makes me smile, but it also makes me remember I'm alone now, Nash-less, and that without him things don't make sense. I head toward work feeling about the same as I did before I tried to make myself feel better.

CHAPTER 28

Somehow I'm both completely full and completely empty by the time I reach the door of Square Peg. And I half wonder if Quinn will want me back after my tantrum and walkout the other day. I pause at the door, fingers on the handle, bracing myself. After a few seconds, I go in. Waving at Quinn, I say hello in a bright high-pitched voice that doesn't sound like me. He stares, holding two faded album covers in mid-sort.

"Whatcha doing?" I throw my pack under the counter and shove my coat on top of it.

Quinn is still watching me, but he looks like he's eaten something nasty.

"New collection?" I say.

Quinn doesn't throw me so much as a tiny sliver of a bone.

"You okay?" I ask.

His cheeks go red, but the cartilage around his nose and ears is white where he's holding it taut.

"Am I okay?" he says, his voice low and soft. He is still

clutching the records, and his knuckles have gone as pale as his nose. "Am I okay?" he repeats. "Am I the one who's been falling apart for days? Am I the one who stormed out of here into the dark and never called to let her boss know she made it home? Am I the one who's about to get fired if she doesn't come over here and give that boss a big hug?" He drops the records and opens his arms wide.

I'm so relieved, I move right into them and let him fold me up and squeeze me for much longer than I am usually comfortable with. My nose burns a little as tears start to form. I will them back down.

"I'm sorry, Maggie. I had no right to pry," Quinn says into my shoulder, his voice muffled by the fabric of my sweatshirt. "I wanted you to know I see that things suck right now. And that I think you deserve better." He releases me and I step back, out of reach of any additional bear hugs he might be moved to impart.

"It's okay," I mumble. "You care. I know. I don't . . ." I'm not sure what else to say. "Anyway, thanks." We both stand there for a minute, unsure how to proceed. "Sooooo, alphabetize or toilet?"

"Yes," Quinn says, and we both laugh.

"Sweeping it is." I grab the broom and head for the far corner of the store, chasing down dust bunnies under the fixtures. But every few minutes, I stop sweeping and watch Quinn.

He keeps flicking at something at the back of his neck, like he can feel my gaze but is trying to shoo it away. Irritated, he turns. "What?" He's brushing now at his nose and hair.

"Nothing." I go back to sweeping.

Quinn turns back to the stack of records.

I glance up, wondering how to begin.

"What?" Quinn turns to look at me again. He sounds irritated, but he's smiling this time. "And don't say 'nothing.' Spill it."

I lean the broom against the record bins and make my way to the counter, not meeting his eye. "I guess . . . I wanted to thank you. Again."

"For . . . ?"

"For, you know, giving a shit."

"Oh, that." He studies me. "I thought you were mad about that."

"No. Not mad, not really. Surprised. And, okay, a little mad that you were right. But not about everything. You weren't right about everything."

"I was right?" Quinn leans forward. "Which part was I right about?"

"About running, I guess."

"So, what are you running from this week?" He pats the stool across from him.

I slide onto the seat, stare at my hands for a second, then dive in. "Nash hates me. Kayla screwed me over. Tom kissed me. He likes me, but only as a friend. And my mom thinks I'm fat."

"Anything else?" he says.

I shake my head.

Quinn claps his hands together and rubs. "Okay. One at a

time. Nash will get over it. My mom always told me I was fat too. Kayla's a bitch." He leans in and puts both hands on my knees. "Let's talk about Tom."

A warm blush rises to my hairline, but then I register everything Quinn just said. "No, wait. Back up. Your mom told you you were fat?"

"Yep. Until I left home at seventeen. No, wait, she still does."

I eyeball Quinn. He's oldish, but he's still pretty good-looking. And definitely not fat. Not even close. "Were you?"

"Nope. Never was. But I believed I was. So inside, I felt fat."

"But you're not."

"But I am inside."

"And that means . . . ?"

"That means I let someone else tell me things about myself that weren't true, and I made them true. And that was a stupid thing to do."

"But my mom's right," I say, indicating my ample frame.

"Was she always right?"

"What do you mean?"

"Let me put it this way: How long have you believed you were overweight? A month? A year? Five years? How long?"

I think about this for a minute, and I realize that I've always thought I was too big. That I took up too much space in the world. "Always," I say.

"And how long has your mom been telling you, in subtle and not-so-subtle ways, that you need to 'watch your weight'?"

I think about this. "Always," I say.

"Chicken? Or egg?" Quinn asks, grabbing my knees again.

"Huh?"

"Which came first? Your mom telling you or you believing it?"

"Being fat came first," I say.

"Bullshit." He's so adamant; I have to consider the possibility that he could be right. "Do me a favor. Go home later and look through some old photo albums. And then you need to ask yourself again: Which came first?" He looks at me a minute longer and then releases my knees.

"Now, Kayla? What did she do?"

I explain about Tom kissing me, and Kayla guessing, and Kayla telling Nash, and how now about a million other people think I did a lot more than kiss him. And I tell him how that little reveal morphed my life into something lonely and painful and frustrating. "How do I fix this? I have no clue how to make it up to Nash," I say.

Quinn taps his forefinger on his chin. "Harsh. I guess it's possible Kayla might have just misunderstood," he says. "But she told a story that wasn't hers to tell, and she needs to apologize."

"Yeah, like that's going to happen," I say.

"You need to make it happen, Miss Maggie!" Quinn says. "You are leaving too many balls in other people's courts. Kayla, Nash, Tom: according to you, they all get to decide what happens to Maggie. You need to get some balls of your own! *Cojones,* that is."

"But—"

"No *but*s. Make Nash see you stumbled, but you're the same

wonderful friend you always were. And make Tom see he's a fool to kiss and run. Make Kayla apologize for being unworthy of your friendship and trust. You need to show them what Maggie Bower is made of. Do it! Make it happen!" Quinn waves me away and switches out the Roxy Music that's been drifting under our conversation. The needle drops and Quinn starts gyrating as Blondie belts out "One Way or Another." I get the message loud and clear.

CHAPTER 29

O nce home, I go right to the hall closet and start pulling out boxes until I unearth the bin with the family photo albums. I settle myself against the wall and choose an older album: Maggie as a baby.

Peering at the photos, I try to be objective, searching for information, evidence that I have always been overweight. The baby I am looking at has round, chubby cheeks and sturdy arms and legs, but no more baby fat than you'd expect to find, well, on a baby.

I discard that album and find one from my preschool years. Maggie at her birthday party hitting a piñata. Not a lithe child, but not overweight either. Maggie riding a bike, muscles flexed and tan. Maggie at the pool, a polka dot two-piece framing a belly that's childish and round but not overly fleshy.

I trace my school photos and class pictures through grade school. I am taller than most. Bigger, but not fatter. I close the book and lean my head against the wall, eyes closed. Chicken? Or egg? That was Quinn's question, and now it's mine too.

I'm not about to start blaming my mom for my weight.

An egg contains the possibility of a chicken, and I knew that I must contain, genetically speaking, the possibility of fatness. But why Fat Maggie instead of Athletic Maggie or Brainy Maggie or Punk Rock Maggie? Why did I choose to push the overweight version of myself out of the egg instead of some other version? I'm still sitting in the hall, my elementary school photo album slung across my knees, when Mom gets home.

"Mags?" she calls. Her book bag thumps onto the kitchen floor and then the two smaller bumps as she kicks off her shoes. "You here?" she tries again. Her head appears at the bottom of the staircase. "What are you doing, sweetie?"

I gesture at the album resting on my knees. "Looking at pictures." I scoot over a bit, making room for her on the wall.

She stands over me for a few seconds, deciding, then slides down and pulls the album partway onto her own lap so she can see it. "Oh, look at that," she says, smiling at my fourth grade school photo.

I make a face.

"I know you hate that picture. But I love it. To me it was the last year you were a little girl." Her finger strokes the rise of my fourth grade cheek. "So long ago," she whispers.

I swallow, trying to muster the courage to ask the question I need to ask. "A little girl," I say, my voice soft. "You mean before I got fat?"

Mom stiffens beside me. "Oh, Maggie." She flips the page and looks at fifth grade. My face has changed. The angles are more pronounced, and the nose is a little big for the face, but I'm still smiling. Flip again, and the angles are starting to get lost in a face that looks more round, less content.

"So here's the thing, Mom," I say. "I've only been overweight a little while, a few years." I turn back the pages of the album. "See, not here." I turn again. "Or here." I turn the last page, landing on my sixth grade photo. "It doesn't really show up until here." I point, and my mom takes her hands off the album. She folds them in her lap. "But I feel fat; I've always felt fat. I am a lot of other things. I'm smart and funny. I'm a good friend and a good cook. I'm kind to animals and small children. But my weight is the only thing about me you ever seem to notice."

"I notice other things," she says.

"No, Mom, you don't."

"I do too."

"Okay, fine. You notice other things, but my weight is the only thing you ever mention to me."

"I'm trying to help."

"Well, stop helping."

She doesn't say a word.

"Mom, I don't blame you. But I need you to leave my fat alone. Don't look at it; don't try to change it. Don't mention it. Don't even think about it."

She laughs a little at this. We sit there, both of us trying not to think about my fat. "I know you mean well, Mom, but I have to understand, why the obsession?"

Mom rubs her eyes, pressing her palms into her sockets, and then she gets up, goes into her bedroom, and returns with a shoebox. She sits, placing the box in my lap. "Open it," she says, and starts gnawing at her nails.

I lift the lid off the box. Inside are photos, old concert tickets, a dried-up corsage, and a few other crumpled and dusty odds and ends. I start to look through the pictures. They all show the same girl, full face, wide smile, but there's a sad something in her eyes. When I look into those eyes, the unfamiliar parts of the girl's face snap together.

"They're mostly from high school, but there's a few elementary school photos in there too," Mom says, her voice quiet.

"Why haven't you showed these to me before?" I ask.

"I don't show them to anyone. Not even your father has seen most of them, although Grandma showed him a couple when we were still dating." She's chewing her thumbnail like a crazy woman now. "I guess I hoped by worrying about your weight, by hoping you didn't end up like me, I could keep it from happening." She lifts out one of the pictures and studies it. Mom at about fourteen, hair feathered, braces. "Growing up was hard. The teasing. The loneliness. I didn't want things to be so hard for you. I thought I could protect you from that, but now you're telling me I've made things worse."

"No, Mom. Not worse," I say. "But I wish I'd known." I gesture to a photo of her at about my age, dressed for some sort of special occasion. She looks pretty.

"Well, that's not something you bring up in casual conversation. 'Oh, Maggie, by the way, I was fat the whole time I was growing up. My first eighteen years were painful and lonely. I thought you'd want to know.' Not easy to wedge in between 'eat your vegetables' and 'do your homework.'"

"I just mean it would have been nice to know why it's so important to you."

Mom takes the photograph out of my hand. "I lost weight twenty-two years ago, and I still feel like this every day," she says, her voice shaking a little. "I couldn't bear the idea of going through that again with you."

"Mom, I'm not you. Heavy or thin, I'm not you, and my life is not your life."

"But it's so much easier . . . You're so lovely, if only . . ." But she doesn't know how to say what she wants to say without telling me to lose weight.

"You don't get it," I say. "Mom, you look beautiful. You've always looked beautiful." I point to the photo in her hand. "You look beautiful here."

And this, I guess, is the right thing to say, because the floodgates open and my mom is sobbing beside me. I sit and let her cry, my hand on her knee. After a bit I get up for some tissues, hand them to her, then settle back against the wall to wait.

When her tears subside, she turns to me, handing back the photo. "I did the best I could," she says.

"I know, Mom. And I turned out okay. Self-esteem mostly in tact. Only minor bouts with teenage pain and suffering. Well done! Time to give both of us a break." I smile, and she kisses my forehead.

"Maggie, you are so much smarter than I was at your age. Actually, I think you're smarter than I am now."

We both laugh, and I rest my head against her shoulder.

"I guess I need to know that you care about other stuff besides what I look like," I say. "I need to know that you see more even if other people don't."

"I do, Maggie. I do." Mom starts in on another round of tears, and I join her.

We've both cried ourselves out by the time Dad comes home and finds us laughing together in the hallway.

"What in the world are you doing?" Dad surveys the wadded-up Kleenex and splayed photo albums.

"A little mother-daughter bonding," Mom explains. Mom and I look at each other and collapse into giggles.

Dad shakes his head and retreats downstairs.

"I'd better go get dinner started," she says, patting my knee. She follows Dad down to the kitchen.

Gathering the albums, I carry them to the closet, but then stop. I like the Maggie in these photos, and I don't want to lose sight of her again. I detour into my room, toss them on the bed, and put on *Body and Soul,* one of my favorite Billie Holiday records. I lie next to the photo albums, flipping through them, choosing pictures from different sections. Arranging the photos in chronological order, I tape them around the border of my mirror and step back so I can see my own history, my own life. It turns out Quinn was right. I like what I see. I smile as the soothing voice of Billie Holiday sings "They Can't Take That Away from Me." I know for the first time that she's absolutely right.

CHAPTER 30

Nothing much has changed the next day except my attitude. Every time Nash looks at me like I'm a ten on the slut-o-meter, or I see Tom with Kayla dripping off his arm, it makes me even more determined to show them they can't mess with me. A small kernel of an idea is forming, a way for me to make it clear I'm not going to play their reindeer games.

I'm holding it together in my classes, except I realize I have skipped too much PE. I'm in danger of flunking, which would mean another semester with Ms. Perry. So I give myself a pep talk and grit my teeth through yet another timed run. I am, of course, one of the last to cross the line. Most of the other students are resting on the bleachers, waiting in bored silence for the stragglers. When I get close to the end, the row of horn-dog wrestlers at the top of the bleachers start grabbing their junk and thrusting their crotches at me behind Ms. Perry's back.

Tom turns to where I'm looking and catches enough of the performance to get the gist. He comes out of his seat in an instant and lunges halfway up the bleachers before I realize what he's doing. He grabs one guy's shirt with both hands and shakes him. The shocked kid's head bounces like one of those bobble-head figures they hand out at baseball games.

"Tom! Don't!" I yell.

He stops, his face showing the strain of reining in his anger. "Did you see what those assholes—?"

"It doesn't matter." I don't need to prove anything. Douche-bags like that never go away.

Tom lets the guy go, and he puffs himself up, bumping against Tom's chest. They face off on the bleachers, testosterone crackling off both of them. I hear the sharp blast of a whistle.

"Mr. Pierce!" Ms. Perry yells.

"Ms. Perry, those jerks—" Tom starts to explain, but I shake my head. I get the feeling he'd like to cast himself as the hero, and he's disappointed that I don't want him to fight my battles for me.

"Miss Bower can take care of herself." I might be imagining it, but Ms. Perry gives me a look that might contain just the tiniest bit of respect.

"Sorry, Ms. Perry. It won't happen again," he says. The final bell rings, and Tom descends the bleachers, walking past me without a word.

I jet out of the locker room after PE, then work on my math homework in the library until the hallways empty out a little. I'm almost to my locker when I spot a pack of guys coming toward me. A couple of the bleacher boys from PE, but the rest of them I don't really know. I avoid eye contact, but one of them leans over and says in a low voice, "Hey, chunky monkey, you open for business?"

He runs his hands over the front of my shirt and then bumps against me, knocking me into one of his buddies on the other side. It's over before I even register what happened, before I even believe it's real.

"Tell your boyfriend we're not finished."

The other guys snicker, but I ignore them and speed walk the rest of the way down the hall. I lean against my locker door, the metal cool against my forehead. My heart is a jackhammer, trying to drill through my chest wall. I pound my fist into the green metal, then slam my locker open. A bright orange flyer falls out and floats to the floor. Picking it up, I scan for information. It's for a party on Friday night. **KICKING IT OLD SCHOOL: A GOOD OLD-FASHIONED '80S KEGGER** the flyer reads. I start to throw it away, but midcrumple I stop and reconsider. Desperate times call for desperate measures. Maybe the new Maggie goes to keggers. Maybe Nash and Tom and Kayla will see me differently if I start doing things differently. Maybe doing the unexpected is one of the ways I show them who I am. There's also the possibility Kayla will be there and the even smaller possibility that I will take the opportunity to kick her ass. I smooth the flyer out and fold it, putting it in my backpack.

Cece's waiting for me when I walk out the doors.

"You walking home?" she asks.

"Yeah."

"Mind if I walk with you?"

I try not to show my shock. "Not at all. Bluff or street?"

"Street?" Cece says. "It'll give us more time."

We walk without talking at first, enjoying the warm sun

on our backs. Halfway up the hill, we both take off our coats. Cece ties hers around her waist like everyone used to do during recess in elementary school.

"So, I'm sorry I got caught up in the Tom and Nash thing. I know you made a mistake, but it's not what it seemed like at first."

"Yeah, it's all pretty much sucked. But I don't blame you for being mad."

"Still, I should have known, as soon as he told me what he'd heard, and that he'd heard it from Kayla. I should have known."

"It's okay. I get it. I know how you feel about Nash."

"Yeah. And he's really, really mad at you."

"I'm kind of getting that message."

We've reached the top of the hill and take a break on a bench near the bus stop. There's a slight breeze, and the ripples on the lake are diamond studded from this angle. "Cece? Can I show you something?"

"Sure."

I unzip my backpack and pull out the flyer. Cece reads it, her eyes widening.

"Are you going?" she asks.

"Maybe."

"Nash won't be there."

"I know."

Cece hands the flyer back. "What's the point? What are you going to do if you go?"

I fold the kegger information and tuck it into my backpack. "I've got to do something."

"You should go," Cece says. "You should go, and if Kayla's there, you should tell her off."

"You really think I can?"

"I know you can," Cece says, grabbing my hand. "But I'm glad it's you instead of me!"

CHAPTER 31

I step into the dark hallway and cringe. The smell of sweaty boys and desperate girls stings my nostrils. Several of Cedar Ridge's finest are already drunk enough to totter on high heels. I swing left into the kitchen. Grabbing a red plastic cup, I inscribe a capital *M* on it with a fading Sharpie and offer the cup to Sean Carp, who's manning the keg. He looks at me, skeptical as he fills the cup halfway with nasty beer and too much foam.

"You sure?" he asks as he hands me the cup.

I nod and head back through the narrow hallway to the living room. I almost spit my first swig of beer right back into the cup. Nash and I never drink, mostly because of how much he hates his mom's drinking. But Nash isn't here, isn't anywhere for me right now, so I swallow a little more beer and step into the main room. In the semidarkness I can see several couples making out in the corners while the as-yet-unattached talk in morphing clumps in the room's center. I roll my eyes again and scout out possible escape routes that aren't blocked by horny couples in mid-clutch.

"Oh my God! Maggie!" someone squeals, and I spill half my beer as I am bumped from behind. No great loss.

I wheel around but stop short. Standing in front of me is a very tipsy Kayla. She's only keeping her balance by draping herself all over Tom. He doesn't look totally sober, but he's got way better balance than Kayla. Two or three of her groupies hover behind them. I take a swig of the beer and paste a smile on my face.

"Hey, guys," I say. "Great party, huh?"

"What are you doing here?" she asks. Kayla clings to Tom like ivy on a tree. He keeps trying to detach her, but this only makes Kayla clutch his arm tighter. Even with Tom as support, she sways a little. Her friends whisper, watching me closely.

"You don't party!" She turns to Tom and says, "Maggie never comes to parties, Tom. Never ever!" Tom has given up trying to get Kayla to stand on her own now. Kayla grins and wags her finger in my direction. "But I've heard you are doing a lot of things you never do. Crossing over to the dark side, I hear. Naughty, naughty!"

I still have my fake smile on, but I have a brief fantasy about throwing the rest of my beer in her face, maybe hitting Tom in the process. It would be unavoidable, really, as close as they're standing. But I don't; I don't say anything. Maybe it's pure chicken-shittery, but now that she's in front of me, I realize I'm not really sure what I want to tell her. I need more time to sort out her mistakes from mine. More time to figure out what, exactly, I'm pissed off at Kayla about. She told people about the kiss, along with some pretty serious elaboration. She embarrassed me and wounded my best friend so deeply he won't even talk to me. But she didn't ruin my life. I did that myself. I'm the one who kissed Tom. I'm the one who let her back into my life.

I lift my cup and drink a toast to Kayla, but she has lost interest by now and is squealing someone else's name. She lurches across the room to her next victim, dragging Tom behind her. Catfight averted for now. Suddenly I feel sick from the sour smell of my beer cup. I need some air.

I make a move for the patio door, but someone throws an arm across it right as I reach to slide it open. "Not leaving so soon, are you?" purrs a voice, and I look up into the face of the boy who groped me and called me "chunky monkey" in the hallway. Jack or Jay or Jake, something like that. He's got at least a foot on me, with the thick neck of a wrestler or steroid user. Or both. His breath smells of beer and something stronger, skunky and acrid, like pot, maybe. He's still upright, but his inhibitions are no longer a factor in his decision making.

I feel the atmosphere shift as a couple other largish bodies move in behind me, corralling me and blocking me from the rest of the room. Gripping my beer, I try not to panic.

"Yep, curfew and all that." I move to duck under his arm, but he's too quick in spite of the booze.

"No, no, no. Not so fast. Let's get to know each other a little better." Jake—at least I'm pretty sure that's his name—runs his fingers along my chin. I shiver, and he seems to take it for excitement. "Did your boyfriend move on to hotter pastures?" His voice still has that purr in it, but there is menace underneath.

"I don't have a boyfriend."

"Whatever. It looks like he's left you to fend for yourself. That's not very nice of him. But it's nice for us. Maybe we should show your boyfriend what happens when he leaves his girlfriend alone at a party."

His friends start to press me toward the sliding door—gentle, but insistent. The two tree trunks in letterman's jackets cross their arms and stand between me and the party while Jake backs me up against the door. I allow it because my skin crawls at the thought of them touching me.

"Alone at last," Jake says.

"Yeah, just the four of us," I say.

J-hole stares at me. "That's hilarious. You and that Tom guy think you're fucking comic geniuses." He puts his hands on the slider and leans in close. I can smell he's put on way too much body spray, and it mixes with the beer and pot smells, turning my stomach. For a minute I sort of hope I puke on him.

"Well, I'm not really in the mood for comedy right now. I'm in the mood for other things. And I've heard you offer just about all of them. Full service."

I freeze.

"I'm here to find out if the rumors are true." He starts sort of mauling my neck with his tongue. He has me boxed in. I squirm, trying for some leverage, but Jake has height and physics on his side. And I get the sense this is not his first time with an unwilling victim. He tries to kiss me on the mouth, but I keep swinging my head around, trying to keep him from making contact. He grabs my jaw, maneuvering my face so his lips can find the mark.

"Hold still," he says. "Just enjoy it."

"I bet you say that to all the girls." I steady my voice, but my hands are shaking. I inch one of them behind me, trying to get a grip on the door handle. I'm still shifting, dodging his lips and looking for an escape route.

"Jesus! I don't even know if it's worth it!" Jake grips my shoulders, trying to get me to hold still. "I shouldn't have to work this hard to get some from a fat cow like you. Seems like you should be honored."

"Yeah, you're probably right." I drop my head, pretending to be defeated. Meanwhile my hand finds the handle, and I brace myself to open the door.

Jake smiles and turns to his buddies to share his moment of triumph. As soon as his eyes are off me, I open the slider, backing through it as Jake falls toward me. But he's tall, and it seems like he's going to land on top of me, so I raise my hands and pull my knee up to protect myself.

The knee connects with Jake's crotch as he stumbles, trying to catch his fall. Jake sucks in a huge mouthful of air and goes stiff, then doubles over in pain, clutching his damaged groin.

"You bitch!" he wheezes.

His friends rush in to help, and I run into the darkness of the yard. Crouching behind some evergreen bush that smells like a mixture of Christmas and cat piss, I gulp air as Jake pulls himself together and hobbles back into the party.

My heart has finally slowed to a reasonable pace when I see Tom come outside.

"Hello?" he says into the darkness from the corner of the patio.

"Shit!" I say, putting my hand over my mouth. Tom is either not the guy I need to see at this moment or exactly the guy I need to see at this moment. Until I know which, I keep quiet.

"Is someone out there?" Tom squints into the yard. He takes a swig of his beer. "Who is that?"

"Screw it," I whisper to myself, then move into the faint light from the living room. "It's me," I say. My hands are still shaking, and I can still smell Jake's cologne. I keep my distance from Tom so he can't tell how messed up I am.

When he sees me, Tom shakes his head and looks off into the darkness. My stomach drops. Whoever he expected to see out here, it wasn't me.

"Yeah, sorry." He turns back to the house. "I saw those guys come inside and thought someone might need help. Anyway, I'll go."

"Tom, wait."

He doesn't turn around, but he doesn't move toward the house either. I take a couple steps closer to him. He finally looks, and now he can see something is wrong. My face starts to crumple, but I force it back to neutral.

"Whoa, Maggie, are you okay?" he says, closing the distance between us in a few long steps. He drops his beer and reaches out to gather me into his arms, and I resist for a minute, but then let him hold me until the shaking stops. "What happened?" he whispers. "Was it those guys?"

I nod.

"Did they try to—"

"Yeah. But then they got bored and moved on to a meaner, drunker version of the usual cow jokes."

"I'd love to be your knight in shining armor, but it looks like you took care of them on your own." Tom pulls away so he can take a good look at my face. He's swaying a little, his face flushed from the beer, and his hair is messy, probably from Kayla running her fingers through it.

"I'm okay. I'm fine," I say, and I think it's the truth, at least for the moment.

Tom smiles, his hands still holding my shoulders, and takes a step closer to me.

I want to let him comfort me some more. But after the beer, and seeing Tom with Kayla, and the wrestling match with the Three Stooges, I can't handle any more drama right now. I cross my arms over my chest against the cold and the crappy night and against whatever it is we've got to say to each other.

"Thanks." I step away. "I'm good now."

He watches me a minute, then shakes his head. "You know, I really like you, Maggie. But the whole thing with Nash got stupid. I wish it could have been better."

"Yeah, I'm really sorry you got stuck with Kayla. That must have been hard on you."

"Shit!" His voice is strained. "Why do you do that? You use all that crap to push everyone away. You duck and dodge anytime the good stuff gets close."

"This is the good stuff?"

"That's what I mean!" Tom keeps throwing his hands around while he talks. His slightly drunk, manic energy directed at me is a little frightening. "Ever since this whole thing started, you joke, and run, and put up every roadblock you can think of to avoid a real conversation." He stops and rubs both hands through his hair, making it stand on end. "Look, I miss hanging out with you, Maggie. I miss our hikes, our talks, all of it."

"I'm the one avoiding real conversation? You're the one who never gets real. Besides, what's the big deal? I thought you just wanted to be friends anyway."

"But I miss you."

I raise my eyes, and Tom's looking at me now. I stare at him a minute, trying to figure out if he's saying what I think he's saying. He closes the distance between us, wrapping his arms around me in one fluid motion.

Then he's kissing me. Again. He tastes like beer and cigarettes and peppermint lip balm. And for a second, I think I might let him keep kissing me. But maybe it's Nash, or seeing Tom with Kayla, or being cornered by Jake, but I realize right now I don't want Tom kissing me.

I put my palms against his chest and shove him away. "Nope. Not happening. I can't do this, Tom. I really, really can't do this."

"Maggie, lighten up. It's a kiss. It's not the end of the world."

"But, Nash—"

"Nash also needs to lighten up." Tom grabs my hands, holding them gently and running his thumbs over my palms. The motion raises goose bumps on my arms, and I silently curse my own nervous system. "Are you saying you weren't enjoying it?" Tom smiles, and my legs seem a lot less solid than they were a second ago.

"Yeah, okay. But a little while ago, you said you wanted to be friends, and now we're . . ." I don't think I can actually say out loud what we were doing.

"I do," Tom says. "So?"

"Do what?"

"Want to be friends."

"Seriously?" I stare at him. "You are the master of mixed signals, Tom."

Tom sighs. He's still holding my hands, but now it feels like comfort instead of seduction. "Maggie, you're great. But this doesn't mean . . ."

I tear myself away from him before he can finish.

"Look, Maggie. We're drunk . . ."

"*You're* drunk."

"Fine, I'm drunk. We're here. It's been a hard week. I thought we were . . . I thought you were just . . ."

"Just what?" I ask. "Just slutty enough? Just lonely enough? Just desperate enough that we could hook up and have it not matter the next day?"

"Look, I'm sorry, Maggie. I really am, but I don't like you that way, not enough to be your boyfriend or whatever. I'm not . . ." Tom rubs his hand hard on the back of his head, making his hair stand out. "I thought you understood. I want to be friends. No more than that."

"Oh, well, forgive me if I'm a little confused. My other friends don't shove their tongues down my throat."

"Sorry. I guess things got a little mixed up."

"It's not things that are mixed up, Tom. It's you. First you flirt with Nash, then me, then Kayla, and who knows who else? And I bet every one of us thought we had a chance with you."

"I tried to fix things. When I told Nash we kissed—"

"Wait, *you* told Nash we kissed? I thought Kayla told Nash?"

"Maybe she did, but I told him first."

"Why the hell would you do something so completely, obviously stupid? And you told me you didn't tell him. I specifically remember you telling me you didn't tell him."

"I'm sorry. I know. It sort of backfired. But I was trying to get Nash to see that I wasn't going to be, that I couldn't be the guy he wanted."

"And so you told him something designed to make him see that I'm not the friend he thought he had? Double heartbreak in one tiny little package. Perfect. Brilliant!"

Tom shoves his hands in his pockets and shivers, glancing back toward the house.

"Look, you've had an exit strategy since the day you got here, so I guess it doesn't matter who you hurt or who you lie to. You won't be around to clean up your own mess anyway."

"I didn't mean to hurt anyone."

I can tell he means it, but it doesn't change things. Tom looks back at the door again, and I can see he wants to escape. I feel the same way.

"Just go, Tom. I'm pretty sure we're done here." I step off the patio and feel my way in the darkness around the side of the house, scratching my arms on the huge arborvitaes along the way. By the time I reach the street, I am crying full out and start to run. I have to get away from the party, and Tom, Jake, and Kayla, and the whole fucked-up situation. The snow starts to fall, the huge flakes sticking to my eyelashes and teary face.

CHAPTER 32

That weekend I hike the shoreline trail twice. With the cold weather, I have it to myself. The smell of cedar and the repetitive sound of water hitting land help me slow my breathing and quiet my brain. Mom leaves me alone for the most part, and so does Dad. I text Nash about a dozen times, but he doesn't answer. I hear from Cece, who wants to know if I went to the party. And Tom. He keeps sending texts that range from apologetic to worried to frustrated, but I ignore his messages. Tom's even more confused than I am. Besides, I need time by myself to think. Time to figure out how I can get my life back. But by late afternoon Sunday, I am a little stir-crazy, so I head to Square Peg.

"Hey, beautiful!" Quinn calls out when I enter the store.

I slouch onto one of the cracked vinyl stools behind the counter.

"What?" Quinn asks, crossing his arms. "What?" he says again when I don't answer, and then leans in. "Seriously, Mags, you look like somebody told you unicorns aren't real. What. Is. Up?"

My mouth forms a surprised O. "Unicorns aren't real?"

"You're hilarious. Now tell me."

I flip through the records on the counter, somebody's pile of classical cello music.

Quinn cues up "Lady Sings the Blues." Billie's voice is gravelly and deep and makes me remember every one of the crappy things that has happened the last couple of weeks.

"Nice." I glare at him. "Kick a gal when she's down."

"Hmmmmm?" Quinn says. "Whatever do you mean? I am doing what I always do, fitting the music to the mood."

I wait for him to say more, but he turns back to the ledger he's poring over.

"And you think my mood is blue? Billie Holiday, heroin-addicted, early death kind of blue?"

"Not yet, but if you settle in there, anything could happen!" Quinn's voice is cheerful. "I'm not going to let you get that comfortable."

"Nice." I try to look bored.

"Hey, someone has to pry you from your bunker of despair. And since your supposed 'best friend' is the one who put you there, I am acting as the proxy bestie."

"Proxy bestie? That's not a thing. You totally made that up. Besides, Nash did not put me in the bunker—I did. With a little help from Kayla and Tom."

"Good point. But whoever put you there, I am here to make sure you don't set up housekeeping."

"For your information, I am not settling in." I look around to make sure neither of the customers is listening, but they both seem absorbed in their individual quests for vinyl. I lean in and whisper, "I went to a party Friday night. A kegger."

Now it's Quinn's turn to make the surprised O, but his astonishment is real. "A kegger? You?" he whispers.

I nod.

Quinn shakes his head, a rare moment of speechlessness.

"I didn't get wasted or anything," I say. "I needed to do something unexpected."

"Mission accomplished."

"I know, I know," I say, covering my face with my hands. The party was a nightmare, but I'm enjoying Quinn's surprise.

He switches out the record. I guess I've earned my way out of the blues, because he puts on Kiss's "Rock and Roll All Nite." Quinn does a little air-guitar riff while extending a Gene Simmons–worthy tongue.

I crack up. "It's just been so weird since all this stuff started. So I thought, 'What's the harm in going to a party where nobody will talk to me?' Check something off my high school bucket list."

"And?" Quinn says.

"And . . . nobody talked to me. It was lame. It smelled of teen angst and desperation."

"That's it? Your first high school kegger and there's nothing to report? You didn't see anybody? Didn't talk to anybody?" Quinn's voice is skeptical. He knows I'm not saying everything.

"Well, not exactly." I wonder if I can find a way to answer without really answering.

"Hmmmmm?" Quinn coaxes.

I slump a little further and start fiddling with the stapler.

Quinn removes it from my hand and puts it back on the counter. "Spill," he says.

"There were some drunk wrestler assholes who got a little too close for comfort."

Quinn makes a face. "You okay?"

I nod. "They assumed I'd be up for it. Apparently the rumor mill has cast me as this week's slut."

"Wow. That's, um— How exactly did that happen?"

"I haven't quite pieced it all together yet. But I have some ideas."

"Well, I hope you did some damage while you were telling them where to shove their attentions."

"I did. I used one of my best moves."

"Elbow to the sternum?" Quinn asks.

"Knee to the groin. Sort of accidentally, but the effect was the same."

"A classic. Well done," he says. "You sure you're okay?"

"I am. Thanks. Disaster averted. At least on that front."

"What else? You're still holding out on me."

"Well . . ." I hesitate. "Tom was there."

Quinn waits.

"And, um, we talked for a minute. In the backyard." I pick at my thumbnail, trying to decide if I want to tell Quinn the rest. "And he was kind of . . . Well, like I said, we talked and stuff." I look at Quinn now, wanting to run, but also wanting him to help me tell him everything.

"'And stuff'?" Quinn asks. But I shake my head, so he changes tunes, again. This is another bone of contention with

Quinn and me. He has no problem listening to little snippets of songs and changing things out every couple of minutes. But I feel the same way about songs as I do about books. Once I start them, it drives me a little crazy not to finish them. I'm sure it drives the customers insane too, but Quinn doesn't seem to care.

This time Quinn puts on "Love Is a Battlefield." "If I were Tom, I'd be just a little miffed." Quinn takes a swig of his coffee.

"Oh, so this is all my fault?"

"He behaves like a decent guy, and you blow him off for your gay best friend who won't talk to you anymore. He's got to be wondering what your freaking problem is."

"When you say it that way, it makes me sound like a complete whack-job. And define 'decent.' He was there with Kayla. He was drunk. And he . . ." I take a deep breath and say it. "We sort of . . . kissed a little. Again."

"What?" Quinn shouts.

"Shhhhh!" I lean in. "We kissed. But it was dumb and I stopped him."

"Because?"

"Because I remembered Nash. And because Tom clarified that he just wants to be friends. But friends who kiss, I guess. Whatever that's supposed to mean."

"Yeah, um, no."

"Duh. Oh, and he's the one who told Nash about the other kiss. Not Kayla. I didn't see that coming."

"Seriously?"

I nod.

"What a tool."

"Yeah. Who knew?"

"No comment," Quinn says.

I pick up the stapler again, and Quinn takes it away from me again. "Besides, I didn't want him to kiss me. Okay, I like kissing him in general. But I didn't want him to kiss me then, not with all that other stuff swirling around us."

"A woman who knows her own mind. I like what I'm hearing."

My cheeks get warm. "Yeah. Sometimes."

Quinn nods. "So what else?"

"Kayla was . . . a little drunk. More drunk than Tom. And I'm pretty sure she's the one who told those Neanderthals I was ready and willing. I wanted to punch her in the head. Hard."

"Did you?" Quinn asks.

"No!" I laugh. "No! Of course not."

"Why not?" Quinn asks. "She deserved to get her butt kicked from here to Texas with that popular-girl, shit-talking, gossip crapola." Quinn chooses another record, placing the needle before speaking. Hall and Oates warn us to watch out for the maneater. "Please tell me you at least gave her a piece of your mind?"

I duck my head and start picking at my cuticle again. I tear off too much, and it starts to bleed. "Not exactly," I mumble. "We sort of talked for a minute, and then she was off with Tom, and her friends were there. She was so clueless and drunk. It was pathetic."

"I'm beginning to understand that when you say 'not exactly,' you actually mean 'not even close,'" he says. "That girl needs to understand what she did. And you need to tell her."

I suck on my bleeding finger, but I don't say anything.

"'Once more unto the breach,' Maggie," Quinn says.

"It's going to take more than cookies and some old blues ballads to fix this, Quinn." I change Hall and Oates out for some Three Dog Night: "One Is the Loneliest Number."

"Har, har." Quinn digs through the RAPs; he's looking for something specific. "So what *is* it going to take, Maggie?"

This stops me. I know he's right. I planned on telling Kayla off at the party, but at the moment, the thought of telling Kayla how much damage she did makes me want to hurl. And now that ship has sailed. What's my plan B?

He puts his hand on my arm. "Time to stand up for yourself, Maggie," he says. "To Kayla. To your mom. To Nash. To Tom."

"I forgot to tell you. I did talk to my mom."

"Well done! And?"

"I told her she has permission to talk about any of my wonderful qualities except my weight. She understands, and she agrees."

Quinn chooses another record: the Smiths telling me shyness can stop me from doing what I want in life. The guy shopping in the Classical section keeps giving us dirty looks, clearly not appreciating the fact that we keep changing out the song every ten seconds.

"Racking wrestlers in their privates is all well and good, but now it's time, Maggie. Time to tame your fear monkeys and make them stop throwing their feces all over your life. Whatever her intentions, Kayla screwed up in a big, bad way. You have to tell her."

On top of the RTP pile I see a way to end this conversation. Donna Summer: "Enough Is Enough." I place the needle, watching Quinn for his inevitable reaction. Quinn hates Donna Summer, and the quaver of her voice causes Quinn to close his eyes, pinching the bridge of his nose. He grabs the needle, scraping it across the record. Both customers look up in alarm.

"Enough *is* enough. At the end of all this, the only person you know for sure will still be there for you is you. So find a way to be true to yourself, Maggie. Follow your bliss and all that." He waves me away and turns back to his accounting. "It's time to do this thing."

"Thanks, Quinn." I grab my backpack. "Love your guts. Gotta go." And as I leave, I know he's right. It's time for badass Maggie to step up to the plate. At this point I've got nothing to lose.

With that I'm out the door, but I don't want to go home yet. I wander through town and find myself at the swing set. I'm not in the mood to swing, but I move myself back and forth a little. The sun is shining, but it's cold enough to see my breath. The lake shimmers and the deep green of the firs looks nearly black against the clear sky. Snow has dusted the trees farther up the hillsides. Leaning back in the swing, I close my eyes and soak in the feel of the sun on my face. I know Quinn's right: I can't make any of these other people happy with me. But I can do something that makes me happy with myself. Suddenly that kernel of idea that's been rattling around my brain takes root.

I stop at the store for supplies, then settle into the kitchen for a marathon baking session. I make dozens of cookies, all my best inventions: chocolate cherry coconut, pecan butterscotch chip, dark chocolate snickerdoodles.

Dad comes into the kitchen around dinnertime. He starts to say something but thinks better of it. I think he can tell I'm not going to make room for anyone else to cook, so he orders pizza and leaves me alone.

Later my mom comes in. "That's a lot of cookies," she says.

"Yep," I say.

"Any idea when we'll have our kitchen back?"

"Soon-ish." I expect Mom to flee in the face of all these baked goods, but she surprises me by tying on an apron.

"Can I help?"

"I didn't know you could bake." Grandma used to let me help her with Christmas cookies, but Mom never baked a single thing that I can remember. I didn't think she knew how.

"There are still a few things you don't know about me, honey."

"True." I point to the mixing bowl in the sink. "That bowl needs to be washed. I was going to start the peanut butter chocolate chunk next." I hand her the recipe, and we work side by side for a while before she speaks again.

"Can I ask what you're going to do with all these cookies?"

"Bake sale."

"Oh? What are you raising money for?"

"Food bank. They always need extra donations around the holidays."

"I don't think you'll have any trouble selling these cookies," Mom says. "They look amazing, honey. Besides, I'm sure Nash will help eat whatever's left over." She's joking, but the Nash-shaped hole in my heart gets a little bigger.

"Not so much lately. I'm not his favorite right now."

"Ahhh, I wondered if there wasn't something," she says. "Want to talk about it?"

"Nope." I pull a pan out of the oven. "But thanks." We finish the cookies, and Mom helps me wrap them after they cool. I go upstairs to make signs and finalize my plans. I've been hiding too long, waiting for the storm to pass. It's time to get out there, even if I get drenched.

CHAPTER 33

That night my mind whirs with all the disparate, crazy revelations I've had in the last couple of weeks. But what, if anything, does it all mean? These unfamiliar versions of people I thought I knew leave me wondering how my perceptions of them could be so convincing, and still so wrong. I think about how people see me. Nash is obviously convinced I'm some sort of backstabbing closet nymphomaniac. Kayla thinks I'm a loser who should be grateful for whatever attention she tosses my way. Tom thinks I'm an immature idiot who runs away from a little fun. None of these things are entirely true, but people are convinced of these truths and act accordingly.

I roll over; the clock glows 1:30. I have to be up in about four hours, but I can't stop thinking. I know this bake sale is a long shot. But I don't really care. I need Kayla to see she hasn't beaten me. And I need Nash to see I'm still the same person I always was. More than that, I need to prove it to myself. I shove my fist into the pillow and look at the clock again: 1:34.

Rolling over on my back, I stare at the sparkles on the ceiling reflecting the light from the streetlamp. I think back through

258 • KRIS DINNISON

the catalog of my favorite Billie Holiday songs, the songs that have gotten me through the last couple weeks. I know what Billie would say about all this: she'd say it's nobody's business what I do. Then I remember that Lady Day's life wasn't a joy ride; in fact, it was more like a train wreck. But she kept singing. That's what I'm trying to do. I look at the clock again: 1:42 a.m.

Sleep comes at some point. When my alarm goes off, getting my eyes open takes some effort. But I realize I feel sort of okay, I guess. Feeling okay is such significant progress over the way I've been feeling that I pop out of bed and get ready with a new sense of purpose.

By the time I get to school, I'm ready for action. I set up my bake sale table in the hallway before school. A few of the skaters buy cookies, and one girl stops by to ask if I've used all organic ingredients. Mostly people pretend I'm not there.

The one bright spot is when Cece buys five cookies.

"Are you going to eat all those?" I ask.

"You know I can't resist your cookies!" she says. "But no, I'm only eating one. The rest I'm using as bait. Like those drug dealers who give out free samples to get people hooked."

"You're an evil mastermind, Cece."

I pack up just before the first bell. I haven't seen Nash, Tom, or Kayla. But the day has just begun.

Back at my locker I find an envelope scrunched into the vents. I have to open the locker and pull the letter through on the inside. I feel a little jolt of excitement, thinking that Nash has finally made contact. Then I recognize Tom's handwriting on the envelope. I rip it open and scan the letter inside.

> *Dear Maggie: After the other night, you probably don't want to talk to me, but to paraphrase the lovely Ms. Holiday, who I know you admire: Ain't nobody's business if you do!* — *Tom*

I grab the books I need and shove them, along with the note, into my backpack. It doesn't seem fair, Tom using Billie against me that way. But the message hits me in the gut and gives me some hope. I dig the note back out of my pack, smoothing it out, and put it in my pocket.

I set up for the bake sale again at noon. More people buy, and fewer people ignore me. Halfway through lunch, I put samples out like Cece suggested. This pushes the final holdouts over the edge. One taste of homemade goodies and all that feeble resistance goes out the window. I even get a few people to sign up to volunteer at the food bank. I've sold about two-thirds of my stock when I hear Kayla's voice.

"Hey, Maggie!" she says.

The hallway is crowded, and I don't see right away where the voice is coming from. I hand some change back to a skater, a guy who's bought several cookies today, and Kayla and her friends move to the front of the crowd standing around the table.

"How'd you like Tara's party? Crazy night. I can't believe you went; I told Tom you never go to parties!" She looks like she's waiting for something, and I wonder if there's a question in there that I missed.

"Anyway, it's so great that you're helping the food bank. I totally want to support you. Which kind is your best seller?"

"I think we're all sold out," I say, smiling.

"What do you mean?" She looks at the table, her forehead wrinkling. "There are plenty of cookies left. I only want to buy a couple. They're for Tom."

"Sorry, these are all spoken for."

"You okay, Maggie?" Kayla asks. "What's going on?"

My stomach clenches in anger, and the red that's been creeping up my neck reaches the top and explodes like some Saturday morning cartoon character.

"Am I okay?" I ask, leaning forward. "Really? You have no idea what the answer to that question might be? Are you really that self-absorbed?"

Kayla's posse stares, and Kayla gapes like a trout on a hook, but only for a few seconds. Then she gathers her wits. Grabbing my elbow, she pulls me up and leads me to a corner where we can talk in private.

"What the hell are you talking about?" she hisses. "I just want to buy some of your stupid cookies. What's your problem, Maggie?"

"My problem is you ran your mouth about things that weren't yours to talk about."

"And?" Kayla is right in my face now.

"And it hurt people I care about, and it was a shitty thing to do. And I think you owe me an apology."

"An apology? All I said was that you liked Tom and that the two of you got together. All true, by the way."

"Really? That's all you said?"

"I'm not responsible if someone takes the story and runs with it." She glances back at her friends, who are straining to hear the conversation. "Maggie, why are you doing this?"

"Are you really going to stand there and pretend you didn't spread the rumors about Tom and me? According to the guys who tried to maul me at the party, I'm the girl who will do it anytime with anyone, and should be grateful for the attention."

"Well, I didn't tell them that."

"Maybe not, but you were the source of the information."

"Not my fault."

"Jesus! Really?" My voice is getting louder now. "Is any of this sounding familiar to you, Kayla? Aren't you having just the tiniest bit of déjà vu?"

Kayla grabs me again and pulls me into an empty class-room, shutting the door behind us.

"What are you talking about, Maggie?"

"I never said a word to you when you sucker punched me in middle school. But you're pulling the same shit now that you did then."

"Are you kidding me?" Kayla says. "This is about something I did to you in middle school?"

"God, Kayla, no. This isn't about middle school. This is about you still acting like you're in middle school!"

"Look who's talking!"

"You're right. Here we are, cozy and close and sharing girl

talk again four years later, and I let you suck me right back in. I'm an idiot, just like I was then. That part is my fault."

"Oh, and I suppose the rest of the stuff in your sad little life is my fault?"

"Kayla, look, I get it. You're so scared people are going to leave you or ditch you or whatever that you'll do anything to feel like you belong. But half the time you're faking it. So you seek me out because your minions bore you."

Kayla crosses her arms. "My minions?"

I just wave her words away. "But you spend so much time pretending that you don't even know what's true anymore."

"It's not like the fact that you like Tom was a secret."

"Maybe not, but in your hands a little piece of information like that gets passed through some twisted game of telephone, where everyone playing knows deep down they've screwed up the original message, but they keep passing it on anyway. And now you're trying to act like none of it matters. But it does."

"I didn't have to fake anything to get Tom." Kayla looks me up and down like I'm a banana slug she stepped on and got stuck to her shoes. But she's spinning her pearl ring, working it around and around her finger. "I think we both know who a guy like Tom would choose."

"Maybe you're right. But I still wouldn't want your life. You scramble twenty-four seven, pretending to be someone you're not, and for what? So you'll be popular? It must be exhausting. And it seems like a crazy way to get people to like you."

Kayla lets out a bitter burst of laughter. "You think being popular means people like you?"

"I liked you."

Kayla stops spinning the ring and looks at me. "I know."

"Then why—Never mind." I take a deep breath and let it out. "Listen, Kayla. I gave you another chance to be my friend. You blew it, again. You're not getting any more chances from me. Now leave. Me. Alone."

I pull open the classroom door and wade through the crowd gathered outside listening. Throwing the rest of the baked goods in a box, I grab my backpack and walk away. My cheeks feel hot, and I'm shaking head to toe. I see Nash's green combat boots out of the corner of my eye, but I head right for the side exit and into the cool air. It takes an hour of walking the bluff to get my heart to stop racing.

When the adrenaline wears off, my mood deflates. I told Kayla off, but I spent all that energy on someone who's really just a minor character in my life. The people I care about most are still in doubt. My heart sags as I think of Nash. I miss him so much. Even if we can forgive each other, I'm not convinced things between us will ever be like they were. And the stuff with Tom is so tangled, I have no idea how to pick all the strands apart again. I stand on the bluff, waiting for some idea of what to do next.

CHAPTER 34

I don't want to go to Square Peg, and I don't want to go home. I don't really want to be anywhere, so I go to the swings. Pumping my legs hard, I launch myself as high as I can into the air, looking for that split second when the swing reaches the end of the arc and starts to fall before I do—weightless and free. The lake and the trees clump together in one dark mass, making it hard to tell where I am in space and how close I am to hitting the ground. After a couple big swings, I have a few moments where the fog lifts, but then I let the chains slow and soon I'm only moving a few inches in each direction, my feet dragging in the gravel trench carved out by hundreds of feet over the years.

"Hey, that's my swing."

I twist around, and there's Nash, standing in a puddle of light by the boat launch.

He walks over and grabs the chain of my swing like nothing ever happened. Like we haven't spent the last couple weeks, the longest of my life, incommunicado.

"I had dibs," he says.

"Well, if you had dibs . . ." I get out of the swing and move to the one next to it.

"Thanks." He sits, pushing the seat back and forth with a gentle, hypnotic motion. "A bake sale for the food bank? Kids stuffing their faces with cookies to feed the hungry? The irony!"

"I had to do something to get your attention."

We swing in silence for a few more minutes, and then Nash dives in.

"I was so hurt."

"I was too," I say. "Hurt. And miserable. And lonely. And pissed off."

Nash keeps swinging.

"And sorry," I say. "So, so sorry! I didn't mean to—"

"No, that's the thing. You didn't. I mean, you did kiss him, which was shitty. But I was really mad because Tom didn't like me. Seriously, just once can't the cute new guy be gay? Is that so much to ask? Anyway, I took it out on you."

"Yeah, you kinda did."

"I'm sorry too," Nash says. "Incredibly sorry. I can't believe how close I came to screwing this up permanently."

"Good. Remember that. Because no guy is worth our friendship."

"I know."

"Good." We move back and forth like twin pendulums on a clock that is winding down. "Kayla—" I start to say.

"Kayla is a sad little future prom queen who sabotaged you in hopes Tom would land in her lap."

"God, I've missed you."

"I know."

We laugh together this time, but my laughter merges with some tears. I'm hiccupy and a little snotty, but I'm grinning from ear to ear. Nash looks me up and down and hands me the crisp cotton handkerchief he always carries.

"Pull it together, Mags." He pulls me off my swing, and we walk, elbows linked, across the park. I rest my head on his shoulder for a minute, and he kisses the top of my head. "I missed you too, friend."

When we get to my house, Mom starts into her usual speech about calling when I'm going to be late, but stops short when she sees Nash.

"Naaaash!" she squeals, giving him a big hug. "Where have you been? We've missed you around here."

"Hi, Mrs. Bower," Nash says. "Mr. Bower," he adds, shaking Dad's hand. "I've missed being here."

I grab a couple oranges from the bowl on the counter.

"That's a great snack . . ." Mom starts in.

"Mom . . ." I say.

"Right. I forgot. Sorry."

When we get to my messy room, Nash gives a fastidious little snort. "Have we been wallowing, Miss Maggie?"

"We have been miserable, Mr. Taylor, as you well know. Now sit while I clean this mess up."

Nash clears dirty clothes off the chair by my desk and perches himself on the edge of it, making as little physical contact with my room as possible. He peruses the photos of me framing my mirror.

"What's this?"

"That? That was a brisk, clarifying walk down memory lane," I say. "I learned some things I don't want to forget."

Nash nods with what I decide is approval. He points to my fourth grade photo. "I thought you hated that one."

I smile, loving him for remembering something like that. "I used to. But in view of recent events, I've come to appreciate its charms."

He nods again.

"So, spill." I resume my cleaning frenzy. "What brought you back into my ever-lovin' arms?"

"The truth is Tom did." Nash examines his fingernails while he says this. "Well, Tom and your fiery and unintentionally public discussion with Kayla today. Anyway, he's pretty upset about how everything happened, and he wanted to know if there was anything he could do to make things right between you and me again, short of dating me, of course."

"Of course." I hurl a big pile of shoes into my closet. They crash and tumble against the back wall. "I can't believe him. What did you say?"

"I told him he could stay away from you," Nash says.

I look at him.

"Kidding, I'm kidding." He smoothes down his hair. "Well, I did say that, but I also said that if Tom was serious about you, I would step out of the way."

I freeze, wondering if I've heard Nash right. "You said that?" I ask. "For real?"

"Yes," he says, his face pinching a bit. "You can have Tom with my full support and approval."

"You'd really do that?"

"Maggie, you're my best friend. I know on the friendship spectrum, I lean toward the 'it's all about me' end, but this last little episode has been ridiculous even for me."

I think about Tom kissing me and know this won't really be behind us unless I tell Nash everything. "In the interest of full disclosure . . ." I fold some T-shirts to avoid eye contact with Nash. "You should know that he kissed me. Well, we kissed. Again."

"Where?" Nash brushes some imaginary lint off his sweater sleeve.

"On the lips. And my neck. And my forehead." I wait for his reaction.

"I meant where did this happen?"

"First time by the lake. You already knew about that. Second time at a party last weekend."

Nash's eyes widen when I mention the party. "And?"

"And I definitely wanted him to. I didn't stop him, not the first time."

"What about the second time?"

"The second time Tom was drunk and he just wanted a warm body. And I told him to stop. He just wants to be friends anyway."

"That sounds extremely friendly."

I laugh. "It was, except for the part when we stopped kissing, and he said he didn't mean it. And then he told me he was the one who told you about the kiss, when I thought all along it was Kayla."

"Oh, Kayla did her part, and more than her share of the damage."

"But why did Tom do that to you? It must have hurt like hell!"

"Yeah, it did. But I think he was trying to find a way to let me down easy. Good intentions, but just between you and me: he's not that great at relationships." He waves his hand like he's shooing a cat off a table. "His loss, Maggie." Nash sighs. "Was it fabulous?"

I nod. "Yep. Pretty much."

"So now you've been kissed."

"I guess, sort of, yeah."

Nash looks a little wistful.

I rush to reassure him. "But not technically. Not by someone who actually likes me. Are you freaking out?"

Nash takes a deep breath. "I was for a second. And it's going to take me some time to get past all the twinges left over from whatever crushy thing I had going with Tom. But I'm also thinking that now that you've crossed the kissing threshold, maybe there's hope for me too?"

"No doubt. That is definitely going to happen." I throw Neshie on the bed. "So, we're okay?"

"Sure. I'm a new and improved Nash. This way if the actual man of my dreams ever does show up in Cedar Ridge, he'll find me much more lovable and irresistible."

I give Nash a hug and sit on the bed across from him. "Did Tom make the book? Your Crushology book?"

"Oh, honey. Tom has his own chapter!" Nash shakes his head. "But it's okay. I'm already kind of getting over him. Mostly."

"This has all been such a shit show!" I flop back on my bed.

"I was so wrong about Kayla, and Tom. The one thing I'm sure of right now is you."

"Good. Because I'm not going anywhere."

"Right back at you." I sit up and look Nash in the eye. "So, what should we do now? What do you want?"

"What do I want?" He's quiet for a long minute, and when he continues, I can hear the longing and ache in his voice. "I just want someone who wants me back. I want to sit on the same side of the booth while we're having coffee. I want to slow dance at my own prom and have a beautiful first kiss, and second kiss . . . I want . . . sweaty palms and jellyfish, the whole thing."

"Yeah," I say. "Jellyfish."

"Do you think I can really have all that?"

"Definitely."

Billie's already on the turntable, so I flip the record over and put the needle down.

"Ain't Nobody's Business" starts playing, and I sing the intro right along with Billie. She's right. No matter what you do, somebody's going to complain and criticize. So you might as well do what you want. For the first time, I believe the words down deep.

Then the music shifts, and Nash and I both leap from our chairs, singing along as loud as we can. "'If I should take a notion, to jump into the ocean, ain't nobody's business if I do-ooo.'"

I realize whatever I decide about Tom, or my weight, or who I'm friends with, or whatever: it's my decision. My business, and nobody else's. Nash and I collapse onto the bed when the song ends. The needle pulses at the inside edge of the record, but both of us are too tired and happy to care. Nash reaches across the bed and links his pinkie with mine.

"Maggie Bower," he whispers. "You are my pinkie partner for life."

I smile and whisper back, "I know."

CHAPTER 35

Nash stays late, and I sleep better than I have in weeks. Mom knows it's been rough, so she lets me ditch school. In the afternoon I realize I haven't told Quinn about Kayla or Nash, so I throw my coat on and head over to Square Peg before my shift starts. As soon as I walk through the door, he can see something's different.

"Something happened!" He claps his hands together. "Tell me. Tell me. Tell me!"

I take off my coat and throw it on the stool. "I told her off."

"Kayla? No joke?" The girl in the R&B section is listening, so he lowers his voice. "What happened?"

"Not much to tell," I say. "She stopped by the bake sale to say hi and buy some cookies. I said I wouldn't sell her any cookies. I also told her she screwed up, that she's really bad at the whole friendship thing."

"Just like that?" he says. "'Hi, Kayla, you're a lame friend'? How'd that go over?"

"Ton o' bricks," I say. "But I told her to leave me alone, that she'd had more than enough chances from me."

"How do you feel?"

"I was shakin' like bacon yesterday, but I feel okay now. I think I feel good." I grin as I realize this is actual happiness.

The bell jingles and Tom walks in. He's smiling, trying to look relaxed, but I can see in his eyes he's not sure if he should be there.

"Hi," he says.

"Hi," I say back.

"Missed you at school." He holds out a Ziploc bag with some deformed cookies in them. "I made you cookies." He looks embarrassed. "I've never really baked before. I know they're kind of ugly, but I think they taste okay."

I take the baggie and peer at the cookies through the bag.

"They're plain old chocolate chip."

"My favorite." I pull one out and take a bite. They're a little burned, but he's got the right idea. And nobody but my grandma ever made cookies for me before. "Thanks."

We stand like that for a minute, and then I put down the cookies and grab Tom's hand, pulling him through the store and into the back hallway. Standing in the narrow hall creates a forced intimacy that amplifies the voltage I feel whenever Tom's around.

"Great speech," he says.

"Oh." I cross my arms over my chest. I can't find a safe place to look when he's standing so close. "You heard?"

"Yep. Me and about a hundred other people."

We both laugh, but it's not easy like it was before.

"So, yeah. Sorry about the other night," he says. "I shouldn't have . . . Well, there's been so much going on, and I was a little . . . I'd been drinking . . . I shouldn't have tried anything."

"Yeah. It was a rough night. I needed a friend, not a make-out session."

"I know. Or I should have known."

"Yeah, you should have."

"And I shouldn't have told Nash about the kiss."

"Yeah, that was a bit of a dick move."

"Yeah, well, I thought it might make things better, but I don't really have an excuse."

"Good. I hate excuses. So I guess an apology will have to be enough."

"I'm sorry."

"Accepted." I tilt my head and look at him a minute; the neon hanging over the counter lights half his face as it penetrates the hallway. "You know, Tom, you're not really who I thought you were."

Tom smiles. "Neither are you, Maggie."

He holds his arms open for a hug at the same time I stick out my hand for a handshake. We laugh, and he settles for the handshake.

"Ahem." Quinn coughs and knocks on the wall near the hallway entrance. "Hate to interrupt, but we have some actual customers. A little help?" Quinn returns to the store.

"Is he mad?" Tom asks.

"Not a chance, but I should get back out there."

"Yeah, okay." Tom smiles. "See you later?"

"Sure." I retreat behind the safety of the counter.

"Nice work, Maggie," Quinn says. "Now if only that dumbass Nash would pull his head out of his butt, it would be a golden day!"

"He already did!" I tell Quinn everything, about Nash and Tom and all the crazy ways things got mixed up and made right again.

"Hallelujah!" Quinn says when I finish. "All is well in Maggie world! You deserve it, hon."

I'm still grinning as Quinn turns to ring up a customer. Some other browsers drift around the store, still looking through the bins, hoping to find an album that will remind them of who they used to be. Over the speakers, the Kinks sing "Ev'rybody's Gonna Be Happy." I don't know if everybody will be, but I think I am. At least for the moment.

ACKNOWLEDGMENTS

This book, like all books, bears the marks of many generous people. Kerry Sparks, agent extraordinaire: Thank you for believing in the work, and in me, when neither was fully formed. You have been a patient mentor and tireless champion. Thanks also to Kate O'Sullivan, my amazing, thoughtful editor: You taught me so much through this process. Both the book and its author are so much better than they were before you got a hold of us. I am so grateful to all the people at Houghton Mifflin Harcourt who helped bring the book into being, especially the copyeditor, Erin DeWitt, who gave the book such thorough attention, and Susanna Vagt, who wowed me with her cover designs.

I would have been unable to write this if not for the support and encouragement of Kelly Milner Halls. Thank you, friend, for being a mentor to me as I became a writer. Kevin Shields, thanks for helping me make sure I got things right for Nash. My gratitude goes out to all the excellent friends and writers who were willing to read for me: Pete Fromm, Beth Cooley, Sheri Boggs, Kerry Halls, Carole Allen, Anne Walter, Ava

Walter, Claire Rudolph Murphy, Mari Hunt, and Jen Menzer. You each showed me ways to make Maggie and Nash's story more complete. Thanks, too, to all the editors who read the book and took the time to offer feedback even though it wasn't right for them. Every piece of that made the book better and helped me become a stronger writer.

To my parents, Tom and Sandi Burns, who always encouraged me to learn and read: thank you. Finally, I am so grateful to my husband, Andy, and my daughter, Kate, for giving me the time and space to write and for believing I could actually do this.